THE MRS. PIGGLE-WIGGLE TREASURY

By Betty MacDonald

Illustrated By Hilary Knight

HarperCollins*Publishers*

THE MRS. PIGGLE-WIGGLE TREASURY

CONTENTS

Mrs. Piggle-Wiggle

Betty MacDonald

Pictures by HILARY KNIGHT

HarperCollins*Publishers*

For Anne, Joan, Mari, Salli Heidi,
Darsie, Frankie and Stevie

who are perfect angels and couldn't
possibly have been the inspiration for
any of these stories.

Contents

1

MRS. PIGGLE-WIGGLE, HERSELF

I expect I might as well begin by telling you all about Mrs. Piggle-Wiggle so that whenever I mention her name, which I do very often in this book, you will not interrupt and ask, "Who is Mrs. Piggle-Wiggle? What does she look like? How big is she? How old is she? What color is her hair? Is her hair long? Does she wear high heels? Does she have any children? Is there a Mr. Piggle-Wiggle?"

Mrs. Piggle-Wiggle lives here in our town. She is very small and has a hump on her back. When children ask her about the hump, she says, "Oh that's a big lump of magic.

Sometimes it turns me into a witch; other times into a dwarf or a fairy, and on special occasions it makes me into a queen." The children are all very envious of the hump because, besides being magic, it is such a convenient fastening place for wings.

Mrs. Piggle-Wiggle has brown sparkly eyes and brown hair which she keeps very long, almost to her knees, so the children can comb it. She usually wears it on top of her head in a knot, unless someone has been combing it and then she has braids, or long wet curls, or long hair just hanging and with a jewelled crown or flowers on top.

One day I saw her digging in her garden wearing the jewelled crown and with her hair billowing down her back. She waved gaily and said, "I promised Betsy (Betsy is one of her children friends) that I would not touch this hair until she came home from school," and she went on with her digging. Mrs. Piggle-Wiggle's skin is a goldy brown and she has a warm, spicy, sugar-cooky smell that is very comforting to children who are sad about something. Her clothes are all brown and never look crisp and pressed because they are used for dress-up. She wears felt hats which the children poke and twist into witches' and pirates' hats and she does not mind at all. Sunday mornings she takes one of the hats off the closet shelf, gives it a few thumps, pulls it firmly down fore and aft and wears it to church. She wears very high heels all the time and is glad to let the little girls borrow her shoes.

Mrs. Piggle-Wiggle, Herself

Mrs. Piggle-Wiggle has no family at all. She says that her husband, Mr. Piggle-Wiggle, was a pirate and after he had buried all of his treasure in the back yard, he died. She just has herself and Wag, her dog, and Lightfoot, her cat.

The most remarkable thing about Mrs. Piggle-Wiggle is her house, which is upside down. It is a little brown house, and sitting there in its tangly garden it looks like a small brown puppy lying on its back with its feet in the air. Mrs. Piggle-Wiggle says that when she was a little girl she used to lie in bed and gaze up at the ceiling and wonder and wonder what it would be like if the house were upside down. And so when she grew up and built her own house she had it built upside down, just to see. The bathroom, the kitchen and the staircase are right side up—they are more convenient that way. You can easily see that you could not cook on an upside-down stove or wash dishes in an upside-down sink or walk *up* upside-down stairs.

In the living room of her house is a large chandelier and instead of being on the ceiling it is on the floor. Of course it is really on the ceiling, but the ceiling is the floor and so it is on the floor and the children turn on the lights and then squat around it pretending it is a campfire. Mrs. Piggle-Wiggle says that her chandelier is the only one in town which is put to any real use. Her bedrooms all have slidy boards in them because if you will look up at your attic ceiling you will see that a slanty ceiling when turned upside

11

down makes a fine slidy board. Also all the wall lights are very close to the floor and handy for the small children. For the first five or ten years after the house was built Mrs. Piggle-Wiggle climbed in and out of her rooms over the high doorways but now she has little steps which are just the thing to practise jumping. She gives the children chalk so they can mark on the rug how far they jump.

Nobody knows how old Mrs. Piggle-Wiggle is. She says she doesn't know herself. She says, "What difference does it make how old I am when I shall never grow any bigger."

Mrs. Piggle-Wiggle's dog, Wag, has puppies every once in a while and so she keeps a long list of names of children who want them on the blackboard in her kitchen. For Lightfoot-the-cat's kittens she has a long waiting list on the blackboard in the dining room.

Mrs. Piggle-Wiggle's back yard is full of big holes where small boys dig for Mr. Piggle-Wiggle's buried treasure and her front yard is full of flowers which the little girls pick, jam into vases and place about her living room or carry to their teachers.

Every child in town is a friend of Mrs. Piggle-Wiggle's but she knows very few of their parents. She says grown-ups make her nervous.

For the first year after she built her house, Mrs. Piggle-Wiggle lived there all by herself except for Wag and Lightfoot, and she was very lonely. Then, one dark, rainy afternoon when she was baking sugar cookies and thinking how much fun it would be if she knew someone besides Wag and Lightfoot to invite for tea, she happened to look out of her kitchen window and there coming up the street in the pouring rain, dragging a big suitcase and bawling, was a little girl. Mrs. Piggle-Wiggle wiped the flour off her hands and hurried right out into the rain and invited the little girl in for tea.

The little girl's name was Mary Lou Robertson and she was eight years old and quite fat, and she was running away from home. She told Mrs. Piggle-Wiggle all this after she had drunk three cups of cambric tea and eaten seven sugar cookies. She said, "I'm running away from home because I hate to wash dishes. All I do is wash dishes. I am just a servant. Dishes! Dishes! Dishes! Wash, dry, put away. That's all I do. My mother doesn't love me at all. She isn't my real mother, anyway. She probably got me out of an orphanage just to wash her dishes." Mary Lou began to cry again, so that the eighth sugar cooky got quite soggy before she finished it.

Mrs. Piggle-Wiggle said, "Isn't she your real mother?"

Mary Lou said, "She says she is but no real mother would make you wash dishes. Wash dishes! Wash dishes!"

"Now that's a funny thing," said Mrs. Piggle-Wiggle. "I mean your hating to wash dishes so much, because you see, I like to wash dishes. In fact I enjoy washing dishes so much that a cause of great sorrow to me is the fact that the only dishes I must wash are for Wag, Lightfoot and me. Three or four dishes a meal, that is all.

"When I wash dishes, Mary Lou, I pretend that I am a beautiful princess with long, golden, curly hair (Mary Lou's hair was jet black and braided into two stiff little pigtails), and apple-blossom skin and forget-me-not blue eyes. I have been captured by a wicked witch and my only chance to get free is to wash every single dish and have the whole kitchen sparkly clean before the clock strikes. For, when the clock strikes, the witch will come down and inspect, to see if there is a crumb anywhere. If there are pots and pans that have been put away wet, if the silverware has been thrown in the drawer, or if the sink has not been scrubbed out, the witch will have me in her power for another year."

Mrs. Piggle-Wiggle looked at the clock and jumped up. "It is ten minutes to four, Princess, and we have so much to do. Hurry, hurry, hurry!" Mary Lou also jumped up and began carrying the tea things to the sink and Mrs. Piggle-Wiggle whisked them in and out of the dish water and Mary Lou dried them and Mrs. Piggle-Wiggle hurried as fast as she could and put the cooky things away and every once in a while she would stop and say, "Hark, Princess, do you hear the thump of the witch's big gnarly cane?" Then Mary Lou, her braids bobbing up and down with excitement, would say, "I hear it, Princess, it is coming closer and closer." Soon the kitchen sparkled, the dishes were washed and dried and put away and every crumb had been swept off the floor. Mary Lou even curled Lightfoot's tail neatly around her legs and smoothed Wag's fur. Just before the clock struck, Mrs. Piggle-Wiggle said to Mary Lou, "Princess, I must leave you now but show the witch your work and oh, I do hope you will be freed!"

Then she went upstairs and pretty soon down the stairs came a terrible old witch with a long black dress, a tall black hat and a big gnarly black cane. Mary Lou was very scared until she saw the sparkly eyes of Mrs. Piggle-Wiggle under the black hat. She showed the witch the kitchen and the witch took out the cooky pans and carried them over to the light to see if they were clean and dry. She got down on her knees, squeaking like a rusty gate, to see if Mary Lou had swept under the stove. She felt inside the teacups to see if there was sugar in the bottoms and she put on her glasses to examine the sink. But she could not find anything wrong so she handed Mary Lou the key to the kitchen door and screeched out, "You are free, Princess, but I will get you again, never fear!" The witch clumped back up the stairs and in a few minutes down came Mrs. Piggle-Wiggle.

"Well," said Mrs. Piggle-Wiggle, "do you see why I like to wash dishes?"

Mary Lou said, "Oh, Mrs. Piggle-Wiggle that was the most fun I've ever had!"

Mrs. Piggle-Wiggle said, "Of course you can have more fun than I can because you have so many more dishes to wash. If I only had more dishes and could take longer I would be a princess with curly, yellow, long hair, apple-blossom skin, blue eyes and a beautiful voice and I would sing sad songs over the dishpan. Also if I had more dishes I would have the witch ride through the night on a broom-stick and I would creep out on the back porch to see if she was coming. I could hear her land with a thump on the roof and I would slip upstairs to see if she was going to slide down the chimney or thump down the stairs. Oh, there would be ever so many exciting things to pretend if only I had more dishes to wash."

After a while it stopped raining and the sun came out and Mary Lou took her suitcase and went home. That night her mother (it really was her mother, of course) almost fainted when she came out to the kitchen exactly twenty-seven minutes after dinner and Mary Lou was sweeping the floor and all the dishes were washed and dried and put away and everything was immaculate. Mrs. Robertson rushed in and called Mary Lou's father and he came out to the kitchen and pretended to fall on the floor with surprise and then he said to Mary Lou's mother, "I like your new maid, madam. In fact, she is so much better than Tillie Slopwash who used to be here that I think we should invite her to the moving picture show some early evening."

Then Mary Lou told them all about Mrs. Piggle-Wiggle and Mary Lou's mother said, "Oh, yes, I remember seeing that odd little house. She sounds like a charming friend and if you are certain that she invited you, you may go over there after school tomorrow."

The next day after school Mary Lou went to see Mrs. Piggle-Wiggle. She took her best friend, Kitty Wheeling, with her, and Mrs. Piggle-Wiggle was very glad to see them and showed them through her upside-down house and served tea and cookies. Kitty said, her mouth full of cooky, "My worst trouble is bedmaking. I just cannot get them smooth. I'd much rather wash dishes like Mary Lou, but Mother won't let me change with my sister, Sally, who washes the dishes, until I have learned to make beds properly. Oh, I just despise to make beds!"

Mrs. Piggle-Wiggle poured herself another cup of tea, gave a saucer of cream to Lightfoot and four cookies to Wag, then said, "If you think you have a hard time making beds, Kitty, imagine how hard it is for me. You see, the Cruel Queen sleeps in my beds every night and inspects them every morning and if *she* finds a single wrinkle, even one as big as a pin, she will have me thrown in a dungeon. Come upstairs and I'll show you how I have to make beds."

They went upstairs and Mrs. Piggle-Wiggle threw the covers clear off the foot of one of her own beds, then she had Kitty help her make it and when they finished it was as smooth as the floor—no wrinkles. Mrs. Piggle-Wiggle said, "The secret is to throw the covers way back. You simply cannot smooth up a bed because if you do there might be a wrinkle down by the foot and of course the

17

Cruel Queen will find it and then DOWN INTO THE DUNGEON!"

Mrs. Piggle-Wiggle took the bed all apart again and said, "Now, Kitty, you and Mary Lou make the bed while I tell the Cruel Queen you are ready for inspection." She went into the closet and shut the door. When she came out just as Kitty and Mary Lou finished the bed, she was no longer Mrs. Piggle-Wiggle but the wicked, haughty Cruel Queen. On her head she wore a glittering jewelled crown. Her hair hung down her back in deep waves. Around her shoulders she had a purple fur-trimmed robe and on her face she wore a smile so cruel it made Kitty's teeth chatter. She stalked over to the bed and lay down. With her gold slippers she felt the bottom of the bed. With her ringed fingers she felt the top and the sides. She stood up and with her scepter she pulled back the spread to see if the pillows were wrinkled. Everything was perfect. The Cruel Queen's face became convulsed with fury. She yelled, "Not a wrinkle! Not a single lump! I am furious! But, never fear, little slaves, my day will come and into the dungeon you will go! Come, my servants, we will go." Mrs. Piggle-Wiggle stalked into the closet.

That was the beginning of Mrs. Piggle-Wiggle's friendship with the children. The next day Mary Lou and Kitty and Kitty's little brother, Bobby, and Bobby's friend, Dicky, went to Mrs. Piggle-Wiggle's for tea, and the next day they came and each brought someone else and pretty soon

every single child in town had been or was going to Mrs. Piggle-Wiggle's house.

She showed Bobby how to sneak out and get the fireplace logs without being caught by the Indians. She showed Dicky how a lawnmower is really a magic machine that mows down the enemy millions and billions at a time. She taught Max how to take out the ashes without making a sound and without leaving a trace to show the train robbers who were on his trail that he and the sheriff had camped there that night.

Mrs. Piggle-Wiggle certainly knew how to make work fun and she also knew that there are certain kinds of work that children love to do even though they do not know how very well. Like painting and ironing and cooking and carpentry.

One day at Mrs. Piggle-Wiggle's there were two little girls baking cookies; one little boy baking a pie and getting flour on the floor and eating most of the dough; a little girl ironing, in a very wrinkly fashion, all of Mrs. Piggle-Wiggle's clean clothes; four boys, with paint on their faces and feathers in their hair, chopping kindling; two boys painting the dog house; three little girls darning old pirate socks of Mr. Piggle-Wiggle's; and pirates, pirates everywhere, digging in the back yard, shooting and yelling, running through the house and grabbing hunks of raw cooky dough.

Mrs. Piggle-Wiggle was sitting over in a corner of the

living room sewing on doll clothes. She was wearing the jewelled crown and Kitty Wheeling was standing beside her throne, which was a chair with a table cloth draped over it, dipping her hairbrush in a glass of water and making Mrs. Piggle-Wiggle's hair into long wet curls.

Kitty said, "Your Highness, shall I use the gold or the silver hairpins?" Mrs. Piggle-Wiggle said, "Oh, let's use the ones with the diamonds in them, hairdresser, they look better with this crown." Just then the telephone rang and it was some mother wanting to know what to do with her little girl who wouldn't take a bath, and that is how Mrs. Piggle-Wiggle got started with her wonderful cures. She told Hubert's mother about the Won't-Pick-Up-Toys Cure; Patsy's mother about the Radish Cure; Allen's mother about the Slow-Eater-Tiny-Bite-Taker Cure; Anne and Joan's mother about the Fighter-Quarrelers Cure; Dick's mother about the Selfish-Boy Cure; Mary's mother about the Answer-Backer Cure; and Bobby and Larry and Susan's mother about the Never-Want-To-Go-To-Bedders Cure.

2

THE WON'T-PICK-UP-TOYS CURE

Hubert was a very lucky little boy whose grandfather always sent him wonderful toys for Christmas. Hubert's mother said that his grandfather sent him these marvelous presents because Hubert was such a dear little boy. His father said that it was to make up for that awful name they had wished on him. Hubert was named for his grandfather. His full name was Hubert Egbert Prentiss.

Hubert liked the presents his grandfather sent him, but who wouldn't? He had an electric train with track that went four times around his bedroom and into the closet and out again and had seven stations and every signal there was and two bridges and a snow shed. He also had a Little-Builder set so large that he could build regular office buildings; and a great big wagon full of stone blocks made into shapes so that he could build big stone bridges for his electric train and stone buildings and even stone barracks for his one thousand and five hundred toy soldiers. Hubert also had a circus with every kind of wooden, jointed animal and clowns and tightrope walkers and trapeze artists. He had a little typewriter, and a real desk and a little radio and two automobiles. He had about a hundred or more airplanes and little cars. He had a fire engine with real sirens and lights and hook and ladders; and so many books that he had to have two bookcases in his room.

Hubert liked all of his toys and he was moderately generous about letting other children play with them, but he never put his things away. When his mother made his bed she had to pick her way around and in and out and over the electric train and track. She had to take circus performers off the bureau and the bed posts. She had to pick up books that had been thrown face down on the floor and she was continually gathering up the Little-Builder set. It used to take her about three hours to do Hubert's room and about one hour to do the rest of her housework.

She would send Hubert up to put his toys away, but all he ever did was to stuff them under the bed or into the closet and in the morning when his mother cleaned his room, there they were for her to pick up.

Mrs. Prentiss was getting a little bored with this.

One rainy Saturday Hubert invited all of his little friends to play up in his room. He had Dicky and Charlie and Billy and Tommy and Bobby. They got out every single toy that Hubert owned and played with them and then, just before dinner, they all went home and left the mess. Hubert's mother didn't know a thing about this until the next morning when she went in to make Hubert's bed. Then she just stood in the doorway and looked. The electric train track went under the bed five times and under the bureau and under the chairs and around the desk and into the closet. All along the track were bridges and buildings of the stone blocks and whole towns built from the Little-Builder set. On the bed and under the bed and on the bureau were the circus tent, the animals, the clowns, the tightrope walkers and the trapeze artists. The floor was littered with books and little automobiles and airplanes and painting sets and chemical sets and woodburning sets and crayons and coloring books and the little typewriter and the printing set and teddy bears and balls and jacks and parchesi games and jigsaw puzzles and soldiers, soldiers, soldiers.

Perspiration broke out on Hubert's mother's forehead and she began to feel faint so she closed the door and slowly went downstairs.

She took two aspirin tablets and then telephoned her

friend, Mrs. Bags. She said, "Hello, Mrs. Bags, this is Hubert's mother and I am so disappointed in Hubert. He has such lovely toys—his grandfather sends them to him every Christmas, you know—but he does not take care of them at all. He just leaves them all over his room for me to pick up every morning."

Mrs. Bags said, "Well, I'm sorry, Mrs. Prentiss, but I can't help you because you see, I think it is too late."

"Why, it's only nine-thirty," said Hubert's mother.

"Oh, I mean late in life," said Mrs. Bags. "You see, we started Ermintrude picking up her toys when she was six months old. 'A place for everything and everything in its place,' we have always told Ermintrude. Now, she is so neat that she becomes hysterical if she sees a crumb on the floor."

"Well, I certainly hope she never sees Hubert's room," said Mrs. Prentiss dryly. "She'd probably have a fit." And she hung up the phone.

Then she called Mrs. Moohead. "Good morning, Mrs. Moohead," she said. "Does Gregory pick up his toys?"

"Well, no, he doesn't," said Mrs. Moohead. "But you know Gregory is rather delicate and I feel that just playing with his toys tires him so much that I personally see that all of his little friends put the toys away before they go home."

"That is a splendid idea," said Hubert's mother, "but I am trying to train Hubert, not his playmates."

"Well, of course, Hubert is very strong and healthy, but Gregory is intelligent," said Mrs. Moohead.

"Is he?" said Mrs. Prentiss crossly, because she resented this inference that her son was all brawn and no brain.

"Oh, dear," squealed Mrs. Moohead, "I think Gregory is running a temperature. I must go to him." She hung up the phone.

Mrs. Prentiss then called Mrs. Grapple. "Hello, Marge," she said. "How's Susan?"

Mrs. Grapple said, "I've spanked her seven times since breakfast and I just heard a crash so she is probably getting ready for another. How's Hubert?"

"That's what I called about," said Mrs. Prentiss. "Can you suggest a way to make Hubert *want* to pick up his toys? His room looks like a toy store after an earthquake."

"Why don't you call this Mrs. Piggle-Wiggle? I have heard she is perfectly wonderful. All the children in town adore her and she has a cure for everything. As soon as I spank Susan, I'm going to call her."

Hubert's mother said, "Thank you very much, Marge. That is just what I'll do. I had forgotten about Mrs. Piggle-Wiggle, but I just know she can help me."

So she called Mrs. Piggle-Wiggle and said, "Mrs. Piggle-Wiggle, I hate to bother you, but you seem always to know what to do about children and I'll confess that I don't know what to do to make Hubert put his toys away."

Mrs. Piggle-Wiggle said, "Hubert is the sweet little boy with all the wonderful toys that his grandfather sends him, isn't he?"

Mrs. Prentiss said, "Why, yes, but I didn't know that you knew him."

"Oh, yes," said Mrs. Piggle-Wiggle. "Hubert and I are old friends. In fact, he is building an automobile in my back yard out of orange crates and empty tomato cans. Hubert is a very good carpenter."

Hubert's mother thought of the two little automobiles with rubber tires, real horns, leather seats big enough for two boys and lights that turned on with a switch, that Hubert's grandfather had given him; and she wondered why in the world he would want to build an automobile out of old orange crates and tomato cans. She said, however, "So that is where he and Dicky go every afternoon. I certainly hope he behaves himself."

"Oh, he does," said Mrs. Piggle-Wiggle. "We are all very fond of Hubert. But this problem of his toys. Let me see." Mrs. Piggle-Wiggle was quiet for some time. Then she said, "I think that the best thing for you to use is my old-fashioned Won't-Pick-Up-Toys cure. Starting now, don't pick up any of Hubert's toys. Don't make his bed. In fact, do not go into his room. When his room becomes so messy he can't get out of it, call me." Mrs. Piggle-Wiggle said goodbye and hung up the phone.

Hubert's mother, looking very relieved, went gaily about her housework, baked a chocolate cake for dinner and did not say a word to Hubert when he came home with ten little boys and they all trailed upstairs to play in Hubert's room.

The next morning when Hubert came downstairs for breakfast his mother noticed that he had a little pan of water-color paint stuck in his hair and his shirt had purple ink from the printing set on one shoulder. She said nothing but tripped upstairs after breakfast and quickly shut the door of his room.

The next morning Hubert's mother had a little trouble shutting the door of his room and she noticed that Hubert had circles under his eyes as though he had not slept very well.

The next morning Hubert was very late coming downstairs and before he opened his door his mother heard a great clatter and scraping as though he were moving furniture. He had Little-Builder bolts stuck to his sweater and two paint pans in his hair. He was so sleepy he could barely keep his eyes open and he had a red mark on one cheek. His mother looked at it closely and saw that it was the shape and size of one of his stone blocks. He must have slept with his head on one of the bridges.

On the seventh day after Hubert's mother stopped putting away his toys, he did not come down to breakfast at all. About eleven o'clock his mother became worried and called up Mrs. Piggle-Wiggle.

She said, "Good-morning, Mrs. Piggle-Wiggle. This is the seventh day of the old fashioned Won't-Pick-Up-Toys cure and I am worried. Hubert has not come downstairs at all this morning."

Mrs. Piggle-Wiggle

Mrs. Piggle-Wiggle said, "Let me see! The seventh day —it usually takes ten days—but Hubert has so many toys he would naturally be quicker."

"Quicker at what?" asked Hubert's mother anxiously.

"Quicker at getting trapped in his room," said Mrs. Piggle-Wiggle. "You see, the reason Hubert hasn't come downstairs is that he cannot get out of his room. Have you noticed anything different about him lately?"

"Well," said Hubert's mother, "he looks as though he hadn't been sleeping well and on the fourth morning he had a red blotch on his cheek just the shape of one of his stone blocks."

"Hmmmmm," said Mrs. Piggle-Wiggle. "He probably can't get at his bed and is sleeping with his head on his blocks for a pillow."

"But what will I do?" asked Hubert's mother. "How will I feed him?"

"Wait until he calls for food, then tell him to open the window and you put a piece of rather dry bread and peanut butter on the garden rake. He will have to drink out of the hose. Tie it to the rake and poke it up to him."

When Hubert's mother hung up the telephone she heard a muffled shouting from the direction of Hubert's room. She hurried upstairs and listened outside the door. Hubert was shouting, "Mother, I'm hungry!"

His mother said, "Go over and open the window, dear. I will send something up to you on the rake."

Mrs. Prentiss took the crusty piece of a very old loaf of bread, spread some peanut butter on it and took it around to the side of the house. Pretty soon Hubert's window was raised about a foot and a hand and arm appeared. His mother stuck the bread on one of the tines of the rake and poked it up at the window. The hand groped around for a while and then found the bread and jerked it off. The window banged shut.

That night when Hubert's father came home his mother told him all about Mrs. Piggle-Wiggle's treatment. Hubert's father said, "Mrs. Piggle-Wiggle sounds all right, but none of this would have happened if Hubert's grandfather hadn't given him so many toys. When I was a boy all I needed to have a good time was a little piece of string and a stick. Why, I—"

Mrs. Prentiss said, "Not that old string-and-stick routine again, John. Anyway now that Hubert has the toys the picture is changed."

Mr. Prentiss hid his face behind the evening paper and said, "Something smells delicious. Is it Irish stew, I hope?"

"Yes, dear," said Hubert's mother worrying about how she was going to serve Irish stew to Hubert on a rake. She finally put a potato on one prong, a carrot on another, an onion on another and pieces of meat on the last three. The window was opened only about three inches but the hand grabbed the food. After dinner Hubert's father tied the hose to the rake and held it up while Hubert put his mouth to the window opening and tried to get a drink of water. It was not very successful but he managed to get a few drops.

Mrs. Prentiss was worried. The next morning she knocked on Hubert's door and said, "Hubert, what are you doing in there?"

Hubert said, "I've got a bear pen made out of bureau drawers and my bed's the mother bear's house and my train runs under my bed thirteen times now."

"Hubert, dear, don't you think you should try and come out soon?" asked his mother.

Hubert said, "I don't wanna come out. I like it in here. All my toys are out and I can play with them any old time I wanna. This is fun."

His mother went downstairs and called Mrs. Piggle-Wiggle. Mrs. Piggle-Wiggle said, "Oh, but he will want to come out. Wait and see."

That afternoon about two o'clock there was music on the street and children's voices laughing and calling and pretty soon, right past Hubert's house, marched Mrs. Piggle-Wiggle and all the children and right behind them came the circus parade. Hubert managed, by putting one foot in a bureau drawer and the other in a freight car of his train, to get up to the window and look out. He waved to Mrs. Piggle-Wiggle and she called, "Hurry, hurry, Hubert! We are going to march all over town and then we are all going to the circus."

Hubert turned around quickly with the idea of getting

to the door and joining the fun, but the freight car went scooting under the bed and the bureau drawer tipped over and hit him smartly on the shins. Hubert began to cry and to try and kick his way to the door. But everything he kicked seemed to hit back. He kicked a building and a big block fell on his toe. He kicked at a Little-Builder office building and it fell over and clouted him on the back of the head. He kicked a book and it hit a lamp which fell and knocked a heavy wooden elephant off the bedpost onto Hubert's shoulder. He could hear the music of the circus parade growing fainter and fainter and so he bawled louder and louder.

Then he heard a tapping at his window. He crawled over and reached out. It was the rake with a note on it. He took the note and opened it. It said:

> The only way you can get out of that trap
> is to put everything away where it belongs.
> If you hurry we will wait for you.
> Your friend,
> Mrs. Piggle-Wiggle

Hubert began by finding the Little-Builder box. He took down an office building and put each piece in its right place. Then he put away the stone blocks, then the train tracks, the circus, the soldiers, the paints, the chemical set, the printing press, the books, the fire engines, the automobiles. He played little games, pretending that he was racing some-

35

one to see who could find the most parts of a game the quickest.

He had to take off the bedclothes and shake them in order to find the soldiers and the circus and then he thought that as long as the bedclothes were off anyway, he might as well make his bed. It was so lumpy when he finished he thought he had left some airplanes in it and took the covers off again and shook them. He made the bed again and this time it was neat and smooth. Hubert was proud.

He was under the desk finding the last piece of the Little-Builder when he heard the music again. He put the piece in the box, put the box in the closet and tore down the stairs and out the front door.

There they came, Mrs. Piggle-Wiggle, all the children and the CIRCUS! Hubert ran out to meet them and nobody said anything about the pan of orange paint stuck in his hair or the word XYPGUN printed on his cheek in purple ink.

Away they went down the street, Hubert carrying the flag and yelling the loudest.

3

THE ANSWER-BACKER CURE

At three o'clock in the after-
noon Mrs. O'Toole put a peanut butter sandwich and a nice
cool glass of milk on the kitchen table for her little girl
when she came home from school. Pretty soon the front door
slammed and in bounced Mary, her red braids switching
like little pony tails. Her mother said, "How was school,
darling?"

Mary said as she gulped her milk and took a large bite of
the sandwich, "Well, this afternoon, Miss Crabtree said,
'Mary O'Toole will stay in at recess and put the paint boxes
away,' and I said"—Mary took another gulp of the milk—

37

" 'You're the teacher here, Miss Crabtree, why don't you put away the paint boxes and let me go out and play?' Everybody in the whole room laughed but mean old Miss Crabtree, and she sent me into the cloak room."

Mary took another large bite and looked up at her mother expectantly to see if she would appreciate how smart she was.

However, her mother said, "That was a very rude thing for you to do, Mary, and I am ashamed of you. When you finish your sandwich and milk you had better go up to your room and stay until dinner. You can concentrate on how rude you were to nice Miss Crabtree."

Mary pulled her mouth down at the corners, squinted up her pretty brown eyes and said, "Why should I?" She kept her mouth pulled down and blinked her eyes rapidly in a most disagreeable way.

Mrs. O'Toole was dumbfounded. Never had her little Mary acted in this horrid way before. She said quietly, "You should because I tell you to, now scat."

Mary walked slowly out of the kitchen switching her skirt and her braids and managing to look impudent even from the back. When she reached the top of the stairs, she called down to her mother, "I'm going because I want to but not because you tell me to," and dashed into her room and banged the door.

That night at dinner, Mary was quite normal but after dinner her daddy said, "Scoot the dishes off the table,

WeeUn. Your mammy's tired," and his dear little WeeUn instead of jumping up and doing what she was told, pulled her mouth down until she looked like a sad Jack-o-Lantern, squinted up her eyes and said, "I'll do it because I want to but not because you tell me to. Anyway, you eat here, why don't you clear the table?" She blinked her eyes rapidly.

Her father looked as though he might be going to give her a spanking, but then he noticed that it was time for the news so instead he went into his study, turned on the radio and lit his pipe.

Mary did clear off the table and she dried the dishes but she kept blinking her eyes and muttering.

The next morning her mother said, "Please hurry with your breakfast, Mary. The children are waiting and you'll make them late for school."

Mary pulled her mouth down and began blinking. She said, "I'm the one that's eating this breakfast, madam!" (She pronounced it "mattam".) Mary's mother sighed and said, "If you only knew how unattractive you look when you talk like that, you would stop right now."

Mary mumbled something into her mush, then grabbed her sweater and slammed out the front door.

Mrs. O'Toole went to the telephone and called her friend Mrs. Ragbag. She said, "Hello, Mrs. Ragbag, have you noticed any change in Calliope lately?"

Mrs. Ragbag said, "Well, no, I can't say I have, Mrs. O'Toole. She seems to be studying hard in school and she eats and sleeps well. Have you noticed anything wrong with her?"

Mrs. O'Toole said, "No, it is not Calliope I'm worried about. It is Mary. Yesterday afternoon she came home from school and she seemed perfectly normal and she looked all right, but she told me how very impudent she had been in school. I punished her, of course. In fact, I sent her to her room to stay until dinner but she was impudent to me. She was rude to her father, too. I just cannot understand it. I thought perhaps all the children were acting this way. She pulls down her mouth, squints up her eyes and blinks. She looks hideous."

Mrs. Ragbag said, "Oh, I am sorry, Mrs. O'Toole, because Mary has always been such a dear little girl. I don't know what to suggest. Why don't you call Mrs. Keystop, you know what a problem her little Chuckie is. She should have some ideas."

Mrs. O'Toole said, "Thank you very much, Mrs. Ragbag, I'll call Mrs. Keystop right now."

So she called Mrs. Keystop but she wasn't at home and the maid, Norah, answered the phone. Norah said, "Sure and Mrs. Keystop ain't home, Mrs. O'Toole, but how is that dearrrrrr little Marrrrrry, the one with the beautiful brrrraids?"

Mrs. O'Toole said, "Oh, Norah, that is just why I called. Mary has suddenly become so impudent. She answers back and she pulls her mouth down and squints up her eyes and blinks. She started yesterday and I'm so upset. I called to ask Mrs. Keystop if she has ever had similar trouble with Chuckie."

Norah said, "Sure and there ain't any trrrouble she hasn't had with that Chuckie. He's so rude he talks back to himself, but I'm thinkin' you'd best call Mrs. Piggle-Wiggle. That little woman has forgotten morrre about children than we'll everrrr know. She even taught Hubert Prentiss to pick up his toys. Now therrrrre's a spoilt child."

Mrs. O'Toole said, "Oh, thank you so much, Norah. I should have thought of Mrs. Piggle-Wiggle in the first place. I'll call her right now."

Mrs. O'Toole called Mrs. Piggle-Wiggle and said, "Oh, Mrs. Piggle-Wiggle, I am so worried about my little girl, Mary."

Mrs. Piggle-Wiggle said, "I know Mary. She has such beautiful red hair and such lovely brown eyes."

Mrs. O'Toole said, "Well, she still has the hair anyway, but her eyes don't look pretty any more. She squints them up, pulls down her mouth and then blinks."

Mrs. Piggle-Wiggle said, "She answers back and is impudent, isn't she?"

Mrs. O'Toole said, "Yes, she is. But how did you know? I do hope that she hasn't been rude to you."

Mrs. Piggle-Wiggle said, "Oh, no, Mary is always very polite to me, but I can recognize the Answer-Backer symptoms. When was she first impudent?"

"Yesterday afternoon right after school. She was rude to dear Miss Crabtree, her teacher, and when I sent her to her room she made this hideous face and said, 'I'll do it because I want to but not because you tell me to!' Mrs. Piggle-Wiggle, she walks in such a way that her braids twitch and even her back looks impudent."

Mrs. Piggle-Wiggle said, "Don't worry so, Mrs. O'Toole. Some of the most charming children I know were once Answer-Backers. Fortunately Mary has only just begun so she can be cured in no time at all. You drop by here after lunch and I will give you Penelope Parrot to keep for a while. Mrs. Garrison has been using Penelope but she has had her for a month now and Garry should be cured by this time. Now, don't worry, Mrs. O'Toole. Penelope is a cure for even the most stubborn cases of Answer-Backish-ness."

Mrs. O'Toole hung up the phone and she felt much better. Right after lunch she went down to Mrs. Piggle-Wiggle's house and got Penelope. Penelope Parrot was a large, cross-looking green bird who blinked rapidly. Mrs. Piggle-Wiggle said, as she handed the cage to Mrs. O'Toole, "Fortunately for you, Penelope will only talk to children."

During the walk home from Mrs. Piggle-Wiggle's house Penelope was quiet in a very cross, blinky-eyed sort of way and when Mrs. O'Toole hung her cage in the kitchen, she hunched down and put her head under her wing. But when

Mary came in from school, Penelope woke up and began preening her feathers. Mary was delighted with Penelope. She said, "Oh, Mother, I've always and always wanted a parrot. Do you think she can talk?"

Mrs. O'Toole said, "She hasn't said a word since I brought her home but I was told that she speaks only to children."

Mary said, "Where did you get her, Mother? Is she for me? May I have her in my room for my very own?"

Her mother said, "I am keeping her for a friend of mine but when you play in your room, you may hang her cage by the window."

Mary brought her milk and cookies over by Penelope's cage and was very surprised when Penelope blinked and said rudely, "Gimme a bite, pig!" Mary broke off a piece of the cookie and poked it through the bars of the cage. Penelope snatched it and said, "Thanks, pig!"

Mary turned to her mother. "She's certainly not very polite, is she?"

Her mother said, "Perhaps she has been around rude people. After all she is only a parrot and repeats what she hears."

Penelope blinked her eyes and said, "Oh, yeah? Oh yeah? Oh yeah?" Mrs. O'Toole looked a little shocked but Mary laughed and said, "May I bring the children in to see her, Mother. May I?"

Before Mrs. O'Toole could answer, Penelope began hopping up and down, blinking and yelling, "Say are you the boss around here? Are you the boss around here? Are you the boss around here?"

Mary's mother said, "I am the boss around here, Penelope, and if you are not more courteous, I'll put a cloth over your cage."

Penelope blinked and muttered.

Mary bounced up and down excitedly. "What will that do, Mother? What will that do to Penelope?"

Mrs. O'Toole said, "If I put a cloth over her cage, she will think that it is night and go to sleep."

Penelope squawked, "I'll do it because I want to but not because you tell me to!"

Mary was certainly surprised at that because she thought that she had made up that brilliant remark. She didn't dare to look at her mother so she put on her sweater and went out to find her playmates.

Pretty soon she came back with five little friends and they spent the afternoon standing around Penelope's cage and laughing at her rude remarks.

This worried Mrs. O'Toole. If Mary thought Penelope was so amusing then perhaps she would imitate her and become ruder than ever. So she called Mrs. Piggle-Wiggle. She said in a low voice so the children in the kitchen could not hear, "Mrs. Piggle-Wiggle, I am rather worried because although Penelope is very rude to the children, they don't mind at all. Mary thinks she is very funny and laughs at everything she says."

Mrs. Piggle-Wiggle said, "Just remember, Mrs. O'Toole, that this is only the first day with Penelope. Let Mary be with her as much as she wishes. Keep Penelope's cage in the breakfast nook when Mary eats her lunch and breakfast and in the dining room at night. Hang her cage in Mary's bedroom when she goes up there to play and have Penelope sleep in Mary's room. I am sure that you do not have to worry. Penelope has never failed me."

Mrs. O'Toole said, "All right, Mrs. Piggle-Wiggle. I'll do just as you say. Goodbye!"

Just before dinner Mrs. O'Toole said to Mary, "Mary, dear, send your little friends home now. It is time for you to set the table." Mary turned to her mother and began pulling down her mouth, squinting her eyes and blinking but before she could say a word, Penelope yelled out, "Say who's the boss around here? Who's the boss around here? Who's the boss, anyway?"

Mary's mother quickly put a cloth over her cage, politely asked the children to leave and sent Mary in to set the table.

When Mr. O'Toole came home from the office, she took the cover off again to show him the parrot and then she hung Penelope in the dining-room window. After dinner Mary's daddy said, "Up on your toes, Miss Molly O'Toole, and scoot the dishes out to the kitchen."

Mary pulled down her mouth, squinted up her eyes,

blinked her eyes but Penelope said, "What am I, a servant? Work! Work! Work! What am I, a servant? Say who's the boss around here?"

Mary's daddy laughed so hard the tears ran down his cheeks, but Mary stuck out her tongue at Penelope who bounced around yelling, "Only snakes stick out their tongues! Only snakes stick out their tongues!"

Mary pulled her tongue in quickly and shut her lips together tight. My, but she thought Penelope was horrid!

Mrs. O'Toole hung Penelope's cage in Mary's room and Penelope squawked and made so much noise that Mary finally said, "Oh, be quiet!" And Penelope blinked and said, "I'll do it because I want to but not because you tell me to. I'll do it because I want to but not because you tell me to."

Mary flounced into bed and turned off the light.

The next morning Mary was very slow. She could not find one of her socks and she couldn't button her dress and finally her mother called, "Mary, hurry, dear, breakfast is waiting!"

Mary pulled down her mouth and squinted up her eyes and said, "Oh, hurry, hurry, hurry. Hurry yourself!"

Penelope had been preening her tailfeathers but when she heard Mary she jerked her head up and said, "Oh, hurry, hurry, hurry. Hurry yourself, slowpoke. Hurry yourself, slowpoke. Hurry slowpoke! Hurry slowpoke! Hurry slowpoke! Hurry, hurry, hurry, hurry!"

Mary said crossly, "Oh, be quiet, Penelope!"

Penelope said, "I'll do it because I want to but not because you tell me to. Say, who's the boss around here? Oh, yeah? Oh yeah? Oh yeah?"

Mary ran downstairs and sat down to breakfast leaving Penelope still shouting, but Mrs. O'Toole ran upstairs and got Penelope and hung her cage by the kitchen window.

When the children called for Mary and Mrs. O'Toole said, "Hurry, dear, you will make your friends late for school," Mary pulled down her mouth and squinted up her eyes and blinked but before she could say a word, Penelope squawked, "I'm the one who's eating this breakfast, mattam! Hurry, hurry, hurry, that's all I hear. Hurry yourself, slow-poke!"

Mary was ashamed to look at her mother, so she rushed off without kissing her goodbye. Penelope yelled after her, "Hurry slowpoke. Bell's ringing! Bell's ringing!"

When Mary came home from school that afternoon she kissed her mother and said, "Mother, I apologized to Miss Crabtree, today, and she said that next week I may be monitor for the scissors."

Penelope yelled, "Who said so? Who said so? Who said so? Who's the boss? Who's the boss?"

Mary turned to Penelope and said, "You are a very rude bird. If you don't hush right now I will put the cloth over your cage."

Penelope blinked and said, "Hush, hush, hush! That's all I hear. I'll do it because I want to but not because you tell

49

me to. I'll do it because I want to but not because you tell me to. Who's the boss around here, anyway?"

Mary's mother said, "I am the boss and I think it is time you went home, Penelope. Mary would you like to return Penelope to Mrs. Piggle-Wiggle?"

Mary said, "Oh, yes, Mother. And may I stay and play?"

Mrs. O'Toole said, "I think you had better come home and practise. Your music lesson is tomorrow, you know."

Mary started to draw down her mouth, squint up her eyes and blink but suddenly she looked at Penelope and so she turned up her mouth, opened her eyes and smiled. She said, "All right, Mother. I'll come right home *after* I return that rude Penelope."

4

THE SELFISHNESS CURE

Dick Thompson was certainly a nice-looking boy and he was smart in school and behaved well at the table BUT whenever his name was mentioned, people said, "Poor, poor, Mrs. Thompson. She has such a problem. Whatever will she do with that child?"

I guess that you would feel simply dreadful if people said a thing like that when your name was mentioned, but Dick didn't. You see, Dick Thompson was a selfish, greedy boy and he cared more about being a selfish, greedy boy than about what people said.

When children came over to his house to play, Dick said,

"Don't touch that, that's MINE! You can't play with that, that's MINE! Put down MY ball. Take off MY skates!"

Each time this happened—at least each time it happened where his mother could hear Dick saying, "That's MINE!" —she would send him up to his room to think about how selfish he was. Dick would go right upstairs for he was very obedient, but instead of thinking how bad it was to be selfish he would sit on the bed and swing his legs and think, "Everything in this room is MINE and nobody is going to touch MY things!"

He certainly was a problem.

One day Dick's mother bought a big box of peppermint sticks. She called Dick into the house and said, "Now, dear, I have bought this large box of peppermint sticks for you, but I want you to share them with your friends. There are about fifty sticks in the box and I want you to divide them with all the children in the neighborhood. Don't forget the *little* children, Dick, and you might send one or two to Old Mrs. Burry, she is so fond of peppermint."

Dick said, "Thank you, Mother, for the fine candy." Then he took the box out of doors and put it in the basket on the front of his bicycle and allowed the neighborhood children to look at the peppermint sticks, but he warned them, "This is MY candy and if anyone touches it I will hit him with MY baseball bat!"

The children in his neighborhood had known Dick for some time and they knew that he meant what he said, but as they looked at the candy they wished and wished they could have just one stick. Dick's mother, watching from the window, saw all the children gathered around Dick and the box of candy in the basket on the front of his bicycle and she thought to herself, "Just look at my little Dick. Dividing the candy with all of his little friends. I just knew he would learn to be generous," and she tapped on the window and when Dick looked around she waved and smiled at him.

Dick waved and smiled back, but unfortunately just then Mary O'Toole, who was quite daring, reached in and grabbed a stick of the candy and CRACK! Dick clouted her on the hand with the baseball bat. In a flash his mother saw what was really going on. She flew out the front door, took Dick firmly by the arm and marched him upstairs, thrust him into his room and slammed the door. Then she went downstairs and out the front door, took the box of candy and told Mary O'Toole to divide it up among all the children, even the little ones and to take one or two sticks over to old Mrs. Burry because she was so fond of peppermint.

There were fifteen children, not counting Dick, and fifty sticks of candy so each child was given three sticks and old Mrs. Burry got five.

From the window of his bedroom, Dick watched Mary divide the candy and he was just furious.

After all the candy had been divided, Mrs. Thompson went into the house and called Dick's father. She said,

"Herbert, I know that you are busy and you don't like to have me call you at the office, but I'm so worried about Dick."

Dick's father said, "What is the matter? Is he sick?"

Dick's mother said, "No, but I just wish he were. It would be so much simpler."

Mr. Thompson said, "Now, dear, I am very busy so perhaps you had better wait until I come home."

Mrs. Thompson said, "Herbert, this cannot wait another minute," and she told him about the candy and the baseball bat.

Mr. Thompson said, "Why not give him a good hard spanking? Tell him that you are going to give him something that he can keep all to himself. Ha, ha!"

"Now, Herbert, this is not a laughing matter and I don't think a spanking will solve a thing. I just don't know what to do or which way to turn," and Mrs. Thompson began to cry, partly because she felt so humiliated over Dick's selfishness and partly because she knew that crying was one way to get action out of Dick's father.

Dick's father said, "Now, now, dear, tears won't help. Let me see—shall I hop into a taxi and come home and thrash Dick?"

Dick's mother only cried louder.

Dick's father said, "I know. I know just what to do. Call that Mrs. Wriggle-Spiggle or whatever her name is. You know, the one who cured Hubert Prentiss."

"You mean Mrs. Piggle-Wiggle. Oh, Herbert, you are so wonderful! I knew you would think of something. I'll call her right away," and Mrs. Thompson blew her nose and cheered right up.

Mothers always do cheer up when they think of Mrs. Piggle-Wiggle because she knows so much about children. After all, she has had about a thousand little boys and girls come to her house to pull taffy, play checkers, bake cookies, drink cambric tea and dig for the pirate gold buried in her back yard, and so she has had plenty of opportunity to learn about childish ailments and the cures for them. She was certainly the person to ask about Dick, the selfish boy, and so Mrs. Thompson telephoned her. She said, "Hello, Mrs. Piggle-Wiggle, this is Mrs. Thompson, Dick's mother."

Mrs. Piggle-Wiggle said, "Hello, Mrs. Thompson, I have rather expected you to call."

Mrs. Thompson said, "You have? Why?"

"Because I know Dick very well," said Mrs. Piggle-Wiggle, "and although he is a dear little boy and the most well-mannered child who comes to visit me, never once forgetting to say Thank you and Please, he is very selfish."

"Oh, I know he is. I know he is," said Mrs. Thompson almost crying because she was so ashamed that Mrs. Piggle-Wiggle should know how selfish Dick was.

Mrs. Piggle-Wiggle said, "Now, Mrs. Thompson, do not feel sad. Selfishness and greediness are just diseases like

55

measles and chickenpox and can be cured very easily but we must start now, before another day passes, because Dick is such a nice little boy and we want everyone to like him as we do."

"Oh, do you like him, in spite of his selfishness?" asked Dick's mother.

"Of course, I do," said Mrs. Piggle-Wiggle. "I love all children but it distresses me when I see a child who has a disease like Selfishness or Answerbackism or Won't-Put-Away-Toys-itis and his parents don't do a thing to cure him."

"But I want to cure Dick," said his mother. "I will do anything to cure him."

Mrs. Piggle-Wiggle said, "The Selfishness Cure is really very simple, but the rules must be followed very strictly. You will have to come down here and get my Selfishness Kit and at the same time I will give you the directions for its use."

"Thank you so much, dear Mrs. Piggle-Wiggle," said Mrs. Thompson. "I will leave right now," and she hung up the phone, slipped on a jacket and ran all of the way to Mrs. Piggle-Wiggle's house.

When she arrived Mrs. Piggle-Wiggle was on the front porch waiting for her. On the porch beside her was quite a large green metal box with SELFISHNESS KIT painted on its side in white letters. Mrs. Piggle-Wiggle invited Dick's mother to sit down and then she opened the kit.

Inside were about twenty-five padlocks of various sizes. There were great big ones about the size of apples, down to little tiny ones not much larger than a penny. Also there were screws and a screw driver; a box of cloth labels that said DICK; a box of blank gummed labels; a small can of white paint; a small can of black paint; a small paint brush; and a pastry bag—this is a large bag with a nozzle on the end which, when filled with frosting, can be squeezed and the frosting comes out the end like toothpaste and can be formed into words.

Mrs. Piggle-Wiggle said, "Mrs. Thompson, these padlocks are for Dick's drawers, his closets, his toy chest, his bicycle, his bedroom door, his night-stand drawer and his toothbrush. As soon as you get home put the padlocks on everything he owns and give him the keys. This is to assure him that HE and HE ALONE can touch HIS things. The name labels are to be sewn in all of his clothes and the gummed stickers are to be put in all of his books—even his school books—notebooks, pencil boxes, and are to be pasted on his ruler, crayons and paints. On each sticker print in large letters with this black paint DICK'S BOOK—DON'T TOUCH! DICK'S NOTEBOOK—DON'T TOUCH! and so forth.

"On every toy he owns you must paint in either black or white paint, DICK'S BALL—DON'T TOUCH! or DICK'S BAT—DON'T TOUCH. Put the name of the toy first and then Don't Touch.

"The pastry bag is to be filled with a simple white frosting and used to mark Dick's sandwiches, his fruit, his cookies and his plate for each meal.

"That's all there is to it. I expect you will be returning the Selfishness Kit before a week has passed."

Mrs. Thompson said, "I do hope so, Mrs. Piggle-Wiggle. Are you sure it will work?"

"It has cured hundreds of other children and I see no reason why it should not cure Dick. A week or even less, I should say."

Mrs. Thompson thanked Mrs. Piggle-Wiggle very much and then, lugging the kit, she walked home. As soon as she had hung up her jacket she began sewing the labels in all of Dick's clothes. He asked her what she was doing and when she showed him he was as happy as could be. "Boy, that will just show people who owns MY clothes," he said proudly.

Mrs. Thompson did not answer but continued to put the labels on every single stitch of his clothing including his socks and his handkerchiefs. Then she opened the kit and took out the tiniest padlock. She fastened Dick's toothbrush to the toothbrush rack with the little padlock, snapped it shut and handed the key, which was not much bigger than a pin, to Dick. "You had better find a ring to hold your keys," she said. "You are going to have about twenty-five of them."

"Boy, that's just wonderful!" Dick said fondling the tiny

key and thinking, "That's MY toothbrush, and now nobody but ME can touch it." He was very happy.

When dinnertime came Mrs. Thompson closed the Selfishness Kit and took it downstairs to show Dick's father. She told him about Mrs. Piggle-Wiggle and he patted her on the back and said that he was sure everything was going to be all right and where was the evening paper.

After dinner they went upstairs to put some of the padlocks on and were surprised to find that Dick, himself, had already put the locks on each of his bureau drawers, his night-stand drawer, his toy box, his closet door and his bedroom door. He had also put stickers on the covers of all of his books, notebooks, coloring books, crayon and colored-pencil boxes, and stamp album. On the stickers he had printed in black paint DICK'S BOOK—DON'T TOUCH! DICK'S NOTEBOOK—DON'T TOUCH! DICK'S CRAYONS—DON'T TOUCH! DICK'S PENCIL BOX—DON'T TOUCH! DICK'S STAMP ALBUM—DON'T TOUCH! He was very proud and asked his father if he didn't think he printed well.

His father said, "You should be able to print well, you have certainly practised enough," and he looked disgustedly around the room at the stickers which labeled everything— DICK'S BRUSH—DON'T TOUCH! DICK'S COMB —DON'T TOUCH! DICK'S WINDOW BLIND— DON'T TOUCH!

He turned to Dick's mother and said, "Perhaps we should

wear stickers, DICK'S MOTHER—DON'T TOUCH! DICK'S FATHER—DON'T TOUCH! I'll bet he'll wear monogrammed underwear when he grows up."

Mrs. Thompson said, "Oh, I hope not, Herbert."

Dick said, "Come on, Mom and Dad, let's mark all the rest of my stuff."

And so they worked until 8:30, marking Dick's bicycle, his baseball, his bat, his pitcher's glove, his catcher's glove, his tool box, his roller skates, his lunchbox, his rubber boots, his raincoat, his Indian suit, his soldier suit, his gun, and his wagon. They even painted DICK'S DOG—DON'T TOUCH! on Rover's collar.

When they had finished and it was time for Dick to go to bed, he kissed his mother and said goodnight to his father and went happily up the stairs, his ring of keys jingling from his belt.

Mr. Thompson sank down into a chair in the living room and lit his pipe. "I trust that Mrs. Piggle-Wiggle knows what she is doing," he said, "because if this cure should not work, our son, Dick, is going to be the most loathsome boy in the whole world."

Mrs. Thompson said, "Oh, no, dear, not in the whole world!"

The next morning they heard Dick clicking and snapping at his padlocks long before they were up. He was a little late coming downstairs because it took time to padlock all of his drawers, his closet door and the door of his room, but he was very happy and his mother noticed that he had pinned one of the name labels on the outside of his sweater. While he was eating his breakfast marked DICK'S BREAKFAST—DON'T TOUCH, his mother marked his sandwiches DICK'S SANDWICHES—DON'T TOUCH, and his apple DICK'S APPLE—DON'T TOUCH! and his cookies DICK'S COOKIES—DON'T TOUCH! His lunchbox had already been marked DICK'S LUNCHBOX—DON'T TOUCH!

After breakfast Dick put the lunchbox in the basket on his bicycle and noticed proudly the large sign hanging from the crossbar, DICK'S BICYCLE—DON'T TOUCH!

At school the children paid little attention to the sign on his bicycle but when he opened his lunchbox and took out the sandwiches marked DICK'S SANDWICHES—DON'T TOUCH! and the apple marked DICK'S APPLE—DON'T TOUCH and the cookies marked DICK'S COOKIES—DON'T TOUCH! everyone laughed and wanted to see them and in the resulting crowding and pushing one of the sandwiches was dropped and stepped on and some of the big boys grabbed the apple and tossed it in the air just above Dick's head shouting, "Throw me DICK'S APPLE. Oh, look, I dropped DICK'S APPLE! I wonder if DICK'S APPLE will bounce." When they finally gave Dick his apple it was bruised and very dirty.

In arithmetic period that afternoon, Bobby Slater across the aisle asked Dick for his ruler and when he saw the label

DICK'S RULER—DON'T TOUCH! he began to laugh and reached over and snatched the ruler off Dick's desk and passed it to Kenny Hatch who laughed and passed it to the girl in front of him and finally Miss Crabtree had to come down and get it. When she saw the sign she laughed, too, but she gave the ruler back to Dick.

After school the boys decided to play baseball in the vacant lot by Dick's house but when Dick brought out his bat and ball and mitts and the boys saw DICK'S BALL—DON'T TOUCH! DICK'S BAT—DON'T TOUCH! they said, "We can't touch anything so let's go home," and they did.

Dick went up to his room to play but he found that somewhere during the day he had lost the key to his closet and that he had locked the key to his toy chest in the chest so he went down and sat on the front porch and listened to the shouts of the children playing in Hubert Prentiss' yard.

The next morning at school during recess nobody would play with him and the little girls followed him and laughed. When they marched into school the children pointed and laughed and laughed and Miss Crabtree came down to see what the trouble was and she almost laughed herself when she saw the sign someone had pinned on the back of Dick's sweater. It said "THIS IS DICK—DON'T TOUCH!"

At lunch time the children crowded around to watch him take out his sandwiches and one little girl said, "He's so

selfish and greedy he has his sandwiches marked so he can't share them." Then the children danced around him and chanted, "Dick's sandwich—Don't touch! Dick's apple—Don't touch! Dick's lunchbox—Don't touch!" Finally Dick took his lunchbox out and put it in the basket on his bicycle but the children followed him and seeing the big sign DICK'S BICYCLE—DON'T TOUCH! they yelled and laughed and sang, "Dick's—don't touch! Don't touch Dick! Dick's—don't touch! Don't touch Dick!"

After school Dick hurried right home, but he had lost the key to his room so he went down to the basement to play with his tool box but every time he saw the large white sign DICK'S TOOLBOX—DON'T TOUCH! he thought of school and the lunchbox and he remembered how the children laughed and jeered and he was ashamed. At dinner when his mother brought him his plate marked DICK'S DINNER—DON'T TOUCH! he said, "Aw, why do you hafta mark my plate? I don't care which one I get."

Mrs. Thompson looked significantly at Mr. Thompson and said, "All right, Dick, we won't mark your plate if you will share your dessert with Rover."

Dick thought for a few minutes and then he carefully broke his chocolate cake into two equal pieces and gave one to Rover who gulped it down and looked grateful.

After dinner Dick told his father he had lost the keys to his room and the closet and so his father took off the padlocks on those doors and on the toybox. Dick said, "Don't put them back, Dad, I don't care who goes into my room or gets into my stuff."

The next morning Dick got up early and scraped the DICK'S LUNCHBOX—DON'T TOUCH! from his lunchbox and took the sign off his bicycle. Then he went in to his mother and said, "Mom, please don't mark my sandwiches. Please, don't mark any of my stuff, Mom." Mrs. Thompson said, "All right, Dick, I only did it to protect you."

Dick said, "I don't care who gets my lunch. Just don't mark it."

At noon all the children gathered around Dick but neither his sandwiches, nor his apple, nor his lunchbox were marked so they rushed out to see his bicycle but there was no sign on it, so they sat down and ate their lunches.

Right after school that night Dick hurried home and scraped the marking off his ball and bat and mitts and then he walked up to where the children were playing ball and tossing the ball, bat and mitts down beside the catcher he said, "Do you want to use these? I don't care," and he went back to his own house.

In a little while Mary O'Toole rang the doorbell and asked Mrs. Thompson if Dick could come out and play. Mrs. Thompson said, "He'd love to, Mary, but first he must return something to Mrs. Piggle-Wiggle."

Mary said, "Tell him to come over to the lot when he gets back and here are some keys he lost."

Mrs. Thompson said, "Thank you for the keys, dear, but thank goodness they belong to Mrs. Piggle-Wiggle, not to Dick."

She took the keys of the big padlocks and the tiny padlock up to Dick who was in his room, busily packing Mrs. Piggle-Wiggle's Selfishness Kit.

5

THE RADISH CURE

U<small>p</small> to the time of this story
Patsy was just an everyday little girl. Sometimes she was
good and sometimes she was naughty but usually she did
what her mother told her without too much fuss. BUT ONE
MORNING Patsy's mother filled the bathtub with nice
warm water and called to Patsy to come and take her bath.
Patsy came into the bathroom but when she saw the nice
warm tub of water she began to scream and yell and kick and
howl like a wild animal.

Naturally her mother was quite surprised to see her little
girl acting so peculiarly but she didn't say anything, just

68

took off Patsy's bathrobe and said, "Now, Patsy, stop all this nonsense and hop into the tub."

Patsy gave a piercing shriek and ran from the bathroom stark naked and yelling, "I won't take a bath! I won't ever take a bath! I hate baths! I HATE BATHS! I haaaaaaaaaaaaaaaaate baaaaaaaaaaaaths!"

Patsy's mother let the water out of the tub and went downstairs to telephone her friends and find out if their children had ever behaved in this unusual fashion; if it was catching and what to do about it.

First she called Mrs. Brown. She said, "Hello, Mrs. Brown. This is Patsy's mother and I am having such a time this morning. Patsy simply will not take a bath. Pardon me, just a minute, Mrs. Brown."

She put down the telephone receiver and went over to Patsy who was standing in the kitchen doorway listening to the telephone conversation and feeling very important.

Patsy said, "What did Mrs. Brown say to do with me, Mother?"

Patsy's mother said, "She hasn't told me yet but while I am finding out you had better march right upstairs and get dressed and then you can pick up that messy, sticky pasting work you left all over your room last night. Don't come downstairs until every single thing is put away."

Patsy's mother picked up the telephone and Mrs. Brown said, "I'm sorry but I can't offer any suggestions because our little Prunella just adores to bathe. Perhaps Mrs. Grotto could help you."

So Patsy's mother called Mrs. Grotto. She said, "Hello, Mrs. Grotto, I just called to ask if you could help me with Patsy. She won't take a bath and I am at my wits' end."

Mrs. Grotto said, "Well, frankly, I don't know what to suggest because our little Paraphernalia simply worships her bath. Of course, Paraphernalia is quite a remarkable child anyway. Why, Thursday afternoon she said. . . ."

"Yes, yes, I know," said Patsy's mother quickly. "Goodbye, Mrs. Grotto, thank you anyway."

Then Patsy's mother called Mrs. Broomrack. "Good morning, Mrs. Broomrack," she said a little too brightly. "I wonder if you would do me a favor?"

"Why, of course, dear, of course!" said Mrs. Broomrack.

"Well," said Patsy's mother, "this morning for the first time in her life, our little Patsy won't take a bath. The very idea seems to make her hysterical and I don't know what to do."

Mrs. Broomrack said, "Why, you poor dear, all alone in that big house with that unmanageable child. Personally, I don't know what to say because our little Cormorant looks forward so to taking a bath. Bathing is his favorite pastime. In fact, sometimes we can't get him out of the tub."

"Why don't you let him stay in, then?" said Patsy's mother.

"Because he might drown!" squealed Mrs. Broomrack.

"Well . . ." said Patsy's mother, as she hung up the phone.

By this time she was feeling rather depressed because it seemed that bathing was the most popular indoor sport with every child in town but her own dirty little girl.

In desperation she decided to call Mrs. Piggle-Wiggle. "She should know about children," thought Patsy's mother. "She certainly has her house crawling with them, day and night."

It certainly was fortunate for Patsy's mother that she thought of Mrs. Piggle-Wiggle, because although Mrs. Piggle-Wiggle has no children of her own and lives in an upside-down house, she understands children better than anybody in the whole world. She is always ready to stop whatever she is doing and have a tea party. She is glad to have children dig worms in her petunia bed. She has a large trunk full of scraps for doll clothes and another trunk full of valuable rocks with gold in them. She is delighted to have children pick up and look at all the little things which she keeps on her tables and when Hubert Prentiss dropped the glass ball that snowed on the children when you shook it, she said, "Heavens, Hubert, don't cry. I'm so glad this happened. For years and years I have wanted to know what was in that glass ball." Mrs. Piggle-Wiggle takes it for granted that you will want to try on her shoes and go wiggling around on high heels.

Which is probably why she was not at all surprised when

Patsy's mother told her about the bath. "I suppose we all come to it sooner or later," she said. "Well, from my experience I would say that the Radish Cure is probably the quickest and most lasting."

"The radish cure?" said Patsy's mother.

"Yes," said Mrs. Piggle-Wiggle. "The Radish Cure is just what Patsy needs. All you have to do is buy one package of radish seeds. The small red round ones are the best, and don't get that long white icicle type. Then, let Patsy strictly alone, as far as washing is concerned, for several weeks. When she has about half an inch of rich black dirt all over her and after she is asleep at night, scatter radish seeds on her arms and head. Press them in gently and then just wait. I don't think you will have to water them because we are in the rainy season now and she probably will go outdoors now and then. When the little radish plants have three leaves you may begin pulling the largest ones."

"Oh, yes, Patsy will probably look quite horrible before the Radish Cure is over, so if you find that she is scaring too many people or her father objects to having her around, let me know and I will be glad to take her over here. You see, all of my visitors are children and dirt doesn't frighten them."

Patsy's mother thanked Mrs. Piggle-Wiggle very, very much for her kind advice and then called up Patsy's father and told him to be sure and bring home a package of radish seeds. Early Red Globe, she thought they were called.

The next morning she didn't say one single word to Patsy about a bath and so Patsy was sweet and didn't act like a wild animal. The next day was the same and so was the next and the next.

When Sunday came Patsy was a rather dark blackish gray color so her mother suggested that she stay home from Sunday School.

Patsy's father, who by this time had been told of the Radish Cure, didn't say anything to Patsy about washing but he winced whenever he looked at her.

By the end of the third week they had to keep Patsy indoors all of the time because one morning she skipped out to get the mail and the postman, on seeing her straggly, uncombed, dust-caked hair and the rapidly forming layer of topsoil on her face, neck and arms, gave a terrified yell and fell down the front steps.

Patsy seemed quite happy though. Of course, it was getting hard to tell how she felt as her face was so caked with dirt that she couldn't smile and she talked "oike is—I am Atsy and I on't ake a ath." She also had to take little teeny bites of food because she couldn't open her mouth more than a crack.

Naturally her father and mother had to stop having any friends in to visit except in the evening when Patsy was in bed and even then they were not at all comfortable for fear Patsy would wake up and call, "Ing e a ink of ater, Addy!" (Really, "Bring me a drink of water, Daddy.")

At last, however, the day came when Patsy was ready to plant. That night when she was asleep her mother and father tiptoed into her room and very gently pressed radish seeds into her forehead, her arms and the backs of her hands. When they had finished and were standing by her bed gazing fondly at their handiwork, Patsy's father said, "Repulsive little thing, isn't she?"

Patsy's mother said, "Why, George, that's a terrible thing to say of your own child!"

"My little girl is buried so deep in that dirt that I can't even remember what she looks like," said Patsy's father and he stamped down the stairs.

The Radish Cure is certainly hard on the parents.

Quite a few days after that Patsy awoke one morning and there on the back of her hand, in fact on the backs of both hands and on her arms and on her FOREHEAD were GREEN LEAVES! Patsy tried to brush them off but they just bent over and sprang right up again.

She jumped out of bed and ran down the stairs to the dining room where her mother and father were eating breakfast. "Ook, ook, at y ands!" she squeaked.

Her father said, "Behold the bloom of youth," and her mother said, "George!" then jumped up briskly, went over to Patsy, took a firm hold of one of the plants on her forehead and gave it a quick jerk. Patsy squealed and her mother showed her the little red radish she had pulled. Patsy tried to pull one out of her arm, but her hands were so caked with

76

dirt that they couldn't grasp the little leaves so her mother had to pull them.

When they had finished one hand and part of the left arm, Patsy suddenly said, "Other, I ant a ath!"

"What did you say?" asked her mother, busily pulling the radishes and putting them in neat little piles on the dining room table.

"I oo want a b . . b . . . ath!" said Patsy so plainly that it cracked the mud on her left cheek.

Patsy's mother said, "I think it had better be a shower," and without another word she went in and turned on the warm water.

Patsy was in the shower all that day—she used up two whole bars of soap and she didn't even come out for lunch but when her father came home for dinner, there she was, waiting for him at the door; clean, sweet and smiling, and in her hand she had a plate of little red radishes.

6

THE NEVER-WANT-TO-GO-TO-BEDDERS CURE

Each evening as the clock struck eight, Mrs. Gray called Bobby and Larry and Susan. She said, "Come, children, eight o'clock and time for bed." She tried to make her voice sound cheerful and gay but actually she felt like groaning, because she knew what was coming.

First Susan, "Oh, we don't want to go to bed now. Please let us stay up a little while longer. Pleeeeeeeeeeese, Mother. Pleeeeeeeeeeeeese!"

Then Bobby, "We are the ooooooooooonly ones in our whooooooooooole neighborhood who have to go to bed at eight o'clock!"

Then Larry. "Mother, nobody, not anybody at aaaaaaaa-aall goes to bed at eight o'clock."

Then Susan again, "But, Mother, we have ooooooooonly just staaaaaaarted this game."

Then Bobby, "Pleeeeeeeeese let us finish this game. *Pleeeeeese!*"

Then Larry, "Just one more turn, Mother. It's my turn, Mother, and I haven't won a game this evening—pleeeeee-eeeeeese!"

Mrs. Gray said, "Now, Bobby, Larry and Susan, you know that if you want to grow up into fine young men and women you must have plenty of sleep. I'm sure they teach you that in school."

"We don't wanna grow up, we just wanna finish this game," Bobby wailed.

And so night after night poor Mrs. Gray argued and pled, and begged her children to go to bed and by the time they had finished whining and complaining it was usually almost nine o'clock. Mrs. Gray was desperate.

Finally one day she called her friend, Mrs. Grassfeather. She said, "Hello, Mrs. Grassfeather, this is Mrs. Gray, and I would like to find out what time Catherine and Wilfred go to bed."

Mrs. Grassfeather said, "Why at eight o'clock, Mrs. Gray, unless their Uncle Jasper comes for dinner and then I usually let them stay up until nine-thirty to hear Uncle Jasper tell about his experiences in the Boer War. That, of course, is strictly Mr. Grassfeather's idea. He not only allows the children to stay up until nine-thirty but he pays them as well for listening to Uncle Jasper while he goes to bed."

Mrs. Gray said, "Do the children like to go to bed at eight o'clock?"

Mrs. Grassfeather said, "Oh, they are very good about it because they know that if they whine and complain I will not let them stay up the next time Uncle Jasper comes over, which is about four nights a week."

As the Grays had no Uncle Jasper, Mrs. Gray realized that Mrs. Grassfeather could be of no help, so she said goodbye and hung up the phone.

Then she called Mrs. Gardenfield. "Hello, Mrs. Gardenfield, this is Mrs. Gray and I called to see what time Worthington and Guinevere go to bed at night."

Mrs. Gardenfield said, "Oh, they go to bed any time after Daddy comes home. You see, Mrs. Gray, Mr. Gardenfield gets home at four-thirty, we have dinner at five-thirty, and the children, Mr. Gardenfield and I all go to bed at six-thirty."

"Six-thirty!" said Mrs. Gray, amazed. "My goodness, that *is* early!"

Mrs. Gardenfield said, "It is not early if you get up at four-thirty."

Mrs. Gray said, "But who wants to get up at four-thirty?"

"We do," said Mrs. Gardenfield and hung up the phone in a huff.

So Mrs. Gray thought and thought and suddenly she remembered that only yesterday Dick Thompson's mother had been telling her about a wonderful little woman named Mrs. Piggle-Wiggle and so, even though she had never seen Mrs. Piggle-Wiggle, she decided to call her on the telephone and ask her to help with her Never-Want-To-Go-To-Bedders.

She said to Mrs. Piggle-Wiggle, "I am Mrs. Gray, the mother of Bobby, Larry and Susan."

Mrs. Piggle-Wiggle said, "Oh, yes, of course. How are the children? I have not seen them since they returned from camp."

Mrs. Gray said, "Mrs. Piggle-Wiggle, Bobby and Larry and Susan are very well and very cooperative until about eight o'clock at night and then they turn into whiny, complaining little non-cooperators."

Mrs. Piggle-Wiggle said, "Oh, yes, I see. They are Never-Want-To-Go-To-Bedders, aren't they?"

Mrs. Gray said, "How on earth did you know?"

Mrs. Piggle-Wiggle laughed and said "Oh that is one of the commonest of the children's ailments. The moment you said they were good until eight o'clock I knew what the trouble was."

Mrs. Gray said, "Do you know anything to do for them? How to cure this hateful disease?"

Mrs. Piggle-Wiggle said "Oh that's very simple. Beginning tonight, don't tell them to go to bed. Let them stay up as late as they want to. You and Mr. Gray go on to bed any time you are tired but leave the children downstairs."

Mrs. Gray said "But their health? That will ruin their health!"

Mrs. Piggle-Wiggle said "Oh I do not believe that a day or so without sleep will harm them and it will certainly cure them. It is really worth a try, Mrs. Gray, but if you have any trouble and the cure doesn't seem to be working, call me."

Mrs. Gray said, "Oh, thank you so much, Mrs. Piggle-Wiggle. I will let you know tomorrow how we are getting along."

That night at eight o'clock the clock struck and Mrs. Gray continued to mend socks and said nothing about bed and Mr. Gray changed the radio and Bobby and Larry and Susan played parchesi.

At nine o'clock the clock struck again and Mrs. Gray put down the socks and took up a woman's magazine. Mr. Gray changed the radio and Bobby and Larry and Susan continued to play parchesi.

When ten o'clock struck, Mrs. Gray yawned and put down the magazine, Mr. Gray snapped off the radio and Larry and Susan and Bobby began another game of parchesi.

At ten-thirty Mr. and Mrs. Gray went upstairs to bed and left the children playing parchesi.

At twelve o'clock Mrs. Gray awoke and at first thought

there were burglars in the house, then she remembered the Never-Want-To-Go-To-Bedders so she tiptoed down the stairs and there were Bobby and Larry and Susan playing parchesi on the living-room rug.

The next morning the children slept until eleven-thirty. About nine o'clock Dick Thompson's mother stopped by to take them to the beach but Mrs. Gray told her they were still asleep.

When the children finally got up they were cross and quarrelsome. When their mother told them about Mrs. Thompson inviting them to the beach they said, "Why didn't she wait for us? Why didn't you wake us up? I think Mrs. Thompson's mean not to wait."

Mrs. Gray said, "I see no reason why Mrs. Thompson and Dick should have their day spoiled waiting for the three little members of the All-Night Parchesi Club to get up. Now come and eat your breakfast and stop complaining."

That night after dinner Mr. and Mrs. Gray went to a moving picture show and left Larry and Bobby and Susan playing tiddly-winks. When the Grays came home about twelve-thirty the children were still up playing tiddly-winks and quarreling about whose turn it was.

The next morning they had a nine o'clock dentist appointment and so Mrs. Gray got them up at eight. Susan was so sleepy she could not eat her mush and Larry yawned so much he choked on his egg and had to be turned upside down and shaken by his legs. Bobby just sat and rubbed his eyes.

Bobby went to sleep in the car on the way to the dentist, Susan went to sleep in the dentist's waiting room and Larry slept all the way home.

That night, after their parents had gone to bed, Larry said, "Why do we hafta stay in the house for all the time? Let's go outside and play."

So they went outside and put on their roller skates and began skating up and down on the dark streets.

Mrs. Milgrim who lived on the corner came out on her front porch in her bathrobe and yelled, "For heaven's sake, don't you children know that it is almost midnight? What on earth are you doing up at this hour?"

Larry said, "We don't have to go to bed any more. We stay up late every night."

Mrs. Milgrim said, "Well, stay up some place else. And be QUIET!" She went into the house and slammed the door.

So the children took off their skates and tiptoed back to the house. They got out the parchesi board but Susan said it was her turn for the pinks and Larry said, "I happen to beg your pardon, but it is my turn."

Susan said, "You had the pinks yesterday and Bobby had them the day before and it's my turn tonight," and she began to cry.

Larry threw the pinks at her and one of them went into the fireplace and they had to strain the ashes through their fingers until they found it. When they finally were ready to play, Bobby was asleep with his head on the board, so Susan and Larry played, jumping their men across Bobby's head, until Susan too fell asleep right in the middle of her turn. Larry woke Susan and Bobby and they all went to bed just as the clock struck one.

The next day there was a matinee at the neighborhood theatre and Mrs. Gray said they could go. It was a wonderful picture, with Indians and cowboys and pioneers, and the children were very excited. But, no sooner had they found their seats and settled back in the nice dark theatre when first Susan, then Bobby and finally Larry fell asleep. They slept peacefully through the Indian picture, a Mickey Mouse cartoon and a newsreel. When the show was over all the other children went home to dinner but Larry and Susan and Bobby slept on. Susan was the first to awake. She sat up and rubbed her eyes. Where was she? Why was it so dark? Oh, how stiff and cramped she was. She poked Larry and Bobby until they too awoke. They were frightened when they realized that they were still in the theatre, now dark and empty, except for two rats nibbling popcorn in the front row. Susan began to cry, "Everybody's gone and left us and we'll have to stay in here until we die," she bawled. Larry said, "Oh, Susan, don't be so silly. All we have to do is walk out the door. Come on, everybody." They groped their way up the aisle to the door but it was locked. They tried all the doors but they were all locked.

Susan began to cry again. "I'm hungry and I want to go home," she wailed.

Bobby said, "I'll bet there's a back way, Larry. Let's look."
They felt their way back down the aisle again and climbed up on the stage. Then suddenly they heard the front door open, a flashlight's bold eye blinked in the darkness and a voice said, "Hey, what's goin' on here? What are you kids doing?"

It was Mr. Murphy, the janitor, and the children were so glad to see him that they ran and clung to his legs and all talked at once. "Oh, Mr. Murphy, we were locked in. We must have fallen asleep in the picture. What time is it? Will you let us out?"

Mr. Murphy laughed at them, let them out the front door and drove them home. Mother and Daddy were in the living room playing bridge with the Andersons and seemed not at all surprised to see the children. Mrs. Gray said, "There's bread and milk on the kitchen table. Please put everything away, when you finish," and went on with her game.

The children ambled out to the kitchen but they were too tired to eat so they went upstairs and flung themselves across their beds. After they had rested for a while Larry suggested that they play burglar. They turned off all the upstairs lights and crept around behind doors and under beds and had a fine scary time until Larry pushed Bobby down the clothes chute and Bobby stuck and Susan screamed and Daddy came upstairs and yanked Bobby out, spanked them all and sent them to their rooms. Susan and Bobby got right into bed and went to sleep but Larry stayed awake until the guests had gone home and their mother and daddy had gone to bed, then he pinched Bobby awake and they both sneaked into Susan's room and pulled off her covers. Larry said, "Let's go downstairs and see if there are any sandwiches or cookies left." Susan was very sleepy but she said, "Oooooooh, aaaaaall right."

They ate about ten little sandwiches, a small dish of salted nuts, two little dishes of candy, some olives and pickles and some chocolate marshmallow cake. They felt very lively after that so they sat down at the bridge table and began playing slapjack. When they finished the last game the birds were singing and they heard the thump of the morning paper on the porch. They scurried up to bed quickly.

The next day was Patsy's birthday. It was a wonderful party with a fishpond and a magician who did tricks and games and balloons and prizes for every child. But Larry and Bobby and Susan did not enjoy it at all. Susan had such big black circles under her eyes that Patsy's mother thought she was sick and would not let her have any refreshments. Bobby was so sleepy he fell asleep just as the magician pulled a rabbit from under his chair and the magician thought Bobby was so rude he gave the rabbit to Hubert Prentiss. Larry fell asleep right at the table. He laid his cheek in his ice cream, closed his eyes and dreamed he was in the North Pole. Patsy's mother called all the others to look at him and he awoke very embarrassed.

That night, when eight o'clock came, Mr. and Mrs. Gray were working on the budget and not saying much and Susan and Larry and Bobby were sitting on the davenport pinching each other to keep awake. At last the clock struck—bong, bong, bong, bong, bong, bong, bong, bong! The children jumped up and rushed over to their mother and father. They said, "It is eight o'clock and time for bed. Please let us go to bed. Please don't make us stay up any more. Pleeeeeeeese!"

Mrs. Gray said, "Why I thought you enjoyed staying up late. I thought all the children in this neighborhood stayed up late."

The children said, "Nobody has to stay up late but us. We just hate it. May we go to bed, pleeeeeeeese?"

Mrs. Gray said, "Very well, children, from now on, if you are good, I will let you go to bed at eight o'clock every night."

7

THE SLOW-EATER-TINY-BITE-TAKER CURE

Once upon a time there was a little boy named Allen. He had curly brown hair and sturdy legs and a very shiny smile. One morning he sat down to breakfast, but instead of picking up his spoon and eating his mush and milk like a good little boy he took a fork and began eating his cereal grain by grain.

When his mother, certain that he had eaten all of his mush, brought him his egg, he was still on the eleventh grain of cereal.

Allen's mother said, "My goodness, you are poky this morning, dear. What is the matter? Is the mush too hot?"

Then she noticed that Allen was eating his cereal with a fork so she took the fork away and handed him the spoon saying, "Now, then, eat properly and hurry or your egg will get cold."

Allen took the spoon but instead of filling it with mush he daintily lifted one grain from the bowl and slowly brought it up to his mouth. His mother watched him for a few minutes and then said, "Well, eat an ice cold egg, if you like, *but* I am going upstairs to sort the laundry and when I come down I want to find every bit of that mush and all of the egg eaten."

Allen's mother went skipping upstairs and left Allen in the breakfast nook. As soon as his mother left the kitchen Allen picked up the fork again and began eating his mush by the grain. In a little while even a whole grain seemed too much so he broke each grain in two, taking only half grains on the fork tines. He was so interested in his little bitty bites that he didn't hear his mother come in and was very surprised when she suddenly whisked away his breakfast and sent him marching up to his room.

At lunchtime Allen's mother made cream of tomato soup. This was Allen's very favorite soup but Allen, instead of eating it up quickly and asking for more, began floating little specks of cracker in the bowl. He floated, chased and ate them one by one.

At two o'clock his mother stopped the little cracker

crumb chase, sadly cleared the table and sent Allen up for a nap.

At dinner that night, Allen cut his meat into such small pieces that his father looked over at him and said, "Perhaps you would like to borrow my magnifying glass? I am sure you are going to need it to see those infinitesimal bits of meat."

Allen's mother said, "He has been like that all day. Eating his mush grain by grain with a fork; floating tiny cracker crumbs in his soup and chasing and eating them one by one and now this meat. What is the matter with you, Allen?"

Allen smiled his shining smile and said, "I guess I'm just a slow eater. I choke if I take larger bites."

His mother said, "Nonsense! You were all right yesterday."

Allen said sadly, "Yes, Mother, but that was yesterday," and he carefully cut a grain of corn into four pieces and delicately put the smallest piece into his mouth.

The next morning he had not improved a bit and though his mother scolded and scolded, he took the smallest slowest bites imaginable and to make matters worse he sighed and gazed around the room between each bite.

Allen's mother was very distressed and not knowing what else to do, she called her friend, Mrs. Crankminor.

"Good morning, Mrs. Crankminor," said Allen's mother. "This is Allen's mother and I called to ask if you have ever had any difficulty with Wetherill about eating?"

"Difficulty?" said Mrs. Crankminor. "Just what kind of eating difficulty?"

"Well," said Allen's mother, "Allen has suddenly taken to eating so slowly that if I didn't take his plate away, I'm sure that it would take him approximately twelve hours to eat an average meal. He eats his cereal grain by grain, his soup drop by drop and his meat pore by pore."

"Goodness, gracious, is the child ill?" asked Mrs. Crankminor.

"No, he says that he feels well and I have taken his temperature and it is normal. I don't know what the trouble is," said Allen's poor worried mother.

Mrs. Crankminor said, "I certainly have no complaint about Wetherill's eating. My only difficulty is in getting him to stop. Yesterday morning before breakfast, he weighed one hundred and eighty-two pounds and his father has begun calling him Blimpy."

"Oh, my," said Allen's mother, "I guess you have a more serious problem than I have," and she hung up the phone.

Then she called her friend Mrs. Wingsproggle. "Mrs. Wingsproggle," she said, "do you have any trouble with Pergola at mealtimes?"

Mrs. Wingsproggle said, enunciating very carefully, "Noooo, not eggsactly, trouble, but we do have to keeup after her to chew each mouthful one hundred tie-ums. Some-tie-ums she is forgetful and only chews her food about ninety-thrrrrrrrrreee tie-ums and one day I caught her stopping at seventy-one."

Allen's mother could already picture how disastrous it might be if Allen heard that Pergola Wingsproggle chewed each bite one hundred times because if she multiplied each grain of mush in a dish by one hundred and took into account the unbelievable slowness with which Allen was able to chew, she realized that he would die of slow starvation before a day had passed. Allen's mother hurriedly said goodbye to Mrs. Wingsproggle and hung up the phone.

Then she called Patsy's mother. She said, "Does Patsy eat everything that is put before her quickly and without urging?"

Patsy's mother said, "Yes, she does, why?"

Allen's mother said, "Because Allen has taken to eating like a scared mosquito, and I don't know what to do."

Patsy's mother said, "Call Mrs. Piggle-Wiggle. She'll know what to do. You remember the Radish Cure, don't you?"

Allen's mother was delighted. She said, "Oh, of course, I do and I'll call Mrs. Piggle-Wiggle right now," and she did.

Mrs. Piggle-Wiggle said, "So Allen has become a Slow-Eater-Tiny-Bite-Taker, has he? I thought he looked a little pale this afternoon."

Allen's mother said, "He is so pale his father calls him his little doughboy, and I know that he hasn't eaten more than a tablespoon of food in the last two days. What will I do, Mrs. Piggle-Wiggle?"

Mrs. Piggle-Wiggle said, "Don't worry about Allen, he'll be all right again in a day or two. Let me see, is it, yes, it is Allen coming down the street right now, so I'll send home the Slow-Eater-Tiny-Bite-Taker dishes with him.

"Use the largest set for Allen's dinner tonight; the medium size for his meals tomorrow; the small size the next day and the very small dishes the last day. Serve him portions of food to fit the dishes. That will be four days in all, counting today, and though he may lose some weight, he will gain it right back. I may send for him on the last day and no matter how he feels, let him come to my house."

Allen's mother said, "Thank you, very much, Mrs. Piggle-Wiggle. I will do just as you say and I will be so happy when he is cured."

"I will send Allen right home with the dishes," said Mrs. Piggle-Wiggle. "Now don't worry. Simply follow my instructions," and Mrs. Piggle-Wiggle said goodbye.

After a little while Allen came home carrying a large wicker basket. "Here's a present from Mrs. Piggle-Wiggle, Mother, and she said for me to be very careful with it." He set the basket on the kitchen floor and commenced to undo the fastenings. His mother said, "No, dear, this is a present for me and I think I'll just put it aside for now. You run out and play until dinner. Goodness, you are pale. Run as fast as you can down to Patsy's house and put some roses into your cheeks."

Allen's mother put the basket on the top shelf in the kitchen and shut the cupboard door which left nothing for Allen to do but go out and play. However, instead of running down to Patsy's, he walked very, very slowly because he was tired from not having had enough to eat.

Just before dinner, Allen's mother took down the basket and opened it. There were four little sets of dishes. The largest set had a plate the size of a saucer, a cup like a small after-dinner coffee cup, a small fork and a little spoon.

The medium size set had a plate like a doll plate, a doll cup, a very small fork and spoon.

The small size set had a plate the size of a silver dollar, a cup like a thimble, a fork like a match and a spoon like a salt spoon.

The tiny size set had a plate the size of a penny, a cup that would hold but a drop, a fork like a needle and a spoon like a pin.

Allen's dinner that night was served on the large set. He was given a baked potato as small as an egg, a piece of meat like a postage stamp, a slice of tomato, and the small cup of milk. Allen was so interested in taking tiny bites that he didn't even notice his new dishes. He ate one third of the potato, one sixth of the meat, one tomato seed and drank about half a cup of milk.

When he asked to be excused, his father looked at his saucer plate still heaped with food and started to say "NO!" but Allen's mother quickly said, "Yes, dear, you may be excused but you must play in your room until bedtime."

The next morning his mother put a teaspoon of scrambled egg and an inch-square piece of toast on the medium size plate and a tablespoon of orange juice in the doll cup. Allen loved the tiny fork and spoon because he was able to take such small bites that in one hour he had eaten but half the egg and one third of the toast. He did drink all of the orange juice.

At luncheon and dinner he ate even less and took even smaller bites. He had turned a very pale green and was so tired he had to sit down all of the time.

The next day his mother brought out the small dishes. On the dollar plate she put three cornflakes, a piece of bacon the size of a snowflake, and a quarter of a teaspoon of egg. In the thimble cup she put ten drops of cocoa.

Allen was so tired that he had to crawl in to breakfast on his hands. He was happy about the tiny dishes, though, and gave his mother a very sickly edition of the shiny smile. He cut the cornflakes into thirteen pieces and ate a part of one. He ate a speck of egg, a nibble of bacon and five drops of cocoa and then crawled in and lay on the couch.

For lunch he had seven drops of soup, two cracker crumbs and enough milk to barely moisten his lips.

For dinner he ate one lima bean and drank four drops of

milk. He crawled up to bed right after dinner. He had to rest eight times on the way upstairs.

The next morning he was so tired it took him almost half an hour to crawl down to breakfast. His mother had the penny plate, the drop cup and the needle fork and pin spoon. On the penny plate she had one grain of egg, two toast crumbs, and two raspberry jam seeds. She had a drop of milk in the cup. Allen was so weak he had to lift the needle fork with both hands but even so he cut the one grain of egg in two and ate only one of the toast crumbs. He drank half the drop of milk and then lay down on the breakfast nook bench.

Just then the telephone rang and it was Mrs. Piggle-Wiggle for Allen. His mother had to carry him to the telephone and hold the big heavy telephone receiver. Mrs. Piggle-Wiggle had great difficulty in hearing his weak squeaky voice and finally had to give up and talk to his mother. Mrs. Piggle-Wiggle said, "It is Allen's turn to exercise the spotted pony and I would like him to come over here right away."

Allen's mother told Allen and he was very excited but he was so weak that his mother had to carry him out and put him in his little red wagon. Fortunately it was downhill all the way to Mrs. Piggle-Wiggle's house and when he got there Dick Thompson and Hubert Prentiss were waiting for him out in front. They lifted him out of his little red wagon and laid him across Spotty's back. Spotty turned his head around and licked the top of Allen's head comfortingly. Mrs. Piggle-Wiggle came out onto her front porch to see him off and it took much self-control for her to keep from laughing as Spotty started slowly off down the street with Allen lying on his back like a bag of cornmeal. All morning Allen lay on Spotty's back, his face buried in his mane, while Spotty paced the streets. Several times women rushed out of their houses and asked Allen if he was ill, if he needed any help. Allen was very embarrassed and squeaked out, "I'm all right," and tried to sit up but he was too weak.

When twelve o'clock came Allen was so tired that he knew he could not stay on Spotty's back another minute so he guided the pony up to his own front gate. Then he rolled off his back onto the grass. He lay there like a wet sock, bawling.

His mother looked out the kitchen window and seeing him lying there she became frightened. She thought Spotty was a spirited horse and that he had bucked Allen off. She ran out and knelt beside him. "Darling," she said, "are you hurt? Did that vicious horse throw you? How many times did he buck?"

Allen smiled weakly at the idea of gentle little Spotty bucking or throwing anyone, but then he began to cry again as he remembered that this was his last chance for a long time to exercise Spotty and he was so weak that he couldn't stay on his back. He finally said to his mother, "Spotty did not buck or throw me. It is just that I am so tired I cannot stay on his back. I rolled off and now I can't get back on and it's my turn to exercise him and I won't have another turn for a long, long tiiiiiiiiiiIIIME!"

Allen's mother said, "Now, see here, Allen. This all comes from your turning into a Slow-Eater-Tiny-Bite-Taker and if you want to ride Spotty this afternoon, you will have to come into the house and eat something."

She tied Spotty to the fence, picked Allen up, carried him into the house and set him in the breakfast nook. He leaned weakly back against the wall and closed his eyes.

His mother began rattling pans and turning on burners and pretty soon she handed him the drop cup filled with cream of tomato soup and the penny plate with two cracker crumbs on it.

She said, "Now drink this soup in one gulp and put BOTH those crumbs in your mouth at once." Allen did as he was told then leaned back and closed his eyes again.

Then his mother handed him the thimble cup filled with milk and a tiny peanut butter sandwich on the dollar plate. She said, "Drink this milk in one swallow and put that whole sandwich in your mouth." Allen did and was surprised to find that he didn't feel quite so tired. He leaned back but he kept his eyes open.

Then his mother handed him the doll cup filled with soup and the doll plate with some cottage cheese on it. "Drink that soup right down," she said, "and here is a large

fork and I want that cottage cheese eaten in two bites."
Allen did as he was told. My, but he was feeling strong! He
could sit up without leaning back and oddly enough he was
very hungry.

His mother handed him the after-dinner coffee cup filled
with milk and the saucer plate with a piece of gingerbread
on it. Allen didn't have to be told how to eat and drink these.
He took large hungry bites and big swishing gulps and the
dishes were empty. His mother said, "Do you feel better,
dear? Have you had enough lunch?"

Allen said, "I feel much better, Mother, but I'm still very
hungry. May I please have a large bowl of soup and a large
glass of milk?"

"Of course, dear," said his mother and she quickly filled
a large bowl with soup and a large glass with milk. Allen
ate every drop of soup and drank every drop of milk and
then jumped up from the table saying, "Oh, Mother, I bet
Spotty's hungry. Shall I take him some soup?"

"No, dear," said his mother. "I think that Spotty would
prefer an apple and some lumps of sugar." So they fed
Spotty and then Allen climbed on his back and rode
proudly away, sitting up very straight and holding on to
the reins with one hand.

When he reached the corner by Patsy's house his mother
called him to come back. He turned Spotty around and
steered him up to the gate and his mother came out with
the basket of Slow-Eater-Tiny-Bite-Taker dishes. "Would

you mind returning these to Mrs. Piggle-Wiggle?" she asked.

"Not at all," said Allen graciously. "Just hand me the basket. I'll put it here in front of me and hold it with this hand. You see, Mother, I only use one hand to steer now."

He carefully arranged the basket, kissed his mother, clucked to Spotty, and away they went, in a very slow walk, toward Mrs. Piggle-Wiggle's house.

8

THE FIGHTER-QUARRELERS CURE

Joan Russell opened her blue eyes and saw that it was morning. She saw also that her twin sister, Anne, was still asleep. Joan reached over and gave Anne a little pinch. "Wake up, Anne!" she said making her voice scary and urgent. "Wake up quickly, there's a big black spider in the bed and it's on your side."

Anne awoke with a squeal, leapt out of bed, stubbed her toe on the box of paints she had left on the floor the night before, banged her funny bone on the door and went screaming into her mother's and father's room. "Mother, Daddy, there's a big black spider in our bed on my side! Motherrrr-rrrrrr! Daaaaaaaaaady!"

Mrs. Russell sighed, sat up and reached for her robe. She said in a low, calm voice, "Anne, you didn't fall for that old trick again, did you?"

Anne grabbed her mother's arm and jumped up and down, squealing, "But Mother, Joan said so. It's a big black spider!"

Mr. Russell turned over and yawned. He said, "Ohhhhh, aaah! Stop jumping and squealing and listen. *If* there is a big black spider in the bed, and it is highly unlikely, then, WHY is Joan lying in there, staring at the ceiling and waiting to be bitten AND TO BE SPANKED!" he added in a loud voice.

Anne stopped squealing and listened gravely to her father but when he finished speaking she said, "But Joan said there was a spider, Daddy. She said there was!"

Her daddy said, "Last one dressed gets the littlest melon!" and he jumped out of bed and chased Anne out of the room, roaring like a lion.

Mr. Russell sang gaily in his shower but Mrs. Russell frowned as she dressed, for from the children's room she could hear, "That's my sock! Give it to me!"

" 'Tis not. It's mine! Give it back!" (*sound of slap*)

"Mother, Anne's slapping me!"

"That's my petticoat. You're putting on MY petticoat. Give it to me!"

" 'Tis not. It's mine!" (*sound of slap*)

"That's mine!"

"No, that's mine!"

" 'Tis not."

" 'Tis too!"

Slap, bang, crash, running steps. "MOTHERRRRRRR!"

Mrs. Russell said to herself, "Quarreling, quarreling, from the minute they get up until they go to bed at night. I do not believe that I can stand another day of it." She ran downstairs and began jamming the oranges into the squeezer.

Mr. Russell came whistling in to breakfast. He said mildly, "Oh, scrambled eggs again. I was hoping for sausages and buckwheat cakes."

Mrs. Russell said, "We had sausages and buckwheat cakes yesterday morning."

Mr. Russell said, "What about brook trout? Bill Smith has 'em nearly every morning."

Mrs. Russell said crossly, "Perhaps that is why he looks like a trout and his wife looks like a great big halibut."

Mr. Russell peered at her over the top of his morning paper. He said, "You know, sweetheart, I think that the children's fighting and quarreling is making you irritable."

Mrs. Russell said, "I think it is too. In fact, it is driving me crazy. Just listen to them."

From the upper hall they could hear, "It's my turn to go down first, Joan!"

" 'Tis not, it's my turn!"

"You were first yesterday, you know you were."

"But last night you traded your first turn for my pink crayon."

"I did not!"

"You did too!"

"Cheater!"

"Double cheater!"

In came the twins. Joan looked at her melon and then at Anne's. She said, "Anne's melon is the biggest. She always gets the biggest and the most of everything."

Anne said, "You had the biggest yesterday. You're just a pig. You always want the most."

Their daddy said, "As a matter of fact, ladies, I have the biggest melon because I was the first one dressed. NOW HUSH!" He glared at them.

The twins sat meekly down to their breakfast. They had taken but two bites, however, when Anne poked Joan and hissed, "I've got the most cereal. Ha, ha, ha!"

Joan hissed back, "Yes, but I have three pieces of bacon and you have only two."

Anne looked and sure enough Joan did have three pieces. She grabbed one but Joan snatched her wrist and in the ensuing scuffle they managed to tip over Anne's milk and spill it all over the front of their nice blue pleated skirts. Their daddy spanked them. Their mother sponged them off and they left for school, red-eyed and miserable, but still quarreling. As they rounded the corner their mother could hear, "That big tablet is mine!" " 'Tis not." " 'Tis too!"

After Mr. Russell had left for the office, Mrs. Russell picked up the telephone and called her friend Mrs. Quitrick. She said, "Mrs. Quitrick, this is Mrs. Russell, the twins' mother, and I want to know if Jasper and Myrtle ever quarrel."

"Oh, my dear," said Mrs. Quitrick, "all children quarrel. Why yesterday Myrtle hit Jasper with her big doll and the eyes came out and then Jasper hit Myrtle with the little hammer out of his nice new tool box and the head came off the hammer and I just told them that I wouldn't have them breaking up their toys that way."

Mrs. Russell said, "But the children, weren't they hurt?"

Mrs. Quitrick said, "Why, I didn't notice. I was so angry at them for breaking their lovely toys and the doll hospital won't be able to put Myrtle's doll's eyes back for two weeks and you know how hard it is to get hammers these days."

Mrs. Russell said, "Well, thank you anyway, Mrs. Quitrick," and hung up. She poured herself another cup of coffee and while she drank it she thought and thought about her little fighter-quarrelers. Then she had an idea. She would call Mrs. Piggle-Wiggle and ask her what to do.

Mrs. Piggle-Wiggle would know if anyone would.

She called Mrs. Piggle-Wiggle and said, "Mrs. Piggle-Wiggle, I am Mrs. Russell, the mother of Anne and Joan."

Mrs. Piggle-Wiggle said, "Oh, yes, the twins. Such darling little girls and so pretty."

Mrs. Russell said, "But they quarrel so, Mrs. Piggle-Wiggle. They begin fighting the moment they open their eyes in the morning and they don't stop until they fall asleep from exhaustion. It is dreadful, Mrs. Piggle-Wiggle. You should hear them!"

Mrs. Piggle-Wiggle said, "Oh, I know. 'That's my sock.' 'No, it's mine.' 'That's my box.' 'No, it's mine.' ' 'Tis not!' ' 'Tis too.' 'You have the most.' 'You're a pig!' "

Mrs. Russell said, "Why, Mrs. Piggle-Wiggle, you must have heard them. I was hoping they didn't quarrel when they were at your house."

Mrs. Piggle-Wiggle said, "No, I haven't heard Anne and Joan but I have heard hundreds of other children. You see Fighter-Quarreleritis is a common children's disease and it is very contagious, but very easy to cure."

"Easy to cure? Oh, Mrs. Piggle-Wiggle, how?" asked Mrs. Russell.

"Well," said Mrs. Piggle-Wiggle. "In the first place, fighting and quarreling are merely habits. One morning a child wakens and feels cross and so instead of smiling at his little brother and saying 'Good morning!' he glares at his little brother and shouts, 'You've got on MY shirt!' The little brother says, 'I have NOT!' because he hasn't. The cross child says, 'You have too. You have too!' and the quarreling has begun.

"The next morning both children have the Fighter-Quarreleritis and they wake and begin shouting rudely at each other. It soon becomes a habit and they forget how to be courteous.

"Now, Mrs. Russell, I believe that if Fighter-Quarrelers could hear themselves as others hear them and see themselves as others see them, they would soon realize how unpleasant they were and would be cured.

"In order to do this with Anne and Joan, you and Mr. Russell will have to pretend to be Anne and Joan. First, however, you must write down every single fighting thing that the children say. Begin with this morning and keep a careful record of the whole day. Say nothing to the twins but, tomorrow, you and Mr. Russell repeat their quarrels. I do not believe that it will be necessary to slap and pinch but be sure to be loud and noisy. Don't laugh and don't let the children know that it is just a game. Look quarrelsome as well as acting quarrelsome. One day usually is sufficient."

Mrs. Russell said, "Every morning Joan tells Anne that there is a big black spider in the bed on Anne's side and Anne comes screaming into our room. Should Mr. Russell and I do that?"

"My, my," said Mrs. Piggle-Wiggle. "That is the way Billy and Tommy Peters used to start the day, only Billy told Tommy it was a cobra. Well, cobra or black spider, you and Mr. Russell do the same. Goodbye and good luck!"

After saying goodbye to Mrs. Piggle-Wiggle, Mrs. Russell sat down and wrote down every word of Anne and Joan's morning quarreling that she could remember. After school she purposely gave one of them a bigger apple than she gave the other and then followed them around and wrote down the quarreling. She stayed in their room while they undressed for bed and took notes. Fortunately the children were very productive and fought about the amount of toothpaste on their toothbrushes, whose turn it was for the shower, whose pillow was softest, the amount of room they had in the bed, who had the most covers, whose turn it was to turn off the light, who had the biggest feet, whose mouth opened the widest, who had the most teeth, everything. My, they were naughty and disagreeable!

When she had finished writing it all down, Mrs. Russell handed a copy to Mr. Russell and told him about Mrs. Piggle-Wiggle. He thought it was a wonderful idea and studied his part carefully.

The next morning Joan opened her blue eyes and was just reaching out to pinch Anne when she heard a commotion in her mother's and daddy's room and suddenly the door flew open and in came Mrs. Russell clutching her bathrobe and squealing, "Anne, Joan, quick, there is a big black spider in our bed and it's on my side!"

Joan said calmly, "How do you know there's one? Did you see it?"

Anne awoke and out of habit she leapt out of bed and ran for the door squealing. Her mother squealed louder and

Anne, surprised, asked her what the trouble was. Her mother began pounding on the bed and yelling, "There's a big black spider in our bed on my side. Daddy said so. He saw it."

Anne said, "But, Mother, if there is a spider why is Daddy in there?"

Her mother paid no attention to her but continued to squeal, "Daddy said there was. I'm scared. Eeeeeeeeeee!"

Joan said, "We'd better go in and look, Anne." So they solemnly marched into their mother's and daddy's room. Mr. Russell was lying in bed gazing at the ceiling. Anne threw back the covers and Joan peered into the bed but all they could see were Daddy's feet, the toes wriggling.

Anne said sternly, "Why did you scare Mother that way, Daddy?"

Mr. Russell said, "Was she scared?" and jumped out of bed and ran into the bathroom shouting at the top of his voice, "Ha, ha, my first turn for the shower!"

At that Mrs. Russell came flying in from the twins' room and began pounding on the bathroom door, yelling, "It is not your first turn! It's mine! You traded me your first turn yesterday for a new golf ball."

Mr. Russell laughed rudely and called out, "Too bad for you. I've got the door locked."

Mrs. Russell kicked at the door and shouted, "Cheater, cheater, cheater!"

Anne and Joan looked at each other. Their eyes were

round with amazement. Anne whispered, "Let's get dressed," and Joan said, "Yes, let's hurry!" and they tip-toed out of the room, closing the door carefully behind them.

While they dressed they could hear their mother and father quarreling. When Mr. Russell came out of the shower, Mrs. Russell said, "You used my towel. That's my towel."

Mr. Russell said, " 'Tis not. It's mine."

Mrs. Russell said, " 'Tis not. It's mine."

Mr. Russell said, "That's MY shirt. You've got on my NEW T-Shirt."

Mrs. Russell said, "Well, you wore my golf sweater."

Mr. Russell said, "Take off MY NEW SHIRT!"

Mrs. Russell began to bawl. She sobbed, "You wore my golf sweater and you promised me that I could wear the shirt. You're a pig."

Mr. Russell said, "All right, baby, wear the old shirt."

At breakfast Mr. Russell took a little ruler out of his pocket and measured the grapefruit and then he took the biggest. Mother snatched it away from him and spilled coffee on the new T-shirt.

Mother served the scrambled eggs and gave herself a large heaping plate and Daddy a small serving. Daddy looked at both plates and said, "Pig!"

"Speaking of pigs," said Mrs. Russell, "it's my turn for the car!"

" 'Tis not," said Mr. Russell. "It's my turn. You had the car last week."

Mrs. Russell said, "I only drove up to the drugstore and back last week and you went clear out to the golf club."

Mr. Russell said in a very disagreeable way, "It makes no difference to me how far you drove, you have had your turn, madam."

Mrs. Russell began to bawl. "I think you're meeeeeeean," she wailed. "Isn't it my turn, girls?" she turned to the twins.

The girls looked at their mother but they didn't answer. Instead they asked to be excused, put on their coats and hurried off to school.

At dinner that night, Daddy took the chops up to the bathroom and weighed them on the scales and then took the two biggest. Mother took the biggest baked potato but she sorted the string beans out one by one so that everyone got an equal share but they were ice cold.

The twins cleared the table and Anne carried in the pumpkin pie. Now, pumpkin pie was the twins' very favorite dessert and so Anne was very careful to walk slowly and put the pie down gently in front of Daddy. But it was wasted effort for Mother reached over and grabbed the pie saying, "I'll SERVE THAT!"

"Oh, no, you won't," said Daddy jerking the pie back.

"Will too," said Mother reaching for the pie, but Daddy jerked it off the table and held it over his head. Mother grabbed his wrist and the pie went SPLAT all over the rug.

The Fighter-Quarrelers Cure

The twins began to cry. They said, "Mommy, Daddy, please stop quarreling. We just can't stand it any more. It's dreadful!"

Mother said, "Why, we thought you enjoyed fighting."

Joan said, "We hate quarreling. We are so unhappy!"

Anne said, "Fighting is terrible. It makes us miserable."

Mrs. Russell took Joan on her lap and Mr. Russell took Anne on his lap and they said, "To tell you the truth, girls, we don't like quarreling either. It is just a habit we caught from you. Why, we must have been quarreling all day."

The twins said, "You have, you have!"

Daddy said, "I'll tell you what we'll do. We'll all join hands and solemnly pledge that there shall be no more quarreling in this house. Then, we'll all walk up to Findley's Drugstore and seal the pledge with ice cream. Does everyone agree?"

"We all agree," they shouted. So they joined hands and said, "I do solemnly pledge that I will not quarrel or fight in this house ever again."

Then they walked up to Mr. Findley's drugstore and had ice cream sodas and even though Anne saw Mr. Findley put three scoops of ice cream in Joan's soda and only two in hers and even though Joan saw Mr. Findley put two scoops of strawberry in Anne's soda and only one in hers, they neither of them said a word. The Fighter-Quarreleritis was cured.

The End

HELLO, MRS. PIGGLE-WIGGLE

HELLO, MRS. PIGGLE-WIGGLE

BETTY MacDONALD

Pictures by HILARY KNIGHT

HarperCollins*Publishers*

CONTENTS

I. THE SHOW-OFF CURE

IT was a beautiful morning. A bluebird sat on a small branch in the flowering cherry tree and swayed gently back and forth. A crocus pushed his golden head through the tender green grass and blinked in the sudden sunlight. Mrs. Carmody hummed as she laid slices of bacon in the black iron skillet. "Spring is my favorite time of year," she said to Mandy the dog who was lying in the kitchen doorway scratching a flea and waiting to trip somebody.

Mrs. Carmody plugged in the toaster, got out the raspberry jam then went to the front hall and called up stairs to her husband, "Jordan, breakfast!" and to her little boy, "Phillip, are you up?"

Phillip who was ten years old and still under the covers, called out sleepily, "Practically all dressed, Mom. Be right down."

Constance, his sister who was eleven and three quarters, yelled from the bathroom where she was testing how lipstick would look when she was thirteen, "Phillip isn't even up, Mom. He won't be down for about ten hours."

Phillip shouted, "Old spy. Tattletale."

Constance said, "Be quiet, little boy. You bore me."

Mrs. Carmody called again louder, "Phillip get out

of bed this instant. Connie, wipe off that lipstick. Hurry, Jordan, dear, while the toast is hot."

She went back to the kitchen and gave the percolator a little shake to hurry it up. Then she walked over and stood by the open back door breathing deeply of the fragrant early morning air. Her pleasant reverie was suddenly broken by Mr. Carmody who came grumpily into the kitchen, tripped over Mandy and stepped heavily into her water bowl which was on the floor beside the stove.

Mrs. Carmody grabbed the sink sponge and began wiping up the water.

Mr. Carmody growled, "Well, that's certainly a nice morning greeting."

Mrs. Carmody said, "Oh, Jordan, dear, I'm so sorry. Did you get wet?"

"It doesn't matter," said Mr. Carmody mournfully. "Nothing matters any more."

"What do you mean 'nothing matters any more'?" asked Mrs. Carmody as she squeezed out the sponge.

"Just that," said Mr. Carmody sadly pouring almost the whole pitcher of cream on his shredded wheat biscuit.

"Are you sick?" asked Mrs. Carmody peering anxiously at him.

"No, I am not sick," he said. "Or at least I'm not physically sick. Just sick at heart."

Mrs. Carmody buttered the toast, put the plates in to warm, stirred the eggs, lifted the bacon on to a paper towel to drain, checked the color of the coffee, refilled Mandy's water bowl, then said, "What in the world are you talking about, Jordan? You don't make sense."

"He makes sense to me," said Connie flouncing into the kitchen. "Because I feel the same way. I'm so ashamed I could die."

"What in the world are you talking about?" said Mrs. Carmody. "Are you ready for your eggs, Jordan?"

"I suppose so," said Mr. Carmody dolefully.

Quickly Mrs. Carmody took the plates out of the oven, divided the eggs into four equal portions, added a dash of paprika, laid on four strips of bacon and two pieces of toast, carried two of the plates to the table and snapped them down in front of her husband and daughter. "Now," she said folding her arms, "tell me what this is all about."

Connie picked up a piece of bacon and began nibbling at it. "Well," she said, "if you really want to know."

"I do," said her mother.

"Well," Connie said, "the point is that Phillip is ruining all our lives and you won't face it."

"Ruining our lives! Phillip?" said Mrs. Carmody. "Don't be ridiculous."

"I'm not being ridiculous," said Connie. "Phillip is such a disgusting little show-off I'm ashamed to bring my friends home any more. What about last night? He disgraced poor Daddy."

Mrs. Carmody gazed at her daughter intently for a minute then said, "Connie, you've got on lipstick again. Go upstairs and wash it off."

"Oh, honestly," Connie sighed heavily. "Every sin-

gle girl in the whole United States of America wears
lipstick but me. I'm just a freak. A poor freak with a
disgusting little brother."

"Yes, yes, I know," said her mother. "Go up and
wash the lipstick off."

When she was sure she could hear Connie's furious
footsteps on the stairs she turned to her husband and
said, "Now, Jordan, dear, what is all this?"

Mr. Carmody said, "Meg, Phillip is an obnoxious
little show-off. Last night was the worst I've ever seen
him, and Bob Waltham is my most important client and
frankly I wouldn't blame him if he never came into
this house again."

"Oh, Jordan," said Mrs. Carmody laughing. "Phillip was just trying to be entertaining."

"Do you call putting a whole baked potato in his
mouth entertaining? Do you call drinking an entire
glass of water without stopping, then choking and
turning purple and spitting water all over the table
entertaining? Do you call looking cross-eyed, touching
his chin with his tongue, wiggling his ears, standing on
his head, reciting the alphabet backwards and forwards
and sideways and upside down, entertaining? Well, I
don't. AND NEITHER DID BOB WALTHAM!"

"Now, Jordan," said Mrs. Carmody. "You know
that Bob Waltham is a stuffy old bore. You've said so
yourself, and after all Phillip is only ten. He's just a
little boy. You shouldn't be so hard on him."

"You mean, *he* shouldn't be so hard on *me,*" said
Mr. Carmody angrily ripping a piece of bread in half.

"Meg, something has to be done about that boy. Now! Today!"

Just then Phillip came rattling down the stairs and skidded into the breakfast room. "Hi, Dad. Hi, Mom," he said cheerfully.

"Morning," said Mr. Carmody grumpily.

"Good morning, Phillip, dear," said Mrs. Carmody.

Phillip sat down, grabbed the sugar bowl and began dumping sugar on his shredded wheat biscuit.

"Not so much sugar, honey," said his mother.

Phillip added two more heaping teaspoons of sugar then dumped the rest of the pitcher of cream on his cereal.

Looking brightly, eagerly at his father he said, "Hey,

Dad, want to watch me put this whole shredded wheat biscuit in my mouth all at once?"

"I DO NOT," said his father.

"Not even if I whistle Dixie with it *in* my mouth?"

"NO!" roared his father.

"Eat your breakfast, dear," said his mother putting a fresh pitcher of cream on the table.

"What if I——" Phillip began.

"STOP TALKING!" bellowed his father.

Connie who had come downstairs and was standing unnoticed in the doorway said, "What a repulsive little show-off! My gosh, Mother, can't you see how disgusting he is?"

"My gosh, Mother, can't you see how disgusting he is?" mimicked Phillip in a high squeaky voice. "Shoot him, Mother! Kill him! Cut him up with the butcher knife. Mommy, he embarrasses me in front of my stupid, ugly, giggling friends."

"Now children," said Mrs. Carmody gently.

Mr. Carmody glared around the table and said fiercely, "I want *absolute quiet!*"

"My gosh, Dad, what's the matter?" asked Phillip. "Are you sick or something?"

"Yes, I'm sick or something," said Mr. Carmody savagely jabbing a spoon into the raspberry jam.

"I'll get you an aspirin," said Phillip sliding out of his chair. "I'll get two aspirins and I'll carry them all the way downstairs on my nose. Watch me."

"SIT STILL!" shouted Mr. Carmody. "Sit still and eat your breakfast and DON'T TALK."

"Well, okay," said Phillip. "But you don't have to be so crabby."

"BE QUIET!" yelled his father.

Phillip gave him a reproachful look, sat down again and began to eat his shredded wheat biscuit.

Mrs. Carmody brought her plate and Phillip's from the kitchen and sat down. She looked out the window at the pale pink cherry blossoms and the clear sky and the fat bluebird swaying on the branch but she no longer felt happy. She took a sip of coffee which was lukewarm and looked around the breakfast table.

Phillip was eating busily but the minute she looked at him he grinned broadly and whispered, "Hey, Mom, want to watch me balance my cocoa cup on my fore-head?"

She smiled, shook her head and motioned for him to be quiet.

"Even if it's clear full of boiling hot cocoa?" She shook her head.

"Even if it has the spoon in it?" She shook her head.

"What a bunch of crabpatches," Phillip said.

"QUIET!" bellowed his father.

Phillip reached for the jam dish and began sulkily emptying it on to his plate.

When breakfast was at last over and everyone had left for work or school Mrs. Carmody heated up the coffee, poured herself a cup and sat down at the table to look at the morning paper. Just as she opened the paper the corner of her eye caught a glimpse of something white on the floor under Phillip's chair. She reached over and picked up a small folded piece of paper. She opened it up, smoothed it out and read:

Dear Mrs. Carmody:
I am having a little difficulty with Phillip. Will

you please call me at your earliest convenience.
Sincerely,
Edith Perriwinkle.

Mrs. Carmody looked at her watch—it was four minutes to nine—perhaps she could get Miss Perriwinkle before the bell rang. She hurried into the hall and dialed the number of the school.

When Miss Perriwinkle heard Mrs. Carmody's anxious worried voice she said, "I didn't intend to worry you Mrs. Carmody—it isn't anything serious—it is just that Phillip has become quite a . . . quite a . . ."

"Show-off," said Mrs. Carmody.

"Well, yes," said Miss Perriwinkle. "I guess that is the right word. I also must admit that he is very entertaining and his little schoolmates think he is very funny and laugh at everything he does. Unfortunately he no longer confines his antics to recess and the schoolyard so I have to take steps. Which is why I wrote the note."

"Well," said Mrs. Carmody, "I should have seen it coming, because we are having our problems with him at home, too. Have you any suggestions?"

"Yes, I have," said Miss Perriwinkle. "I think you should call Mrs. Piggle-Wiggle. You've heard of her haven't you?"

"I've heard the name," said Mrs. Carmody. "Is she some sort of doctor?"

"Oh, my no," said Miss Perriwinkle. "She is just a very nice little woman who loves and understands children and has a very magic way of curing their bad habits. Her telephone is Vinemaple 1-2345."

"Just a minute while I get a pencil," said Phillip's mother.

Of course she couldn't find a pencil but she did finally find a broken green crayon with which she wrote down Mrs. Piggle-Wiggle's telephone number on the back of the gas bill.

Mrs. Carmody's hand was shaking as she dialed the number but Mrs. Piggle-Wiggle had such a warm friendly voice that Mrs. Carmody got right over her nervousness and told her all about Phillip.

Mrs. Piggle-Wiggle laughed and said, "Isn't it a shame that children can't be all evened up? I mean some are show-offs and some are shy and some are quiet and some are noisy and some laugh too much and some cry too much. Oh, I could go on and on but loud or quiet, shy or show-offy, timid or boisterous, children are wonderful and I love them all."

"So do I," said Phillip's mother. "And actually, Mrs. Piggle-Wiggle, Phillip's showing off doesn't bother me. But his daddy says he is obnoxious and his sister Connie says he is disgusting and this morning his teacher Miss Perriwinkle told me that he is getting out of hand."

"Well," said Mrs. Piggle-Wiggle, "if it were only his older sister who complained about Phillip I would be inclined to let time work things out, but as long as Phillip is annoying his daddy and Miss Perriwinkle who is one of the best fifth-grade teachers in this county, then we had better take steps."

"Take steps?" quavered Phillip's mother. "What do you mean by steps?"

"Oh, it's very simple," said Mrs. Piggle-Wiggle.

"Have Phillip come down after school and I'll give him a bottle of Show-off Powder. For the next few days sprinkle a little on him before meals, especially when you are having company, and just before he leaves for school in the morning. I'm sure you won't have any more trouble."

"But what is this show-off powder? Will it hurt Phillip?" asked Mrs. Carmody fearfully.

"Show-off Powder is guaranteed to be harmless," said Mrs. Piggle-Wiggle. "But it will stop showing off. You see it makes the show-off invisible."

"Invisible!" wailed Phillip's mother. "You mean I won't be able to see my own little boy?"

"Not when he's showing off," said Mrs. Piggle-Wiggle matter-of-factly. "Nobody will be able to see him. But when he stops showing off and is normal he'll come back into focus."

"Are you sure?" asked Phillip's mother.

"Oh, my yes," said Mrs. Piggle-Wiggle. "Now don't worry about it, just send Phillip up after school. I know that everything is going to be fine. Good-bye and *don't worry.*"

But Mrs. Carmody did worry. She worried as she washed the breakfast dishes and tidied up the house. She worried as she made out the grocery list and sorted the laundry. But she worried the most when she was straightening up Phillip's room.

"What if this powder makes Phillip disappear and then something goes wrong and he won't come back," she sobbed as she took two apple cores, three funny books, a slingshot and an empty box of Smith Brothers' cough drops out from under Phillip's pillow.

Phillip's room was so messy and she was in there such a long time picking up and imagining terrible things that she finally decided not to send for the magic Show-off Powder. That old powder was far too dangerous to use on a sensitive intelligent little boy like Phillip and anyway Phillip's showing off was really very clever and maybe some day he'd be on the stage. Then the front door crashed open, a loud voice yelled "Mom. Hey, Mom, where are you?" and Phillip was home from school.

Mrs. Carmody rushed downstairs and sure enough there was Phillip very much alive and visible, sitting at the kitchen table wolfing down gingerbread and milk. His back was toward his mother but she could see that one sleeve was ripped out of the sweater. "Phillip," his mother said, "what in the world happened to your sweater?"

"Fell off my bike," Phillip said through a mouthful of gingerbread.

"Oh, sweetheart," his mother said running to him, "did you hurt yourself?"

"Oh, not much," Phillip said. "Kind of tore my pants though and ripped one of my new school shoes. See." He held out one leg and showed his mother a pant leg ripped jaggedly to the knee. He held out the other and showed her his brown oxford with a large tear over the instep. He also had a cut over his eye, a skinned place on his nose and blood on his chin.

"Oh, Phillip," his mother said, "you might have been *killed!* Were you hit by a car?"

"Uh, uh," Phillip said.

"Did some big boy push you?"

"Gosh, no," Phillip said.

"Well, then what did happen?" his mother asked.

"Oh, nothin'," Phillip drained his glass of milk. "Can I have another piece of gingerbread, Mom?"

"Certainly," said his mother, "but first I want to know about the accident with your bicycle."

"Well," Phillip said, "if you wanta really know. I was sitting in the basket of my bike ridin' down Mission Hill backwards singing 'Polly Wolly Doodle' and I saw the bread truck comin' and I guess I didn't turn soon enough and I ran into the Wallaces' iron fence and I caught my shoe on the pedal and my pants on a picket and I hit my eye on the handle bars and I don't know what else happened. But, boy, you should have heard the kids and that ole breadman laugh!"

"No doubt," said his mother drily. "Now you go upstairs and change your trousers and your shoes. Bring me the trousers to mend. Take the torn shoe down to Mr. Rizotta and ask him if he can put a patch on it. And on your way home stop at Mrs. Piggle-Wiggle's, she has something for me. Do you know where Mrs. Piggle-Wiggle lives?"

"Sure I do," Phillip said. "We play down there all the time. What's she got for *you?*"

"Never you mind," said his mother. "Just don't forget to stop by there. Now scoot."

A little after five-thirty, Mrs. Carmody happened to look out the kitchen window and saw Phillip coming up the drive followed by a crowd of children. On his head he was carrying his shoe, balanced on the toe of the shoe was a small jar, sitting on the jar was a little green frog. When Phillip saw his mother's face at

the window he called out, "Hey, Mom, lookit! Watch
me I'm going to jump over the wheelbarrow with all
this stuff on my head."

"Phillip, don't," his mother called.

But he couldn't hear her and she watched horrified as
he made a run for the wheelbarrow, caught his foot in
the garden hose and fell backwards into the rhododendron bush. The small jar from Mrs. Piggle-Wiggle
flew up in the air, and landed on the concrete with a
crash. Mrs. Carmody dashed out, knelt down and
began picking little pieces of broken glass out of the
spilled white powder. Having extricated himself from
the rhododendron bush Phillip said, "Gee, Mom, I'm
sorry I busted it. I didn't mean to."

"Don't talk," his mother said briskly. "Go in and
get me a clean white envelope out of my desk and the
spatula off the stove. Hurry."

While Phillip was gone Mrs. Carmody carefully
pushed the white powder into a little mound and held
her hand over it to keep the wind from blowing it
away. When Phillip brought her the envelope and
the spatula she scooped up all the powder into the envelope. All but about a half a teaspoonful—this she
carefully lifted into the palm of her hand and blew at
Phillip.

"Hey, what do you think you're doin'?" he said, rubbing his eyes and coughing.

"Something very wise, I'm sure," said his mother.

Just then Mr. Carmody's car turned into the driveway. Immediately Phillip jumped up into the wheelbarrow and yelled, "Watch me, Dad. I'm goin' to

stand on my head in the wheelbarrow. I'm goin' to stand on my head and say the alphabet backwards."

Mrs. Carmody looked at the wheelbarrow but it was suddenly empty. There was no one there. Not only that but there was no sound either.

Mr. Carmody got out of the car and said, "Where's Phillip? Wasn't he here just a moment ago?"

"Yes he was," said Mrs. Carmody, smiling a secret smile.

"Well, I want him to put the hose and that wheelbarrow in the garage," said Mr. Carmody.

"I'll tell him," said Mrs. Carmody. "He should be back in a minute or so." She and Mr. Carmody went into the house and closed the kitchen door.

Phillip, quite red in the face from standing on his head in the wheelbarrow and hoarse from reciting the alphabet backwards and forwards, called after them, "Hey Mom and Dad. Lookit me." But they didn't even glance at him. They acted as if they didn't even hear him. "Hey you kids, lookit me," he called to the children who had followed him home from Mrs. Piggle-Wiggle's. But nobody answered. They just turned and walked out of the yard. Slowly he righted himself, climbed out of the wheelbarrow and went into the kitchen.

"How come you and Dad didn't watch my trick?" he asked his mother who was busy at the stove.

She said, "We didn't see you doing any tricks. Now go and put away the hose and the wheelbarrow and sweep up that broken glass. Dinner will be ready in about five minutes and it's your favorite."

"You mean frankfurters and baked beans and brown bread?" Phillip asked.

"That's right," said his mother.

"Hot diggety," said Phillip.

Reaching into the broom closet his mother took out the broom and dustpan and handed them to him. "Here," she said, very relieved that he was visible again. "Sweep up that glass first."

Phillip took the broom, held it up over his shoulders and began making loud zooming noises. "Hey, Mom," he yelled, "watch me, I'm a jet plane. Here I go for a take-off."

As he said "Watch me," he began to disappear—with "take-off" he was gone.

Humming contentedly his mother took the lid off the steamer and poked the brown bread.

At dinner he disappeared three times. The first time was when he turned his chair around, crouched down on the seat and said, "Look at me! I'm a big gorilla in a cage. Toss me a banana somebody." He disappeared just after "toss me."

Mr. Carmody almost jumped out of his chair. "Meg, Meg," he yelled at Mrs. Carmody. "The boy's gone. There must be a trap door under that chair."

"Don't get hysterical, Jordan," said Mrs. Carmody. "He'll be back." And he was, in about two minutes.

The next morning after he was dressed Phillip climbed on the bannister and yelled at Connie, "Hey, Connie, lookit! I'm sliding down the bannister frontwards sitting up." Then he disappeared and didn't come back into focus until everybody else had finished breakfast and his poached eggs were quite cold. His mother noticed he had a large purple bump over his left eye. As he slid into his chair Phillip said, "Nobody in this whole darn family cares what happens to me. My whole skull is probly cracked but a lot you care."

"QUIET!" roared Mr. Carmody.

Mrs. Carmody said, "Eat your eggs dear, it's getting late." As she spoke to him she leaned over and sprinkled some of the show-off powder in his hair.

Turning around and giving her a suspicious look Phillip said, "Whatcha doin' to my hair, Mom?"

"Just smoothing it down," said his mother smiling dreamily.

During geography while Miss Perriwinkle was standing with her back to the class drawing a map on the blackboard, Phillip stood up on his seat, wiggled his ears, looked cross-eyed, looked like an ape and scratched himself, all sure-fire tricks for making his classmates giggle. Nobody laughed at all. In fact nobody even looked at him because he wasn't there.

During recess he put a whole package of bubble gum in his mouth and blew a bubble bigger than his head but even though the children were all right around him nobody pointed or laughed or said one thing. Because of course they couldn't see him. Then the bubble burst and got Phillip's hair and face all gummy, then the children laughed because he was back in focus again

but Phillip didn't think it was funny at all especially when the school nurse rubbed his face and neck and head with benzine which burned.

After school he didn't feel very funny, his head hurt and so did his elbow so he rode his bike home sitting on the seat the ordinary way. Bobby Westover and Billy Markle rode beside him and they talked quite solemnly about baseball, except once when Billy rode fast down Mission Hill with no hands yelling "Help, help, I'm out of control. My engine's conked out—my landing gear's stuck. Call the crash crew." Bobby and Phillip laughed like anything until Mrs. Allen backed out of her garage and almost hit Billy who couldn't stop and ran into a tree.

Mrs. Allen turned pure white and shook and was very mad. She said, "Billy Markle, I'm going to call your mother up and tell her what a little show-off you are! You almost got killed and you almost wrecked my car and you have practically given me a nervous breakdown."

Billy who was crying said, "Well lookit me. My shirt's tore and my nose is bleedin' and my bike's wrecked."

Mrs. Allen said, "Go on into the kitchen. I'll fix you up but don't bleed all over my clean linoleum."

Bobby and Phillip called good-bye to Billy but he didn't hear them. As they rode down the hill around he corner toward Phillip's house, Phillip said, "Poor dumb Billy. What a show-off!"

II. THE CRYBABY CURE

MRS. FOXGLOVE was baking brownies. Thick chewey chocolatey nutty brownies. The kind her four children loved. She slid the last pan into the oven, lifted Solomon the black cat down off the kitchen stool where he was drooling up at Alma Gluck the canary, and sat down herself.

It was a very dreary February day. The sky was gray, the snow in the yard was gray and slushy and a cold raw wind was swooshing around the house. Mrs. Foxglove hoped that the children had not left their galoshes on the school bus and had remembered to put on their mittens. She was especially worried about Melody whose eyes and nose always seemed to be so red and chapped.

She sighed and stroked Solomon who had jumped into her lap. Then she pushed him off onto the floor and opened the oven door. The brownies were baking beautifully. She switched the bottom pans to the top shelf and the top pans to the bottom shelf, then closed the door and put the milk on to heat for the children's cocoa.

She was just stirring in the cocoa when from way down the street she heard a noise like a fire siren. Woo-ooooooooooo ooooo, weeeeeeeeeeeeeeeeeeee, bawwwwwwwwwwwww went the noise getting louder and closer. Mrs. Foxglove sighed and opened the back door. Cornell, her oldest boy who was eleven came dashing up the back steps, gave his mother a hug and said, "I smell brownies. Zowie!"

Harvard, who was nine, stamped the snow off his galoshes and said, "Another hundred in spelling, Mom. How many brownies can I have?"

Emmy, who was six, said, "I lotht another tooth today but I can chew brownieth. How many can I have?"

Melody who was eight came shuffling up the walk her mouth so wide open her mother could almost see her stomach. "Moooooother," she bawled. "The kids are teasig be. Baaaaaaaaaaaaaaaaaaaaaw."

Mrs. Foxglove said, "Hurry up, Melody, I want to shut the back door before the house gets cold."

"I cad't hurry," Melody sobbed as she wiped her red nose on her sleeve. "I fell dowd and by dee hurts so I cad hardly walk."

"All right then," said her mother. "I'll shut the door and you can take as long as you like." She closed the door.

Instantly a wail like a dying hyena filled the air and Melody came charging up the back steps and threw herself against the back door yelling, "Let be id. I'b freezig."

Mrs. Foxglove opened the door and Melody who had been leaning heavily against it fell into the kitchen. Emmy and Harvard and Cornell who were sitting on the floor taking off their galoshes laughed uproariously. Melody lay stretched out on the floor like a squashed spider bawling. Mrs. Foxglove pushed her aside a little with her foot and shut the door.

Immediately Melody screamed, "You kicked be. By owd mother kicked be."

Mrs. Foxglove said, "Melody, dear, I only pushed you a little with my foot so I could close the door."

Solomon walked over and licked her ear with his rough little tongue.

"Ouch," she shrieked. "Solobon scratched be. Right here on by ear."

"He did not," Emmy said. "He jutht licked your ear. You old bawl-baby."

"By ear, it's bleedig," Melody snuffled. "I'll probably get rabies."

"Gee, Mom, isn't she awful?" said Cornell. "She's the biggest baby in the whole school. Nobody likes her."

"They do so," said Melody sitting up and wiping her eyes with her mittens."

"Aw they do not," said Harvard. "They call you Old-Wet-Washrag-Foxglove."

"That's what *you* call be," said Melody. "Did you hear that, Mommy? He calls be Old-Wet-Washrag-Foxglove all the tibe." She began to cry again.

Mrs. Foxglove said, "Oh, my goodness I smell the brownies. Out of my way everybody. Pick up your things and take them into the coat closet."

The children gathered up their galoshes and coats and mittens and caps and hurried out of the kitchen. All but Melody who was lying on her back on the floor her mittened hands scrunched into her eyes, crying.

Mrs. Foxglove opened the oven door, pulled out a pan of brownies and poked a broom straw down into it. The broom straw came out clean and so she knew they were done. The cocoa was almost boiling so she took it off the burner and set it aside. She was setting out the cups when she noticed Melody. She said, "Come on, chickabiddy. Stop that snuffling and take off your things. The brownies are all done."

Melody hiccupped several times but didn't move.

Mrs. Foxglove reached down, took hold of her arms and lifted her to her feet.

Melody bellowed, "Ouch, ouch, you're hurtig be."

Her mother gave her a little shake. "I am not hurting you and I'm good and tired of your being such a big crybaby." She took Melody by the shoulders, turned her in the direction of the front hall and gave her a little push.

Melody crumpled into a soggy ball and began to sob hysterically, "You're so bead to be I cad't sta'd it. You shake be and jerk be and push be."

"Oh, go up to your room and stay there until you can be cheerful," said Mrs. Foxglove crossly. "Now scat."

Snuffling and glupping Melody went. Only she didn't scat. She shuffled very very slowly.

Her mother watched until she reached the doorway then sighing with exasperation went back and began pouring the cocoa.

Emmy came skipping into the kitchen. She hugged her mother around the knees and said, "You're the best Mommy in the whole world. Can I have sixth brownieth?"

Her mother bent down and kissed her on top of her

head and said, "Let's start with one."

Then Harvard and Cornell came in with Hiboy, the dog, and for a while Mrs. Foxglove was so busy that she didn't have time to think about Melody. Then the telephone rang and it was Mrs. Popsickle and she wanted to know if Emmy and Melody and Cornell and Harvard could all come to her twins', Trent and Tansy, birthday party next Saturday. Mrs. Foxglove said certainly they would love it and Mrs. Popsickle said they were to wear play clothes and come at eleven because Mr. Popsickle was going to take them to Playland and then to a movie.

As soon as Mrs. Foxglove hung up the phone the children all sounding like owls began whoing and whatting and whenning and when Mrs. Foxglove told them that it was a birthday party on Saturday which was only the day after tomorrow, and that they were going to Playland *and* a movie the boys whistled through their teeth and said Zowie and Hot Diggety and Emmy said, "I'm going upstairs right now and get Bruno all dressed."

"Oh, Mom," Cornell said, "don't let her take that dumb old teddy bear. All his stuffing's hanging out."

Emmy said, "I take Bruno every place I go, Mithter Cornell, and he can't help it becauth hith thtuffing is coming out. Tho there."

Harvard said, "Oh, tho there yourthelf!"

Quickly Mrs. Foxglove said, "Boys, I want you to go down and finish up that play table you're making me. But remember, put *all* of Daddy's tools away when you finish."

"I will," Harvard said. "I always do. It's old

Cornell that always leaves stuff out."

"Oh yeah?" Cornell said. "What about the hammer you left over at Fetlock Harroway's?"

"Come boys," said Mrs. Foxglove. "You'd better get started it's almost four-thirty."

When the cellar door had closed behind the boys Mrs. Foxglove turned to Emmy and said, "Emmy, dear, if you'll run upstairs and get Bruno I'll sew his stuffing back in and while I'm doing that perhaps you would like to wash and iron his clothes."

After Emmy had gone upstairs Mrs. Foxglove was scrubbing out the cocoa pan when she heard somebody sniffing behind her. She turned to find Melody, her eyes swollen to tiny slits, her nose as red as a radish, her cheeks blotchy, her lips dry and cracked, standing in the doorway. Melody said, or rather choked out, "I dotice you're washing the cocoa pad and I didn't get ady and I suppose the browdies are all gode, too."

"Your cup of cocoa is right there on the breakfast table," said her mother cheerfully. "And there are lots and lots of brownies in the cookie jar. However, you can't have anything until you wash your face and cheer up."

"I dod't thick I want adythig adyway," Melody said sadly and went back upstairs.

Mrs. Foxglove groaned. What was she going to do with Melody? What was the matter with her? Perhaps she had better call Dr. Pillsbury. She went in to the back hall and dialled Dr. Pillsbury's number. His nurse answered and said he was busy but would call her back in a few minutes. Emmy came in. From one hand she was dragging Bruno by one leg, from the other a laundry bag of his dirty clothes. Mrs. Foxglove sent her upstairs for her workbasket and then the phone rang and it was Dr. Pillsbury who, when he heard about Melody, said that he would stop by on his way home.

Bruno was all mended with new black shiny shoe-button eyes and Mrs. Foxglove was ironing his best blue-and-white-checked rompers and the boys were sanding the play table with the electric sander when Dr. Pillsbury arrived. He said, "What a busy happy family. Do you happen to have a cup of hot coffee, Martha?"

"Made it especially for you," Mrs. Foxglove said handing Emmy the rompers and turning off the iron. "Take Bruno and his clothes upstairs and tell Melody to come down."

As she poured Dr. Pillsbury his coffee and put some brownies on a plate she said, "Tim, I'm awfully worried about Melody. She cries all the time over everything. Do you think it could be rheumatic fever?"

"Does she have a fever?" asked Dr. Pillsbury taking two brownies.

"No, she doesn't," said Mrs. Foxglove. "In fact she seems very well but she is so sad. *Everything* makes her cry. She cries so much and her face is so red and swollen all the time she looks as if she had been stung by a million bees."

Dr. Pillsbury slowly stirred his coffee and said, "If I can find nothing wrong with Melody physically, then I would suggest that you call Mrs. Piggle-Wiggle."

"Will she know what to do?" Mrs. Foxglove asked.

"She certainly will," said Dr. Pillsbury. "She knows more about children than anybody in this town."

"Well, I know she cured Cornell's table manners and she stopped Emmy's tattling but I didn't dream she could do anything about crying."

"I'll bet she can," said Dr. Pillsbury. "My goodness, Martha, these brownies are so good it's criminal. I want you to make me a solemn pledge you won't give Eunice the recipe. I'm much too fat as it is."

Mrs. Foxglove laughed and looked very happy, then Melody came shuffling and snuffling downstairs. By this time her face was sort of purple plum color, her nose was like a ripe strawberry, and her mother couldn't see her eyes at all.

Dr. Pillsbury said, "Come here so I can see how heavy you are."

Slowly, slowly, hiccupping with every step Melody walked over to him. He lifted her up and sat her on his knee. Then he said, "Whew, you're quite a chunk for eight years old! Stick out your tongue."

Dr. Pillsbury looked at her tongue, looked down her throat, looked in her ears, listened to her lungs and heart, poked at her stomach and took her temperature. When he had finished he said, "Sound as a nut except for a very advanced case of acute eight-year-old sadi-tis. Better call Mrs. Piggle-Wiggle before a certain party's tear ducts wear out."

After Dr. Pillsbury had gone Mrs. Foxglove sent Melody and Emmy next door to Mrs. Rocket's house to borrow an onion, while she called Mrs. Piggle-Wiggle.

Mrs. Piggle-Wiggle laughed when she heard about Melody and said, "Oh, I've got the most wonderful cure for crybabyitis. It's a tonic that tastes delicious, sort of like vanilla ice cream with caramel sauce, and it works very quickly. In fact if you would send Harvard and Cornell over for it right now, I think we could have Melody cured before Trent and Tansy Popsickle's birthday party Saturday."

"Oh, do you think so?" asked Mrs. Foxglove almost crying herself, she was so happy.

"Certainly do," said Mrs. Piggle-Wiggle. "Tell the boys I sent in and got those new Super Secret Outer Space Other Hemisphere Ten Way Wrist Communicators they wanted. That will make them hurry."

"Oh, thank you, thank you, dear Mrs. Piggle-Wiggle," said Mrs. Foxglove.

"Tell the boys to hurry," said Mrs. Piggle-Wiggle. "It's getting dark and the streets are slippery."

When Mrs. Foxglove called to Harvard and Cornell and told them she wanted them to run an errand for her they groaned and said, "Way over there, golleee" and "My Gosh, just when we're busy sandin' this ole table" and "Why can't somebody else in this family ever run any errands?" Then she told them about the Super Secret Outer Space Other Hemisphere Ten Way Wrist Communicators and they were upstairs jamming on their galoshes and coats in two seconds.

Then Melody and Emmy came back from Mrs.

Rocket's with the onion and Melody was bawling because she had gotten slush in her galoshes and Mrs. Rocket's dog had jumped on her and it was too cold outside and her eyes hurt.

Mrs. Foxglove helped her off with her coat and took her upstairs and put cold cloths on her eyes. The cloths weren't very cold but Melody screamed in pain each time her mother touched her until Mrs. Foxglove finally said, "I declare you must *like* to look like a stewed tomato."

Emmy laughed but Melody immediately began to cry. Mrs. Foxglove sent her to her room to stay until dinner was ready.

When Mr. Foxglove came home he was very cheerful especially when he found that Mrs. Foxglove had chicken and dumplings for dinner. Then Melody came sobbing down stairs to report that somebody had used her toothbrush, she could tell because it was wet.

Her daddy said, "Are you sure it isn't just wet with tears?"

Melody said, "After all, Daddy, I dod't brush by eyes with by toothbrush."

"Very logical," he said putting his arm around her, "but of late you have been as soggy as a bath sponge and dampness rubs off, see?" He held her off so she could see the big wet spot on his jacket where her head had rested.

"In fact," he said as he rubbed at the spot, "you are one of the juiciest children I've ever cuddled."

Melody began to bawl. Opening her mouth wide and scrubbing at her eyes.

Mr. Foxglove handed her his handkerchief and said, "Come on now, Missy, that was only a joke and you know it. Dry those eyes or the place where they used to be and let's have dinner. Where are the boys?"

"They'll be here in a minute, Juniper, in fact I hear them now," said Mrs. Foxglove.

Cornell and Harvard burst in the back door, their cheeks crimson from the cold, their eyes dancing with excitement. Thrusting their wrists at their mother they said, "Mom, just look what Mrs. Piggle-Wiggle sent away and got for us. Super Secret Outer Space Other Hemisphere Ten Way Wrist Communicators. Aren't they keen? Lookit, see all the signs of the zodiac and the dials."

Mrs. Foxglove looked at the SSOSOHTWWC and said, "Now for heaven's sake be very careful how you use those things. I don't want to be deluged with people from another planet."

"Oh, don't worry, Mom," Harvard said. "We got all the directions right here in this little book."

"Didn't Mrs. Piggle-Wiggle give you something else?" asked Mrs. Foxglove.

"Oh, yeah, she gave us this little bottle," Cornell said as he rummaged through the pockets of his jacket taking out nails, string, four peanuts, two rocks with gold in them, a note to his mother telling her about a PTA meeting which had happened two weeks ago and to which she had gone anyway, several nuts and bolts, two gray licorice drops and finally a small bottle wrapped in brown paper.

After she had sent the boys up to wash Mrs. Fox-

glove carefully unwrapped the bottle. It was labeled
"CRYBABY TONIC—one teaspoonful as needed."
Mrs. Foxglove pulled out the cork and smelled it. It
smelled delicious. She called Melody who was standing in the front hall dabbing at her streaming eyes with
her father's handkerchief, to come out to the kitchen.
She poured the tonic into a rather large teaspoon and
very briskly told Melody who was leaning mournfully
against the stove, to open her mouth.

Melody began to cry. "I don't wad to take ady bad
tastig bedicid," she sobbed. "I'b dot sick."

"This isn't bad tasting, it's delicious," said her
mother taking advantage of her opened mouth to force
the spoon in.

Melody gulped down the medicine and then said,
"Id's good. I like id. Cad I have sob bore?"

"Not now," said her mother. "Perhaps another teaspoon before you go to bed. Now help me carry in the
salad plates."

The first thing Mrs. Foxglove noticed about the effect of the Crybaby Tonic was that all the redness and
swelling disappeared from Melody's face.

"She's probably already cured," thought her mother
happily.

The chicken and dumplings were delicious. Everybody was having a very good time until Cornell who sat
next to Melody sneaked a chicken bone down to Hiboy
who was *never* supposed to be fed at the table but was
usually lying under it ready in case somebody should
spill. Anyway in reaching for the bone Hiboy put one
paw on Cornell's knee which was covered with jeans,

and the other on Melody's knee which was bare. Hiboy didn't mean any harm but dogs do have toenails and he may have scratched her a little but certainly not enough to warrant the banshee howl she let out. "Owwwwwwwwww, wooooooooooow, weeeeeeeeee!" she wailed.

Then the strangest thing happened. Out of her eyes gushed two regular faucets of tears. They filled her dinner plate with water, soaked her table mat, soaked her napkin, made a little lake in her lap, poured down her legs and filled her shoes. In fact in no time at all there was a huge puddle around her chair.

"My gosh, Mom, look at old Melody," said Cornell, his eyes as big as dollars.

"Mom, Dad, quick stop her," said Harvard as Melody's gushing tears ran across the table and into his lap.

"Melody, you big dummy," said Emmy, "you've cried all over Bruno'th clean romperth."

Mrs. Foxglove said, "Juniper, do something quick! The water's clear over here under my chair."

Mr. Foxglove yelled at Melody who was now soaking wet from head to toe, "Stop crying. Close your mouth. Smile!"

Melody did and the tears stopped. Everybody stared at her in wonder. "I've never seen so many tears in my whole life," her father said. "How in the world did you do it?"

"I don't know," Melody said. "I just started to cry and the tears came out."

"I'm going to rent you out to water lawns," her daddy said.

"Salt water kills grass," Cornell said.

Mrs. Foxglove said, "Instead of talking nonsense let's all get busy and wipe up this water."

After everything had been wiped off and dried out as much as possible, Melody went upstairs and changed into her pajamas and bedroom slippers, and her mother gave her another plate of dinner. The rest of the meal was devoted to talking about Melody's amazing new achievement. By the time it was over she began to feel very important. In fact she didn't see any reason why such a remarkable child should help with the dishes.

Harvard said, "Listen, Wet Washrag, it's your turn to do the pots and pans."

Melody said, "Don't you dare call me Wet Washrag, Harvard Foxglove, or I'll tell Daddy that you broke

Mr. Maxwell's greenhouse window."

Cornell said, "If you tell on Harvard, Melody, I won't take you on the roller coaster with me next Saturday when we go to Trent and Tansy's party."

"What party?" asked Melody.

"The party Mrs. Popsickle is giving for Trent and Tansy's birthday and Mr. Popsickle is taking us all to Playland and to a movie show," Emmy said. "And it *is* your turn for the pots and pans, Melody, you know it is, it's right on the chart."

"Oh, all right," Melody said.

Everything was going very well until Harvard and Cornell started duelling with two big spoons and in jumping around Cornell stepped hard on Melody's toe. She opened her mouth like a yawning hippopotamus and began to bawl. Instantly two faucets of tears gushed out of her eyes and soaked her pajamas, bedroom slippers, Emmy's dish towel, and Solomon who was rubbing against her legs.

"Help, help, Daddy, make her stop," yelled the boys.

"Smile," shouted Emmy.

"Ooooooooooooooooooo, wooooooooooo!" she wailed and the tears poured out faster and pretty soon the kitchen floor was covered with water.

Then Mr. Foxglove came striding out and pushed Melody over to the sink and held her there so her tears would go down the drain. He told Melody to stay there by the sink until she decided to stop crying. She wailed, "But I'b all wet. I'll catch deumodia and die."

"That is your problem," said her father coldly. "You can either stop crying, smile, stop the tears and change into dry things or you can spend the rest of the night standing there at the sink."

Mr. and Mrs. Foxglove were playing Scrabble, Emmy was asleep and Harvard and Cornell were supposed to be doing their homework, when Melody finally stopped crying and sloshed upstairs to change into dry pajamas and slippers. When she finally came down to say good night, her mother took hold of her chin, looked at her anxiously and said, "Do you feel all right, dear?"

Melody smiled rather sheepishly and said, "I feel kind of cold but not a bit sick."

Her mother kissed her and told her to go in the guest room and get Grandmother Dowson's down quilt.

Mr. Foxglove kissed her and said, "For heaven's sake, don't cry in your sleep. You'll drown."

Melody slept well and the next morning when she awakened she felt very happy especially when she remembered that the next day was the birthday party, and the next day after that was Sunday and Pergola Wingsproggle was going to give her a yellow kitten. Also the sun was shining. Also that tonic her mother gave her before breakfast was so delicious.

Everybody was cheerful at breakfast and Mrs. Foxglove told the children she would drive them to school and would drive Daddy to work as she had to have the car. All the children were smiling when they got out of the car at school and Mrs. Rexall, the principal, said to Old Joe, the janitor, "I'm delighted to see that little Melody Foxglove has at last cheered up."

Melody was very cheerful all morning and she got

one hundred in spelling and an A on her story about "My Kitten." Then came lunchtime. She and Emmy and Kitty Wheeling and Susan Gray and Sally Franklin were all sitting together at a table giggling and whispering and having fun when Benji Franklin who was a great tease, leaned over from the table where he was sitting and grabbed Melody's gingerbread.

Without even thinking about the night before Melody opened her mouth and began to cry. Immediately the tears poured out. They filled up her soup bowl, soaked her peanut butter and jelly sandwich, soaked Emmy's sandwich, filled her lap with water, poured onto the table and made a river that flowed into Kitty Wheeling's gingerbread and then into her lap.

The children all began to yell, "Look at Melody. Look out for the tears. Move over I'm getting wet. Help, a flood. Call the fire department!" and other silly things.

Melody got up and ran sobbing out of the lunchroom down the hall and out into the play court which was empty. There was nobody there because they were all inside eating lunch. Melody stood right in the middle of the court and cried and cried and cried and cried. She cried because she was wet. She cried because Benji took her gingerbread. She cried because she was alone. But mostly she cried because it was her habit to open her mouth and bellow when any tiny thing didn't suit her.

Well, she cried and cried and cried and pretty soon the whole courtyard was flooded and the water was up past her ankles. She didn't care she hated everybody and everything in the whole world. She cried and cried and cried. Pretty soon the water was clear up to her waist and lunchtime was almost over and little Emmy was up in the schoolyard which was much higher than the play court, calling down to her, "Smile, Melody. Smile quick or you'll be drownded."

Melody sobbed, "I cad't sbile. I'b too sad." Gallons and gallons more tears rushed out.

Then Kitty Wheeling called down, "Melody, quick, stop crying it's almost time for the bell."

"I dod't care," cried Melody. "I dod't like school adyway." The tears were almost up to her chest now.

Then Pergola Wingsproggle and Emmy and Kitty and Sally and Susan and Mrs. Rexall began whispering and pretty soon Pergola disappeared. Melody kept crying. The tears were almost up to her chin. And then Pergola called out to her, "Melody, quick, look what I've brought you."

Melody looked and Pergola was holding up a darling little orange kitten.

"A kitten. A little kitten of my very own," Melody said and she stopped crying and smiled. The tears stopped. Slowly she made her way across the play court. Once she tripped and had to swim dog paddle. When she finally got out, Pergola showed her the kitten which she couldn't hold because she was too wet. It was adorable with long soft hair and big round blue eyes. She said, "Oh, Pergola, thank you, thank you. It's adorable."

Mrs. Rexall said, "Here, I'll carry it for you, Melody. Now come with me to the teachers' room. I'll dry

you off and Old Joe can dry your clothes down by the furnace. The rest of you children can skip along to class."

After she had taken off her wet clothes, Mrs. Rexall dried her off with a towel and wrapped her in a blanket. Then she handed her the kitten and told her to lie there on the couch until her clothes were dry.

The kitten curled up inside Melody's arm and the blanket was soft and warm and pretty soon they were both asleep. She woke up when Mrs. Rexall came in with her clothes all wrinkly but dry and then there was Mommy to drive the children home and school was over.

That night when Melody kissed her mommy and

daddy good night she said, "I'm never going to cry again. No matter what happens. Not ever." And she never did. *And* at Trent and Tansy Popsickle's birthday party Melody and Betsy Wilt were in the Ferris wheel and something happened to the motor and the Ferris wheel stopped and wouldn't start and there they were right on the very top. Both the little girls were awfully scared but when Betsy began to cry, Melody said, "Crying never helped anything, Betsy. As long as we're up so high, let's see if we can see our houses. Look, way over there, past the saw mill chimney and right up behind the school, isn't that your house?"

Betsy wiped her eyes on her sleeve and looked where Melody was pointing and sure enough it did look like her house. Then she noticed that she could see Little Willow Lake. Then she saw the building where her father worked. Then they both thought they saw Melody's house.

"And I think I see my kitten, Butterball, asleep on the garage roof," Melody said. Just then the Ferris wheel started.

When they got off Mr. Popsickle was waiting for them. He said, "What, no tears? By George, such bravery deserves an ice-cream soda. What flavor will it be, ladies?"

"I'll take chocolate with chocolate ice cream," Melody said.

"Me too," said Betsy. "I've already had strawberry and vanilla."

While they were eating their sodas Mr. Popsickle said, "I thought girls always cried when they were scared."

"I did cry," Betsy said. "But Melody said that crying never helped anything."

"It doesn't either," Melody said. "I know because I used to cry a lot when I was littler."

III. THE BULLY

NICHOLAS SEMICOLON was ten years old. He was a husky boy, very strong and large for his age. All parents like to have large healthy children and Mr. and Mrs. Semicolon would have been very proud of Nicholas except for one thing. One shameful thing. Nicholas was a bully. He hit children littler than he was. He teased and hit girls. He teased and hit puppy dogs. He scared cats. He even threw stones at birds and once he tipped over the stroller of a one-year-old baby left outside the grocery store.

For a long time Mr. and Mrs. Semicolon didn't know about Nicholas. They knew he was large for his age. They knew his friendships with other children didn't last very long. They knew he had not been asked to several birthday parties. But they thought that Nicholas was big and strong and handsome and needed older more intelligent children to play with. In fact just the night before this story opens after Nicholas had kicked the cat, stepped on Josephine, the dog's tail and gone swaggering up to bed, Mrs. Semicolon said to Mr. Semicolon, "Forthright, have you noticed how fine and big and strong little Nicky has grown?"

Mr. Semicolon who was reading about stocks and bonds in the evening paper said, "Sure outgrows his shoes fast. Two new pairs last month."

"I know," said Mrs. Semicolon dreamily, "his feet are just enormous. They're almost as big as yours."

"Good," said Mr. Semicolon brightening up. "Maybe he can wear out those oxblood brogues I got in Chicago last winter. They never did fit and I paid a lot for them."

"Do boys wear brogues?" asked Mrs. Semicolon.

"What difference does it make?" said Mr. Semicolon. "They're shoes and they're new. After all Abe Lincoln went barefoot."

"But, Forthright, dear," said Mrs. Semicolon anxiously, "Nicky is a patrol boy and he needs new patrol boots."

"Nonsense," said Mr. Semicolon. "Shoes are shoes. They are only meant to keep your feet off the cold ground."

The next morning rather hesitantly Mrs. Semicolon went into Nicholas' room carrying the large sturdy brogues. She said, "Look what Daddy got in Chicago, dear."

Nicholas took one of the shoes, examined it carefully then to his mother's surprise said, "Zowie, what strong shoes! Can I wear 'em to school today?"

"I was thinking more of Sunday school," said his mother, "but I guess one day at school won't matter."

Nicholas who was still in his pajamas slipped a bare foot into one of the shoes. He smiled happily. "Kind of big but boy they're strong and heavy."

Mrs. Semicolon heaved a sigh of relief and went downstairs to make the pancakes.

When Nicholas came clumping in to breakfast Mr. Semicolon said, "New shoes, eh, son?"

"Yeah," said Nicholas. "New and strong. I bet if I kicked with these ole shoes it would just about break somebody's leg."

Mr. Semicolon who was reading the paper and not listening said, "Mmmmmmmmmmmmmmmmm."

Mrs. Semicolon who was turning the pancakes said, "How many sausages, Nicky dear?"

"Ten sausages and fourteen pancakes," said Nicholas gulping down his orange juice.

"My what a big strong hungry boy you are," said his mother happily.

Then breakfast was over and Nicholas had gone clumping off to school in his new shoes that really didn't fit and Mr. Semicolon had left for the office in his new shoes that did and Mrs. Semicolon poured herself a hot cup of coffee and sat down at the telephone to call up her friends. She had finished talking to Mary Hex when the telephone rang. It was little Roscoe Eager's mother and she was so mad she was choking. She said, "Carlotta Semicolon, if you don't do something about that big bully I'm going to call the sheriff."

"What big bully?" asked Mrs. Semicolon innocently.

"What big bully!" shrieked Mrs. Eager. "You know perfectly well what big bully."

"I don't either," said Mrs. Semicolon. "I don't know any big bullies."

"Oh, yes you do," said Mrs. Eager, "because the biggest meanest cruelest bully in the whole United States is your own son, Nicholas Semicolon."

"You mean my Nicky?" asked Mrs. Semicolon.

"Yes, your Nicky," said Mrs. Eager. "This morning on his way to school he kicked little Roscoe in the shins with his big new shoes and now Roscoe is home lying on the davenport with bandages clear up to his knees and his legs are still bleeding and for all I know both leg bones are shattered."

"How horrible," wailed Mrs. Semicolon. "How terrible. Shall I call the doctor?"

"I already have," said Mrs. Eager coldly. "He's on his way over. But what I want to know is what you intend to do about Nicholas."

"I'll punish him of course," said Mrs. Semicolon, "but I just can't understand it. It doesn't sound a bit like Nicky."

"But it does," said Mrs. Eager. "It sounds exactly like him. Hitting children littler than he is. Kicking dogs. Jerking toys away from babies. Tipping over little girls' tricycles. Pulling cats' tails. Now I have to go, I hear Roscoe moaning for me."

"Jessie, dear, I'm so sorry," said Mrs. Semicolon. "I'll come right over and bring some coloring books and some sugar cookies I baked yesterday."

At first after she hung up the phone Mrs. Semicolon cried a little, then she remembered the new brogues, blew her nose, wiped her eyes and called Mr. Semicolon.

When he answered she said angrily, "Well I hope you're happy!"

"About what?" he asked.

Mrs. Semicolon began to cry. "It's those darned old brogues that didn't fit Nicky anyway," she sobbed.

"What in the world is the matter?" said Mr. Semicolon.

So, Mrs. Semicolon told him about Mrs. Eager's telephone call.

Mrs. Semicolon said, "It never would have happened if it hadn't been for those brogues. I'm going to give them to the Goodwill."

Mr. Semicolon said, "Listen to me, Carlotta dear, it is not the shoes that are at fault, it is Nicky. After all the shoes didn't grab his feet and force them to kick a little boy in the shins, did they?"

"No, I guess not," sniffed Mrs. Semicolon.

"Well, then," said Mr. Semicolon, "the important thing is not the kind of shoes he kicked with, it is the fact that he kicked and a boy smaller than he. Isn't that right, dear?"

"Yes," said Mrs. Semicolon.

"Well, then," said Mr. Semicolon, "when young Nicholas comes home from school you send him up to his room to think things over and I will deal with him when I come home."

Then Mrs. Semicolon remembered about kicking the dogs, jerking toys away from babies, tipping over little girls' tricycles, pulling cats' tails. So she said, "But kicking with the brogues isn't the only thing, Forthright. Mrs. Eager also told me . . ." and she told him all the rest of Nicky's bad actions.

When she had finished Mr. Semicolon said, "I won't *have* a bully for a son. I think I'll go over to school right now and deal with that young man."

"What will you do?" asked Mrs. Semicolon faintly.

There was a pause, quite a long pause on the other end of the wire, then Nicky's father said, "Why don't you call Mrs. Piggle-Wiggle?"

"Oh, Forthright, how clever of you," said Nicky's mother. "I'll call her right away. She'll know just what to do. She always does."

A few minutes later Mrs. Piggle-Wiggle, who was out in her back yard gathering hazel nuts for her two gray squirrels, Taylor and Philbert, heard the phone ring. When she picked it up and said hello, the voice on the other end was so sad and ashamed when it said,

"Hello, Mrs. Piggle-Wiggle," that she knew at once who it was.

Then Mrs. Semicolon started to tell her about Nicky's kicking and hitting and jerking and pushing and tripping little children, but Mrs. Piggle-Wiggle said in her very gentle voice, "I know, Mrs. Semicolon. You don't have to tell me. I know all about it."

"Do you mean the other mothers have called you up?" said Mrs. Semicolon.

"No, no," said Mrs. Piggle-Wiggle, "but Nicky has been coming over here to play for a long time. I've watched him grow from a rather sickly weak child into a fine, strong, healthy boy. You should be *proud* of him, Mrs. Semicolon."

"I was," said Mrs. Semicolon, "until this morning. Now, after what I have heard I wish he was sickly and weak still."

"Not really," said Mrs. Piggle-Wiggle. "It's much nicer to have a fine healthy son. Easier, too. All you want is to have Nicky behave in as fine and strong a way as he looks."

"What I don't understand," said Mrs. Semicolon, "is why Nicky should act in the dreadful way he does. Neither his father nor I have ever bullied *him.*"

"Of course you haven't," said Mrs. Piggle-Wiggle. "Neither have I but he acts the same way down here. And, if it is any comfort to you, so did Billy MacIntosh until last week when his mother gave him Bully-baths."

"What in the world are they?" asked Mrs. Semicolon.

"They are just evening baths with a little weakening powder sprinkled in them. With each bath the bully gets weaker and weaker until finally, as in the case of Billy MacIntosh, his two-year-old brother could push him down and sit on him."

"Is he all right now?" asked Mrs. Semicolon.

"Just fine," said Mrs. Piggle-Wiggle.

"How wonderful," said Mrs. Semicolon. "Shall I start the Bullybaths tonight?"

"I was just thinking," said Mrs. Piggle-Wiggle. "In the case of Nicholas I'm not sure the Bullybaths would be the right cure."

"But why?" asked Mrs. Semicolon. "They worked with Billy MacIntosh."

"I know they did," said Mrs. Piggle-Wiggle, "but Billy MacIntosh has little sisters and brothers. No, I think that Nicholas would be better off with Leadership Pills."

"Leadership Pills?" asked Mrs. Semicolon. "What are they?"

"Just little green pills that taste like peppermint," said Mrs. Piggle-Wiggle, "but they bring out wonderful hidden qualities of leadership, especially in only children. Does Nicholas have a playroom or a place where he can bring his friends?"

"Well, he has a very nice bedroom," said Mrs. Semicolon.

"I'm sure he has," said Mrs. Piggle-Wiggle. "But I was thinking more of a place in the cellar or garage or even a tent house in the back yard."

"Oh, I know, I know," said Mrs. Semicolon excitedly. "There is a little old studio out in back. It was built for the artist brother of the people who used to live here. We've used it for garden tools and peat moss and the lawn mower and once Nicholas kept a rabbit there but we could move the garden tools into the cellar and I could have it all fixed up for Nicholas."

Mrs. Piggle-Wiggle said, "Why not let Nicholas fix it up himself?"

"Do you think he could?" asked Mrs. Semicolon.

"Let's wait and see how the Leadership Pills work," said Mrs. Piggle-Wiggle. "If you will send Nicholas over when he comes home from school I'll give him a little bottle to bring home. Give him one pill every day for a week but don't expect miracles. The qualities of leadership are not something you attain overnight. Keep in touch and don't worry."

The very first thing Mrs. Semicolon did after she had hung up the phone was to go out in the yard and look at the old studio. It was late autumn, almost winter and the little old path that led from the back porch past the parsley patch, around the chrysanthemum bed, under the gravenstein apple tree, around the strawberry barrel, past the compost pile to the chestnut tree under which was nestled the old studio, was ankle deep in leaves. They made a nice crumpled newspaper sound as Mrs. Semicolon walked through them. The little old studio needed a coat of paint and the porch was sagging. The front door was hard to open.

Inside was the usual gardener's litter. Spilled peat moss, empty buckets, coffee cans half filled with bone meal and lime. A broken bamboo rake. The power lawn mower. Empty seed packages. Empty flower pots. Nicky's first little bicycle; his last big tricycle; and a Christmas tree stand.

Mrs. Semicolon looked around her and sighed. She wondered if she shouldn't forget what Mrs. Piggle-Wiggle had said and have Old Mac, the handyman, clean the place up. Then she heard the phone ringing and it was Mr. Semicolon wanting to know if she had gotten hold of Mrs. Piggle-Wiggle and what she had said and she had just finished talking to him when Roscoe's mother called to say that the doctor said he was just bruised, and then by the time she had tidied up the house and had a sandwich, it was three-thirty and almost time for Nicky to come home from school.

She fixed a plate of sugar cookies and a glass of milk and a big shiny red apple and put them on the kitchen table. Then she went upstairs and washed her face and combed her hair and put on her grocery store skirt and sweater. She was just finishing her shopping list when she heard a commotion out in the street. She ran to the front window just in time to see Nicky lift his geography book high over his head and bring it down clunk on the skinny little eight year old back of Sylvia Crouch. Quickly Mrs. Semicolon rapped on her window and called out, "Nicky Semicolon, stop that this minute!"

Nicky glanced at his mother then lifted the book up for another blow.

Mrs. Semicolon dashed out of the house, grabbed the book and said, "Aren't you ashamed of yourself? A big boy like you hitting a little girl."

"Well she started it," Nicky said.

"I did not either," Sylvia shrieked. "You took the apple away from my little sister and you pulled my hair."

Mrs. Semicolon said, "Nicholas give Sylvia back her little sister's apple at once."

"I can't," Nicholas said smiling sheepishly. "I ate it."

"All right then," said his mother. "March right into the kitchen and get the apple I put out for you and give it to Sylvia."

Slowly reluctantly Nicholas went in and got the apple. But instead of handing it to Sylvia he threw it at her hard. It hit her in the stomach. "There's your old apple," he said laughing.

Mrs. Semicolon grabbed him by the shoulders and shaking him said, "Nicholas Semicolon, apologize to Sylvia and then go right up to your room at once."

Nicholas not looking at all sorry, said, "Aw, I'm sorry I guess. But I hope your ugly little sister chokes to death on the apple."

Mrs. Semicolon grabbed his arm and hustled him into the house. She was just sending him up to his room when she remembered about Mrs. Piggle-Wiggle and the Leadership Pills. She said, "Go out and get in the car, we're going to the store and then we're going to stop by Mrs. Piggle-Wiggle's for a minute."

In the grocery store Nicholas pushed the basket and Mrs. Semicolon chose the groceries. They got along very well until Mrs. Semicolon left him and the basket up by the dog foods while she went to find the garlic salt. She was on her way back when she heard a child crying. She hurried to where she had left Nicholas and found him pushing his heavy loaded basket as hard as he could into the almost empty basket of a little boy not more than six. The little boy was crying.

Nicholas was laughing and getting ready to give his heavy basket another mighty shove, when a firm hand grabbed him by the collar and sent him spinning into the Mity Pup dog food. One can of Mity Pup hit him on the head. Another landed on his toe. Another cracked him on the wrist. "Ouch," he yelled. "Look out what you're doin'."

"I know what I'm doing," said his mother. "Now stand up and see if you have broken any of that poor little boy's mommie's eggs."

Sulkily Nicholas got to his feet, limped over and opened the box of eggs. Three were cracked. Mrs. Semicolon gave the little boy her box of eggs and took the cracked ones, then she made Nicholas apologize and with his own allowance buy the little boy a box of animal crackers. She didn't let him out of her sight after that, until she got to Mrs. Piggle-Wiggle's house. Then she waited in the car while he went in to get the Leadership Pills.

The yard, the front porch, in fact Mrs. Piggle-Wiggle's whole house was alive with children. They were swinging, digging, sewing, building, painting, singing, teeter-tottering. All busy and happy, until Nicholas opened the gate. The first thing he did was deliberately to bump into and tip over a little boy on a tricycle.

Then he stepped on the fingers of a little girl sitting on the steps playing jacks.

His mother was glad to see that when he came out of the house with the bottle of pills, the little girl who had been playing jacks hit him with a big stick and then ran in the house and slammed the door. Nicholas started after her but his mother honked the horn and shouted at him to come and get in the car.

On the way home she told him how disgracefully he had acted but he only hummed and smiled and acted very unsorry. She gave him one of the Leadership Pills even before she unpacked the groceries, and sent him up to his room to study his geography and think about his loathsome actions. She also told him to take off his brogues and put on his bedroom slippers. He said, "I like these big new shoes. They kick hard."

Well, at dinner that night even though his mother kept looking at him hopefully there was not much evidence of leadership on Nicholas' part unless you can call being the first to the table and eating the most, leadership. However, he didn't step on Josephine's tail and he didn't kick the cat and he did walk quietly in his bedroom slippers.

Mrs. Semicolon was drinking her second cup of coffee when she suddenly remembered poor little Roscoe and the crayons, coloring books and cookies she had promised him. She called Mrs. Eager to see if Roscoe was still awake and when she found he was, she put the things in a basket and was just putting on her coat when Nicholas said, "Let me take the things over, Mother."

Knowing how Mrs. Eager felt about him and also realizing that Mr. Eager who was noted for his violent temper was home, she said, "Are you sure you want to?"

"Yes," said Nicholas in a strange quiet voice. "I'll go change my shoes."

After he had left with the basket Mrs. Semicolon said, "Forthright, I'm worried. I know that it is right that Nicky should take those things to Roscoe and apologize but I'm worried about Hilton Eager. You know what a terrible temper he has. What if he should hit Nicholas?"

"Serve Nicky right," said Mr. Semicolon, unfeelingly.

"I suppose you are right," said Mrs. Semicolon in a worried voice. She cleared the table, washed the dinner dishes, fed the cat, fed Josephine, wrote a note to the milkman, and mended a tear in Nicky's play jacket. Nicky still hadn't come home. She and Mr. Semicolon played a game of cribbage. Mrs. Semicolon usually beat him all to pieces but tonight she was so worried she couldn't count.

Finally Mr. Semicolon said, "Come, come, Carlotta, stop worrying. Nicky's all right."

"But what about Hilton Eager and his terrible temper?"

Just then the front door opened and Nicky came in. He was whistling. His mother called out, "How was Roscoe, Nicky?"

"Oh, he's okay," said Nicky. "We played a couple of games of darts."

"How are his legs?" asked his father.

"They're pretty scratched up," said Nicky. "I'm going to ride him to school on my handle bars tomorrow."

"Did you apologize to him?" asked his mother.

"Yes I did," said Nicky cheerfully. "He was real nice about it but his dad gave me an awful bawling out. For a couple of minutes I thought he was going to sock me Mrs. Eager wouldn't speak to me at all, at first. But after I apologized she made us some cocoa. She's awful nice. Well, I got two more pages of geography to do. Good night."

Rather self-consciously he kissed his mother and father. Something he hadn't done for weeks. In fact ever since he had become a big swaggering bully.

The next morning at breakfast Mrs. Semicolon gave Nicholas another Leadership Pill. Later she was pleased to see how carefully he helped Roscoe onto the handle bars of his bicycle.

When he came home from school he said, "Say, Mom, these brogues are really too heavy for school. Do you s'pose I could have some new patrol boots?"

"I'll ask your father," she said.

After he had changed into his play clothes his mother asked him where he was going and he said, "I told Sylvia I'd help her patch the tire on her bike."

In about half an hour he was back with Sylvia, her little sister, and Roscoe. Leaving them outside on the porch he came in and whispered excitedly to his mother who was making apple turnovers, "Say, Mom, would you care if I gave my old trike to Sylvia's little sister? Hers is all rusty and anyway it's too little and Sylvia and Roscoe and I are going to paint it up for the baby."

"I think that would be very nice," said Mrs. Semicolon. "Your old tricycle is out in the garden house. Say, that would be a good place to paint the other tricycle. You could put all that garden stuff down in the cellar."

"Oh, boy," Nicky hugged his mother so hard he got flour in his hair. "By the way," he said as he went out the door, "I asked a boy in my room to come over and play. His name's Jimmy Gopher. He had to go home and ask his mother. Send him out to the garden house when he comes."

Jimmy Gopher, who came streaking up on his bicycle about ten minutes later, was as big and strong and husky as Nicky. He also had red hair and freckles. Mrs. Semicolon was a little worried for fear he and Nicky might not be nice to the smaller children who now included Sylvia, her little sister, her little brother, Roscoe, the Adams twins who were only four and Priscilla Wick who was seven. She kept looking out the kitchen window anxiously but everything seemed to be very peaceful. For a while they all carried things from the garden house to the cellar. Then Sylvia came in for a broom and dustpan. Priscilla Wick wanted a pan of water and a cloth to wash the windows. Jimmy Gopher wanted to know where the turpentine was and Roscoe wanted some steel wool to take the rust off the tricycle.

About four-thirty Mrs. Semicolon put nine apple turnovers on a plate and was about to carry them to the children when she heard a commotion and looked out to see Jimmy Gopher put out his foot and trip Priscilla

who was carrying the pan of water. She fell flat, slopped
water all over her play coat and began to cry. Jimmy
laughed uproariously. Hurriedly Mrs. Semicolon went
to the cupboard and got one of the Leadership Pills.
Picking up the plate of turnovers and the pill she
opened the back door. She couldn't believe her eyes or
her ears. Nicky, her own Nicky, the former bully, was
helping Priscilla to her feet and wiping her tears. He
was also saying sternly to Jimmy, "Listen, Jim, Priscilla's littler than you and she's a girl. Nobody in our
club hits girls or little kids. If you want to hit somebody, hit me *if* you can."

Jimmy said sulkily, "Aw, I didn't hurt her. She's
just an old baby."

"I am not," Priscilla said. "I'm the pitcher on the neighborhood baseball team but you got my play coat all wet and I'm going to tell my father and he'll make mashed potatoes out of you."

Sylvia's little sister said "He will, too. He's big."

Mrs. Semicolon said, "How about a hot apple turnover?"

"Hot diggety, Zowie, oh boy," the children cried as they crowded around her.

She gave them each a turnover but before she gave Jimmy his she tucked a Leadership Pill inside the crust.

While the children were eating their little pies, she took Priscilla's coat in and put it on the hall radiator to dry and got one of Nicky's play jackets for her to wear.

There was no more trouble, and just before the children had to go home for dinner Sylvia came excitedly in and asked Mrs. Semicolon to come to the studio and see her little sister's old tricycle which they had painted a beautiful bright red with silver handle bars and silver spokes on the wheels. The old garden house looked beautiful. The windows were shiny clean. The floor was swept and Nicky and Jim had made a table out of two sawhorses and some old boards. "This is our worktable," they told her proudly.

Little Roscoe Eager said, "We got a club, Mrs. Semicolon, and we're all members and it's to fix bicycles and stuff like that."

Priscilla said, "We're going to call it 'The Neighborhood Children's Club.' "

"Nick's the president," Jimmy said, "and I'm the supervisor because I'm awful good at mechanics and fixing things."

"I'm the secretary," Sylvia said. "I'm going to keep notes and make lists of the work we have to do."

"I'm the treasurer," Priscilla said. "I collect the dues and take the money when we sell lemonade and stuff like that."

"I'm the salesman," Roscoe said. "I go around and find work for us to do."

"We're the helpers," said the Adams twins and Sylvia's little sister. "We run home and get Daddy's hammer."

"Well, I'll be in charge of refreshments," said Mrs. Semicolon.

"And so will I," said Mrs. Eager who had come over to find Roscoe and had been standing on the stoop listening. "I think The Neighborhood Children's Club is such a wonderful idea I'm going to bake brownies for tomorrow's meeting."

"And," said Mrs. Semicolon, "I'm going to scout around and see if I can't find some furniture for the clubhouse. I'm sure I've got an old kitchen table and four chairs up in the attic."

"And, Mom, would you care if we had a fire in the fireplace on cold days," Nicky asked, "if we put up a firescreen and were very very careful?"

"I have an old grate they can have," said Mrs. Eager. "And if they burn coal and use the firescreen I think it would be quite safe, don't you, Carlotta?"

"Nick and I'll watch out for the little kids," said Jimmy earnestly. "After all we're the oldest and biggest."

Well, The Neighborhood Children's Club grew and grew. Different mothers gave them furniture—they even had an old couch—and some dishes and cookies and apples and cider and peanuts and popcorn. Mr. Semicolon built the boys a fine tool bench and gave them some of his older tools. Even Mr. Eager, who was a very good carpenter, controlled his terrible temper and came over and helped them build a porch. The Adams twins' mother, who used to be an artist, painted them a beautiful sign with smiling little children holding up red letters that spelled out "The Neighborhood Children's Club."

The day they put up the sign they invited Mrs. Piggle-Wiggle over for tea. Mrs. Semicolon had made a coconut cake and Mrs. Eager brought over a big plate of fudge. There was a nice fire in the fireplace and pink-and-white-checked tablecloth on the old kitchen table which Sylvia and Priscilla had painted pink. The only trouble was that the paint wasn't dry and the tablecloth stuck, in fact they never could get it off, but it certainly looked pretty that day.

Just before she went home Mrs. Piggle-Wiggle went in to see Mrs. Semicolon. Mrs. Semicolon said, "Oh, Mrs. Piggle-Wiggle I'll never be able to thank you. Never."

Mrs. Piggle-Wiggle said, "Don't thank me. Thank Mr. Piggle-Wiggle for leaving me that old sea chest full of magic cures for children. It was one of the finest things he ever did."

"Oh, by the way," said Mrs. Semicolon, "I have quite a few Leadership Pills left. Let me get them for you."

"Why don't you just keep them," said Mrs. Piggle-Wiggle. "I have lots more and with new children moving into the neighborhood and a clubhouse in your back yard, they might come in very handy."

"Well, I have used them on two of the older children, I mean besides Nicky," said Mrs. Semicolon. "Oh, Mrs. Piggle-Wiggle, I'm very proud of Nicky. He's so patient and kind to the little children."

"Of course he is," said Mrs. Piggle-Wiggle. "Down inside he probably always was. It is just that sometimes with children, especially boys, their bodies grow faster than their patience and kindness. All Leadership Pills do is even things up. Of course having that wonderful clubhouse helps a lot. Busy children are happy children, and happy children are seldom quarrelsome."

As Mrs. Piggle-Wiggle walked off down the street

in the dusk, her dog Wag on one side, Lightfoot the cat on the other, Mrs. Semicolon wiped her eyes with a corner of her apron and said to nobody in particular, "There goes the most wonderful little person in the whole world."

IV. THE WHISPERER

ON FRIDAY AFTERNOONS Miss Weathervane read to the fourth-grade class. She usually read for about half an hour but if the story was very interesting and the children were quiet and well behaved she often read longer. This Friday she was reading from a book of Japanese folk tales, a story called "The Man Who Bought a Dream."

As she was reading "Sssssssssssss, ssssss, Teeheeeeeheeee," came from the far corner of the schoolroom. Miss Weathervane stopped reading. She said, "When Evelyn Rover and Mary Crackle stop whispering I shall continue."

But Evelyn and Mary were so busy whispering they didn't hear her. Their desks were opposite each other and by leaning across the aisle they could put their heads together and whisper and giggle very conveniently. They were whispering about Evelyn's birthday party which was next Saturday and how Evelyn's mother had told her to invite every little girl in her class but she just wouldn't ask that awful old Cornelia Whitehouse who lived in a trailer and got her clothes from the St. Vincent de Paul rummage sale. "Ssssssssssss, ssssssssssss, teeheeheeteeheehee," they hissed and giggled while the class waited impatiently for Miss

Weathervane to go on with the story.

Finally Miss Weathervane put her pencil in the book to hold the place, stood up, rapped on the desk with her ruler and said in a loud clear voice, "EVELYN ROVER AND MARY CRACKLE! COME TO THE FRONT OF THE ROOM AT ONCE!"

The two little girls jumped guiltily, then stood up and walked up to Miss Weathervane's desk. Mary was embarrassed and a little bit frightened. But Evelyn tossed her pony tail which was held with two "sterling silver" barrettes, shuffled her party shoes which she wore to school every day and lowered her eyelids in an attempt to look superior and bored. Mary who was her very best friend and admired everything she did, wished she could be like Evelyn and not be scared of her teacher and look haughty like a princess.

Miss Weathervane said, "I'm sure the class would appreciate it if you girls would tell us all what is so important that it can't wait until after story time."

Mary blushed and hung her head.

Evelyn said boldly, "I'd like to tell you Miss Weathervane, I really would, but I promised my mama I wouldn't because it's about my birthday party and everybody isn't invited." She turned around and looked meaningly at poor little Cornelia Whitehouse then at Mary, who simpered.

Miss Weathervane said sharply, "As long as the party is not school business I would prefer that you did not discuss it during school hours, *especially* when I am reading. Also I would like to have you both stay after school and write a report on the stories we have read this afternoon. Now take your seats."

Mary slunk to the back of the room and sat down. She didn't look at any of her classmates. But Evelyn looked triumphantly around the room then slowly sauntered back to her seat. Her pony tail switched impudently behind her. After she had sat down, she banged open her desk and made as much noise as she could getting out a pencil and some paper for her book report. Mary watched her admiringly and giggled behind her hand.

Miss Weathervane sighed. She opened up the book and went on with the story. She looked up at the class.

They were all smiling happily. Especially Cornelia Whitehouse whose pale cheeks were flushed and her eyes shining with joy.

"You enjoyed the story, didn't you, Cornelia?" asked Miss Weathervane gently.

"Oh, yes," said Cornelia sighing. "It was just wonderful."

From the back of the room came the squeaky twitter of giggles followed by the snakelike hiss of whispering. Mary and Evelyn had their heads together again, their hands cupped by the mouths, their eyes on Cornelia. Miss Weathervane said sharply, "Class dismissed, all except Mary and Evelyn."

When Mary and Evelyn finally finished their reports and brought them up to the teacher's desk, Miss Weathervane said, "Have you girls ever thought how you would feel if you had no father and no pretty clothes? Especially if two of your classmates whose fathers had fine positions, whispered about you and giggled and didn't invite you to their birthday parties?"

Mary hung her head and picked at the buttons on her sweater.

Evelyn said, "I wouldn't care."

"But you would," Miss Weathervane said. "You'd care more than anyone in this class because you are a vain little girl and clothes are very important to you."

"My mama says I have natural style," Evelyn said. "She says I'm going to be a fashion model when I grow up."

Mary said, "Me, too."

Evelyn laughed condescendingly. "Oh, Mary, don't

be silly," she said. "You couldn't be a model, you're too fat."

Miss Weathervane said, "Some day you will learn, Evelyn, that a kind heart and humility are more important to beauty than a 'natural style.' Now run along both of you. I have papers to correct."

All the way home from school Evelyn and Mary giggled and whispered about Cornelia and her raggy old clothes, Miss Weathervane and how mad they had made her, the party, boys, and how Karen Elroyd always wanted to play post office, wasn't that awful? When they got to Mary's house which was next door to Evelyn's, a big black cloud slid suddenly over the sun and large drops of rain began to splat onto the sidewalks. "Ooooooooeeeeeee," they squealed and pulled their school coats up over their heads. Mary's mother who was on her knees by the fence weeding her perennial bed, called out, "Hi, girls, how was school?"

"Oh, it was okay," Mary said, then cupping her hand in front of her mouth she whispered to Evelyn, "Don't tell her about staying after school."

"I won't," whispered Evelyn.

"Whispering's rude," remarked Mary's mother conversationally from behind a clump of phlox.

"Gollee, your mama sounds mad," whispered Evelyn behind her hand to Mary.

"Oh, she's not mad," whispered back Mary. "She just doesn't like whispering."

"Sssssssss, sssssss, sssssss," said Mary's mother wiping her hands on her blue jeans. "You sound like a couple of old snakes. Maybe I'd better go downtown and buy some snakefood and throw away that fresh chocolate cake I have for you in the kitchen."

"Chocolate cake!" shrieked the little girls. "Goody. That's neat." They ran into the house and slammed the back door. Mrs. Crackle went on weeding, in spite of the raindrops which were coming down faster and faster. By the time she had finished the perennial bed her hair was soaked, rain was running into her eyes. But Mary's mother smiled happily. It was a warm spring rain and would be wonderful for the garden. She put the hoe on top of the weeds and trowel in the wheelbarrow and was just going to push it into the garage when she noticed a forlorn little figure leaning on the gate. She said, "Hello, there. Are you one of Mary's little friends?"

Cornelia Whitehouse, for that was who it was, said, "Well, I'm in Mary's room at school. My, you have a pretty yard. I just love gardens. We live in a trailer and can't have one."

Mary's mother said, "Then your daddy must work in the big factory."

"Not my daddy, he's dead," the little girl said. "My mom works there. One of the ladies at the plant who works with Mom owns the trailer and lets us live there."

"Oh, my goodness, what's the matter with me?" said Mary's mother. "Here we are standing out in the rain and getting all wet. Let's go in the house. Mary and her little friend Evelyn are in the kitchen eating chocolate cake I just baked." She walked over and pushed open the gate but the little girl hung back.

"Hurry," said Mary's mother pushing the gate open

wider. A big gust of wind came whooshing around the house and the rain came down even faster. Still the little girl hung back. Mary's mother reached out and took her hand and pulled her into the yard. "Come along," she said smiling. "Let's hurry before those little pigs eat up all the cake." Pulling Cornelia along with her she ran up the path, on to the back porch and into the kitchen.

"Look," she said to Mary and Evelyn who were sitting at the kitchen table eating large wedges of chocolate cake, "I've brought a little friend for you."

"Where'd you find *her?*" Mary asked ungraciously.

"She came sailing in on a big gust of wind," her mother said.

Mary and Evelyn gave each other sly looks, put their heads together and began to whisper.

Mrs. Crackle said sharply, "Mary, where are your manners? Introduce your little friend and invite her to have some cake."

Mary looked at Evelyn who cupped her hand over her mouth, leaned over and whispered something in Mary's ear. Mary giggled. Evelyn giggled. Cornelia flushed.

Mrs. Crackle said, "MARY CRACKLE STOP THAT WHISPERING THIS INSTANT. It is rude and unkind and I won't have it. Now Mary stand up and greet your little friend and introduce her."

Slowly, sulkily Mary stood up, and said, "Mother I'd like you to meet Cornelia . . . uh . . . uh . . ."

"Ragbag," said Evelyn in a loud whisper. Both girls burst into giggles.

Mrs. Crackle said, "Mary, go up to your room and stay there! Evelyn you may go home. Cornelia let's you and me have a cup of tea and a piece of cake."

"Oh, that's all right," said Cornelia in a very low voice. "I better go."

"You'll do no such thing," said Mrs. Crackle. "Hurry up, Mary, go up to your room. Here's your coat, Evelyn, now scat."

Mary said, "But Evelyn hasn't finished her cake, I think it's rude to send her home before she finishes."

"I'll handle the manners in this family," said her mother. "Now you march."

Mary went sulkily out of the kitchen and Evelyn slammed the door hard as she went out. Mrs. Crackle cut two hunks of the fresh gooey chocolate cake, poured boiling water in the teapot and then she and Cornelia sat down. As they ate she asked Cornelia about school and her trailer house and if she had any little girls to play with which she hadn't and Cornelia asked her about flowers and how to grow them and how long it took for them to bloom.

They were just finishing their tea party when there was a knock at the back door and it was Evelyn who said that her mother had sent her over to apologize which she did very ungraciously and then she said, "Cornelia, Mama says I *have* to invite you to my birthday party. It is a week from tomorrow at twelve o'clock."

"Oh, thank you," said Cornelia smiling. "Thank you Evelyn, ever so much for asking me."

Evelyn did not smile back. She opened the back door, started out, then turned and said, "Try and wear a clean dress if you have one." She slammed the door and was gone.

Cornelia's face turned very red and two big tears splashed down on to the crumbs on her plate. Mary's mother said, "It's sometimes very hard for me to remember what a nice little girl Evelyn used to be. Now, I've got an idea about the party. I think it is a pretty good one but if you don't like it you just say so. This is it. We both like gardening and I have a big garden and need help with the weeding and transplanting, so, why don't you come here after school every day and help me in the garden and for payment I'll get you a new dress to wear to Evelyn's party."

Cornelia said, "Oh boy! I'll come tomorrow right after school. I'll run all the way."

"That won't be necessary," Mary's mother said laughing. "But you had better bring along some old jeans and shoes—weeding is pretty dirty work. Now as soon as I put these dishes in the sink I'll drive you home."

Cornelia said, "I'll clear up the dishes, Mrs. Crackle. I'd like to." She jumped to her feet and began carrying the plates and cups to the sink.

Mary's mother said, "Thank you very much, Cornelia. I'd appreciate that. I'll just run up and get out of my gardening clothes, then I'll drive you home."

After she had changed her clothes Mrs. Crackle went into Mary's room and asked Mary, who was sitting glumly by the window looking out at the rain, if she wouldn't like to go with her when she drove Cornelia home.

Mary said, "Can Evelyn come, too?"

"No she can't," said Mrs. Crackle crisply. "She was very rude to Cornelia this afternoon and anyway I can't bear her silly giggling and whispering."

Mary said, "Evelyn Rover is my very very best friend in all the world and I love everything about her and if you don't want her along then I don't want to go. What did Cornelia have to come over here for anyway? Nobody likes her."

Mrs. Crackle said, "She is lonely. Her mother works and when she comes home from school she comes home to a little empty trailer in a shabby miserable little trailer park. How would you like to live like that?"

"I wouldn't," Mary said. "I think it's awful and I'm sorry for her and I'm ashamed I said anything about her clothes."

"Of course you are," Mary's mother said putting her arm around her. "Now run in and wash your face and hurry because it's getting late and I have to go to the store."

When they got downstairs Cornelia had finished the dishes and was rinsing out the dog's water dish. Mrs. Crackle thanked her and Mary said, "Gosh, everything looks neat, Cornelia. I wish you'd come over every afternoon."

"She's going to for a while," said Mrs. Crackle. "She's going to help me in the garden."

Mary looked surprised but before she could say anything Robby and Billy, her two little brothers, came crashing in the back door. Robby was carrying a baby robin and Billy a part of an old nest. Robby said, "Mom, look at the poor little robin. We found him lying on the sidewalk right in front of Armstrong's and I bet their old cat knocked him down."

Billy said, "His poor little old nest was lying right beside him and there was an eggshell in it. Do you think if we fixed the nest up and put it in our room he'd stay in it?"

"I'm sure I don't know," said Mrs. Crackle. "Let me see the bird." Gently she took the baby bird from Robby and put him down on the kitchen table. He slumped down and put his head under his wing. Mrs. Crackle said, "I wonder what's the matter. Frankly I don't know much about baby birds."

"I do," said Cornelia. "I had a baby robin last year. I think this little bird's hungry. You boys go out and dig him some angleworms and I'll fix him a box, just the way I did for my bird."

"Where do you find angleworms?" Robby asked.

"In the compost pile out by the garage. There are lots of angleworms out there," said Mrs. Crackle.

"How do you feed birds?" Mary asked.

"As soon as the boys get the worms I'll show you," Cornelia said. "But first we have to fix a box. We need an old shoe box and some cotton."

Mrs. Crackle said, "There's a shoe box on the shelf of my closet, and a roll of cotton in the top drawer of the linen closet. Mary, you run up and get them."

Mary put her hand over her mouth and whispered to

Cornelia, "Come on up with me and I'll show you my charm bracelet. I have a little silver telephone with a receiver that really comes off the hook."

Cornelia cupped her hand over her mouth and whispered back, "Tomorrow when I come over, I'll bring my pictures of movie stars. I've got over a hundred."

Mary whispered, "Over a hundred! How neat! Bring them for sure."

"Sssssssssss, sssss, ssssssss," said Mrs. Crackle. "Here come the boys and you haven't fixed the nest."

Mary and Cornelia ran upstairs and Cornelia had the box fixed in just a jiffy. When they came downstairs Robby and Billy were standing by the bird whom they had named Admiral after Admiral Byrd, trying to get him to take his head out from under his wing and eat a fat nervous worm that was thrashing around on the kitchen table.

Cornelia cupped her hand over her mouth and whispered to Mary, "Aren't boys dumb? They don't even know how to feed a bird?"

Mary giggled "Teheeteeheeteehee." And whispered, "Boys are dumb and worms are disgusting. Ugh!"

Robby and Billy said, "Aw, quit your whispering and giggling and show us how to feed the bird."

Cornelia walked over to the table and picked up the worm.

Mary squealed, "Eeeeeeeek, don't touch him Cornelia."

Cornelia said, "He's just an old angleworm. Here," she picked up the worm and began tickling Admiral with it. After a little bit the robin lifted up his head,

saw the worm, opened his mouth and Cornelia dropped the worm in. He gulped a few times then opened his mouth for more. This time Robby dropped the worm in. Then Billy. Then Cornelia, then Robby, then Billy. And finally Mary.

Then Mrs. Crackle said that she just had to go to the store and did the boys want to come or stay and dig worms for their bird. They, of course, elected to stay home and feed the bird and so Cornelia and Mary and Mrs. Crackle went to the store and drove Cornelia home.

When Mary saw the ugly old unpainted trailer with the trash-littered yard where Cornelia lived she felt very ashamed of the way she and Evelyn had acted. Impulsively she whispered to Cornelia, "How would you like to be in Evelyn's and my secret society? We call it the Hush Hush Club."

"Oh, I'd just love it," Cornelia whispered back.

"I'll see you at school tomorrow morning, then," whispered Mary.

"Okay," Cornelia whispered. And she was so used to whispering that she whispered, "Thank you for the cake and for taking me home," to Mrs. Crackle and then they all laughed and Mrs. Crackle said, "You girls had better watch out you might forget how to speak out loud."

On the way home Mary told her mother how sorry she felt for Cornelia and how she had asked her to be a member of the Hush Hush Club. Mrs. Crackle told Mary about Evelyn's party and how hateful Evelyn had been and how she had asked Cornelia to help her in the garden in exchange for a new party dress. Mary said that she thought her mother was just wonderful and leaned over and hugged her.

Mrs. Crackle smiled happily to herself because, even though Mary hadn't stopped whispering, she certainly was being her own sweet friendly self again and Mrs. Crackle could hardly wait to tell Mr. Crackle.

The next morning was beautiful with sunshine and birds singing and Admiral Byrd still alive and peeping. Right after breakfast Evelyn knocked at the back door. She was wearing a new green dress with a huge full skirt, new green slippers, a new green sweater and she had a green ribbon tied around her pony tail.

Mary said, "Oh, Evelyn you look adorable. Just adorable."

Evelyn blinked her eyes and said, "Oh, I don't think so."

Mary's mother said, "Don't forget your spelling book, Mary, and remember you're going to walk home with Cornelia tonight."

Evelyn said, "Cornelia! That ragbag. How come?"

Mary cupped her hand around her mouth and whispered, "I feel awfully sorry for her, she lives in a dumpy old trailer and she's going to help Mother in the garden."

Evelyn cupped her hand around her mouth and whispered, "I don't feel sorry for her. I think she's goopy. Her clothes are dirty. I'm just furious Mama made me ask her to my party."

Mr. Crackle said crossly, "Sssssss, sssss, ssssssss. The two little town gossips . . ."

Mary said, "Oh, Daddy! Come on, Evelyn we have to hurry." She whispered to her again, "Ssssssss. Sssssss. Ssssss."

"Oh, go on to school," said Mrs. Crackle crossly. "I'm sick to death of your whispering and giggling."

After the little girls had gone she poured Mr. Crackle and herself another cup of coffee. As he stirred sugar into his cup Mr. Crackle said, "Something has to be done about those two dreadful little females."

"But what?" asked Mrs. Crackle. "What would you suggest?"

"I guess we'd better call Mrs. Piggle-Wiggle," said Mr. Crackle.

"I guess we'd better," said Mrs. Crackle. "And right now."

But of course she didn't get to call Mrs. Piggle-Wiggle "right now" because Robby and Billy had to leave for school while Admiral was still hungry, so Mrs. Crackle spent the entire morning digging in her compost pile for angleworms. By the time she finally got Admiral filled up she was so tired she had to sit down and have a cup of coffee. Then she had to wash the breakfast dishes and make the beds and dust the living room.

She was just finishing when Mrs. Rover knocked at the door and to Mrs. Crackle's surprise said, "Elizabeth, I'm worried to death about Evelyn. She's gotten so mean lately. She whispers and gossips all the time and I was just shocked when she told me she hadn't invited that poor little Cornelia to her party. She never speaks in a normal tone of voice any more. It's sssss,

sssss, from morning till night. Carter and I are nearly frantic."

Mrs. Crackle said, "It's just as bad over here if that is any comfort to you. In fact Cantilever calls Evelyn and Mary the Town Gossips. He wants me to telephone Mrs. Piggle-Wiggle. I was just about to when you called."

"You mean that funny little woman who lives down on Vinemaple?"

"Yes, that's Mrs. Piggle-Wiggle and she knows more about children than anybody in town and she has all sorts of magic cures for their bad habits."

"Well, for heavens sake let's call her right away," said Evelyn's mother. "Maybe she can tell us how to get rid of Mary and Evelyn's meanness before the party. If she can't I do declare I don't think I'll have the party."

When Mrs. Piggle-Wiggle heard about Evelyn and Mary she said, "There must be an epidemic of whispering going around. I'm almost out of Whisper Sticks."

"Whisper Sticks?" asked Mrs. Crackle. "What are they?"

"They're magic candy sticks," said Mrs. Piggle-Wiggle. "Two or three sucks and you can't speak above a whisper. Also, they have a very nice flavor—sort of raspberry cherry and children love them, especially little girls."

"How long does this not speaking above a whisper last?" asked Mary's mother.

"Usually all day," said Mrs. Piggle-Wiggle. "Depends upon how fast the child eats the Whisper Stick.

How many do you think you and Mrs. Rover will need?"

"I really don't know," said Mary's mother. "What do you think?"

"I should say seven," said Mrs. Piggle-Wiggle promptly. "Three each for Evelyn and Mary, and one for Cornelia."

"But Cornelia doesn't need any," exclaimed Mrs. Crackle.

"She will," said Mrs. Piggle-Wiggle. "As soon as she gets friendly with Mary she'll start whispering, they always do. I'll send the Whisper Sticks home with Billy and Robby, they have a Cub Scout meeting here today."

"Oh, thank you so much, Mrs. Piggle-Wiggle," said Mary's mother gratefully.

"No trouble at all," said Mrs. Piggle-Wiggle. "Please call and let me know how everything turns out."

"Oh, I will," said Mary's mother.

Then she told Evelyn's mother all about the Whisper Sticks and she was delighted, in fact they were both so happy and talked so much about the wonderful cure they began to think it had already happened. It was a great disappointment to them when Evelyn and Mary came walking up the street their arms around each other's waists, their heads together, whispering for all they were worth while behind them looking forlorn and friendless sagged Cornelia.

"Just look at that," said Evelyn's mother stirring her coffee angrily. "Those two hateful little old things with

their heads together sayin' mean things about that poor
little Cornelia."

"Of course we don't know that they are," said Mary's
mother passing the cake. "But it certainly looks that
way. However, Cornelia came over to help me with
the garden so the way Mary and Evelyn treat her
doesn't make much difference today. If you'll pardon
me just a minute I'll go out and get her started. I do
hope she brought her jeans."

Jumping to her feet Evelyn's mother said, "I'm going
right home and make that poor little thing a ham sandwich. She's nothing but a bundle of little bones."

Mary's mother said, "Make her a peanut butter sandwich right here. Pour a glass of milk and cut her a big
piece of cake, too, will you? I'll go out and bring her
in."

Stepping outside, Mary's mother called, "Cornelia.
May I speak to you?"

Instantly Evelyn and Mary who had separated for a
minute, put their heads together and began Ssssssss,
sssssssssssing again.

Briskly Mrs. Crackle said, "You too, Mary. Come
here I want to speak to you."

Cornelia came running but Mary and Evelyn parted
slowly like two sticky caramels being pulled apart, gave
each other long meaningful looks, then doubled up in
giggles. When Mary finally started up the back steps,
Mrs. Crackle couldn't help giving her a hard little
spank.

"Hey, that hurt," Mary said, looking surprised.

"I meant it to," said Mrs. Crackle. "It's to remind

you that you and Evelyn were rude and hateful just now. Go upstairs and change your clothes and lend Cornelia a tee shirt. She forgot to bring one."

Cornelia had forgotten a tee shirt but she hadn't forgotten her scrapbook of movie stars. She and Mary whispered and giggled over it upstairs while they were changing their clothes and downstairs while they were eating their sandwiches and cake. Then while Cornelia pulled weeds Mary sat in the wheelbarrow and looked at the pictures and she and Cornelia giggled and whispered about them.

After a while Evelyn came over to see what they were doing but Mary wouldn't show her the book and she and Cornelia whispered and giggled so rudely that finally Evelyn yelled out, "Oh, you make me sick, old fatty and ragbag. I hate you both!"

"Sticks and stones may break my bones but names will never hurt me," chanted Cornelia as she deftly pulled the grass from around the delphiniums.

Mrs. Crackle and Mrs. Rover watching the children from the breakfast-room window, were ashamed to see how hateful they were acting. Then Mary had to go to her music lesson and when she had gone Evelyn came over and she and Cornelia giggled and whispered over the book of movie stars.

Mrs. Crackle and Mrs. Rover thought that Billy and Robby would never get there with those Whisper Sticks. But they did, finally and as soon as they had changed their clothes and taken Admiral out to the compost pile for his afternoon snack of about a hundred worms, Mrs. Crackle gave Evelyn and Cornelia each a Whisper Stick. "Oh, thank you very much," both girls said as they quickly peeled off the paper.

"Um, this candy *is* good," said Cornelia happily licking her stick. "What kind is it?"

"I'm not sure who makes the candy," said Mrs. Crackle, "but I've been told it is delicious."

"Oh, it is," said Evelyn biting off a chunk. "It is sssssssssssssssssss."

Mrs. Crackle couldn't hear the rest of what she said because her voice disappeared and she spoke in a faint whisper, like tissue paper in a Christmas box.

"What did you say, Evelyn?" asked Cornelia. Her voice had grown low and very quiet. A perfect library voice.

"Speak louder, Cornelia, I can't hear you," Evelyn said, but nobody could hear her because her words came out a soft whish like the rustle of a silk petticoat.

"What did you say?" Cornelia asked, but Evelyn couldn't hear her because her voice was now the soft crooning of a mother putting a baby to sleep.

Then Mary came home from her music lesson. "Hi Evelyn, hi Cornelia," she called out happily.

"Ssssssss, sssssss," said Evelyn. She sounded like the wind blowing through prairie grass.

"Sssssss, sssssss," called out Cornelia, who now sounded like the tiny singing of a teakettle.

"If you kids are going to whisper about me I'm going in the house," Mary said angrily.

Mrs. Crackle said, "How about a stick of candy?"

"I'd love one," said Mary. "I'm starving."

Her mother gave her a stick of the candy and she

eagerly pulled down the waxed paper and began sucking.

After about three sucks she turned to her mother and said, "Miss Prince says that I can have two new pieces next time." She looked happy but she gasped out her words as if she had been running for about a hundred miles.

"That's fine dear," said Mrs. Crackle. "Perhaps she will let you try 'The Witches Dance.'"

"Oh, I hope so," said Mary, or rather buzzed Mary, because now she sounded like a bee on a screen door.

Cornelia on her knees in the delphinium bed, sat back on her heels and said, "I'm almost through here, Mrs. Crackle, what do you want me to do next?"

Mrs. Crackle didn't answer her, in fact didn't even look at her, because all she could hear was a thin little hissing sound like a leak in the hose. Cornelia repeated what she had said, this time shouting as loud as she could. This time she sounded like dried peas rattling in their pods.

Mary, seeing that Cornelia was talking and not being able to hear her, of course, decided that she was whispering to Evelyn. Angrily biting off a piece of her candy stick Mary said, "I told you kids that if you didn't stop whispering I would go in the house, and I mean it."

Of course Evelyn and Cornelia didn't pay any attention to her because all they could hear was a thin little noise like a faraway broom sweeping a faraway floor. Evelyn said, "As soon as Cornelia finishes her gardening let's go over to my house and make caramel apples

—Mama lets me make them any time I want."

She waited for excited squeals but Cornelia, who was gazing up at Mrs. Crackle waiting for instructions, didn't even turn her head. Mary who was stamping angrily toward the house didn't turn around and Mrs. Crackle who was grown up and should have had good manners walked into the house behind Mary. Of course nobody heard her, for who can hear a spring breeze riffling through the apple blossoms?

Evelyn flounced out of the wheelbarrow, slammed down Cornelia's movie star book, stamped out of the yard and slammed the gate. Then she called back, "I hate you all! You are all rude and horrible and mean and if you come to my birthday party, I'll stamp on your presents and slam the door in your faces."

Cornelia who hadn't seen Evelyn go and had gone back to her weeding looked up and seeing nobody said to herself, "That's funny. I heard a little noise like somebody brushing sugar off a shelf. But there is nobody around so it must have been the trees." She took another suck of her candy stick, wrapped it up and put it in her pocket, and went on with her weeding.

In a few minutes Mary came out and sat down in the wheelbarrow. She said, "I thought you were my friend. How come you were whispering to Evelyn?"

Cornelia said, "You're whispering too softly, I can't hear you."

Mary said, "I can see your lips move but no words come out. What's the matter?"

"What did you say?" Cornelia asked.

"I said, 'I CAN SEE YOUR LIPS MOVE BUT

NO WORDS COME OUT! WHAT'S THE MAT-
TER?' " Mary shouted.

Cornelia said, "Why do you whisper? Nobody is
around to hear us."

"I'M NOT WHISPERING!" Mary screamed.

"Stop whispering!" Cornelia said.

"I CAN'T HEAR YOU!" Mary yelled. "TALK
LOUDER."

"I'M TALKING AS LOUD AS I CAN. IN
FACT I'M SCREAMING," screamed Cornelia.

Then because Cornelia had put her candy away
while she was weeding and hadn't had a lick for quite
a while, her voice began to come back a tiny bit. In
fact Mary could make out, "I'm screaming."

She said angrily, "You are not screaming. You're whispering as softly as you can. I think you're mean. I got you into the Hush Hush Club and now you're whispering about me."

As far as Cornelia was concerned all that was coming out of Mary's mouth were faint little gasping breaths. She had no idea what she was saying or trying to say. In fact she thought Mary was teasing her and pretending to talk the way the members of the Hush Hush Club did to nonmembers. Furiously she said, "Okay then, be mean, I don't care. Anyway I'm going in the house to talk to your mother."

She got up and ran into the house.

Then Evelyn who had been sitting on her front steps sulking and licking her Whisper Stick, saw Mary alone and called out, "Hey, Mary, come on over. I'm going to make caramel apples."

Of course Mary couldn't hear her any more than she could hear the leaves rubbing against each other in the chestnut tree at the end of the block. But Evelyn who had no idea that she was whispering because her voice sounded perfectly normal to her ears, thought Mary didn't answer because she was mad at her. She began to cry. Her tears made big wet marks on her new green dress and new green slippers. She didn't care. She was lonely and unhappy.

So was Mary who was still standing by the wheelbarrow.

Then Corinthian Bop, the most popular boy in their room, came wheeling around the corner on his bicycle. Evelyn quickly wiped away her tears, straightened out her skirt and called out, "Hi, Corry!"

Corinthian looked at her but as he couldn't hear anything, he rode right on by muttering, "Stuck-up old thing." Then he saw Mary.

She smiled and said, "Hi, Corry, want to see our baby bird?"

Naturally he couldn't hear her, but as she had smiled he stopped, got off his bike, leaned it against the fence and sauntered into the yard. "Whatcha doing?" he asked Mary.

"Oh, nothing," she said, but as he couldn't hear her he said louder, "I SAID WHATCHA DOING?" Mary said, "Want to see our baby robin? His name's Admiral Byrd and he's adorable but he eats worms, ugh."

Corinthian said, "What are you whisperin' for? Your silly old girl friends aren't around."

Mary said, "I'm not whispering. I'm talking in a perfectly normal tone of voice."

Turning and walking out of the yard, Corinthian said, "Aw you make me sick."

"I don't know what's the matter with you," Mary said. "I'm not whispering. I'M NOT."

"Don't talk if you don't want to," Corinthian said as he got on his bike. "You don't have anything to say anyway." He rode away.

Mary began to cry. Cornelia came out of the house and began weeding the flower bed by the porch. Mary walked over to her and said, "What's the matter with me? Nobody can hear what I say." Then she had an idea. She rushed into the house and got a pencil and a pad of paper. On it she wrote, "Something is the matter with my throat. Nobody can hear what I say. Call the doctor." She took this note in to her mother who, with Mrs. Rover, was going through fashion books looking for a dress for Cornelia.

Mrs. Crackle read the note and said, "There's nothing wrong with your throat, Mary. It is just that you have been whispering so much lately your vocal cords have decided that you didn't like them and have taken a little vacation."

"But when will they be back?" wrote Mary.

"When you stop whispering," said her mother. "I imagine that if you took a pledge to stop whispering entirely, except on very necessary occasions such as speaking in the library and telling nice secrets about birthday presents and things like that, your voice would be back at work tomorrow morning."

"What about Cornelia and Evelyn?" wrote Mary. "They whisper all the time."

"They are suffering from the same disease you are," said Mrs. Crackle. "Now I'll tell you what to do. You go and tell or rather write down what I have said and show it to Cornelia and Evelyn. Then you write out a pledge giving a solemn oath that you promise never to gossip and to whisper except when absolutely necessary."

"But Mother," Mary scribbled excitedly, "how can we have the Hush Hush Club if we don't whisper? That was the main purpose of the club. Everything was secret."

"Then I think it is high time it was broken up," said

her mother. "I don't approve of little whispering secret groups. Perhaps you can think of a better kind of club to organize."

"What about a Picnic Club?" asked Evelyn's mother. "You could go on picnics every Saturday and we mothers would provide the lunches."

"That would be fun," said Mrs. Crackle. "And on rainy days you could write plays and act in them."

Mary thought for a minute or two then wrote, "I'll have to see what the other members think."

Her mother said, "Well, write a note to the two that are here now and tell them to come in here I want to talk to them. And," she added, winking at Mrs. Rover, "I wouldn't eat any more of that candy stick if I were you. Candy is very very hard on tired vocal cords. Tell the other girls that, too."

After Mary had gone out to get Evelyn and Cornelia, Mrs. Rover said to Mrs. Crackle, "You know, Elizabeth, I do believe that those children have learned a lesson. I don't think we're going to have to use the rest of those Whisper Sticks. You'd better send them back to Mrs. Piggle-Wiggle."

"Better yet, I'm going to give them to Miss Weathervane," said Mary's mother. "She told me that the whispering during Friday story time had gotten so bad she had almost decided to give up reading to the children altogether. I'm going to tell her to break the Whisper Sticks up into little pieces and give each whisperer one before the reading starts."

"What a wonderful idea," said Mrs. Rover, "and you know what, Elizabeth, I'm going to take one Whisper Stick and keep it on hand just in case any whispering breaks out at the party. Oh, that party is going to be a big success now! I can hardly wait. But don't you really think that pink would be better for Cornelia, she is so pale."

"Whatever you say," said Mary's mother. "You're the one who knows about fashion. Now I had better call Mrs. Piggle-Wiggle and thank her."

V. THE SLOWPOKE

"HARBIN!" called Mrs. Quadrangle. "Breakfast! I'm making waffles, so hurry, dear."

"Coming, Mom," Harbin answered. But unless "coming" means sitting on the bed in your underwear watching a beetle crawling on the screen, Harbin wasn't.

After he had watched the beetle for five or ten minutes, Harbin slowly reached out and picked up a sock. He looked at the sock fixedly almost as if he were waiting for it to say something to him, then let it slide out of his fingers. It fell across his shoe. He lay back on his bed, folded his arms behind his head and gazed up at the ceiling. There was a brown stain just over his head where the roof had leaked the winter they had the hurricane. The stain looked just like a map of South America. Harbin was trying to figure out where the Amazon River and those little fish that ate a man right down to his skeleton in three minutes were when his mother called again, "Haaaaaaaaaaaaarbin! Breakfast!"

"Coming, Mom," he answered. The spot really looked more like Africa he decided. Boy, he'd sure like to go to Africa! He bet that if he went to Africa he'd find a diamond the very first thing. A diamond as big as a

lump of sugar and he'd give it to his mom. No, he guessed he'd give it to Miss Hackett, his teacher. Miss Hackett was pretty and she was sure a lot better than old Crabpatch Wilson. Wow!

"Harbin Quadrangle!" his mother's voice sounded very impatient. "Your waffles are getting cold and soggy, the other children are all through breakfast and your daddy's ready to leave for the office. If you're not down here in two minutes I'm coming up."

Harbin sat up and reached down for the sock. He had it halfway on his foot when Mr. Pierce, the large black family dog, came into his room. "Well, hello, old boy," said Harbin letting go of his sock which now dangled from his toes. "Shake hands with me old boy."

Mr. Pierce wagged his tail and licked Harbin's face but he didn't want to shake hands. When Harbin reached for his paw he backed away. Harbin said, "Say, Mr. Pierce, I bet you've forgotten how to shake hands. Come on I'll teach you. Now first you sit. Sit boy! Come on, Mr. Pierce sit! MR. PIERCE SIT! Good boy. Now, give me your paw. No, don't lie down. Sit. Sit boy. Sit Mr. Pierce. SIT BOY! Come on, leggo my sock. Mr. Pierce, come back here with my sock. Mr. Pierce, come back here!"

But Mr. Pierce didn't. He trotted happily downstairs and laid Harbin's sock at Mr. Quadrangle's feet.

Mr. Quadrangle said, "What's this, Mr. Pierce, a blue grouse?" He picked up the sock and held it over Mr. Pierce's head. Mr. Pierce wagged his tail proudly.

Mrs. Quadrangle who was braiding Janey's hair said, "Let me see that sock a minute, Donald?"

Mr. Quadrangle handed it to her. She looked at it for a minute, told Janey to stand very still until she got back, then with the sock in her hand she marched out of the dining room and up the stairs.

In the meantime Harbin had fallen back on his bed and was lying in the jumbled mass of bedcovers and school clothes daydreaming about helping the Canadian Mounted Police capture the most dangerous criminal in all the world. Harbin also in uniform of course, because he was a secret member of the Mounties. Suddenly his mother's exasperated voice was saying, "Harbin Quadrangle, it's almost a quarter to eight and here you are not even half dressed. What's the matter with you?"

The brave little Mountie was jerked unceremoniously off the bed and clunked to the floor. "Now," said his mother. "Get dressed immediately, while I watch you."

Harbin fumbled around in the blankets for his tee shirt and sweater. Impatiently his mother pushed him out of the way and quickly found the clothes. Jerking the tee shirt then the sweater down over his head she said, "I certainly have enough to do in the morning without having to dress a great big eight-year-old boy. Now where are your jeans?"

"Well, uh, well uh," Harbin looked vaguely around his room.

His mother ripped the blankets off the bed and sure enough there were the jeans down by the foot. While Harbin put them on she went into the bathroom and filled the basin with warm water.

As soon as she was out of the room Harbin slumped back to the bed. "Wolves," he said to his shoe which he had picked up and was holding. "Boy wouldn't I love to have a wolf of my very own. I bet if I was nice to him and fed him meat and petted him a lot he'd be . . ." But he never found out what the wolf would be because his mother yanked him into the bathroom and began scrubbing his face and neck.

"Owwwwww, owwww, you're takin' the skin off," howled the brave little Mountie, trying to shield his face with both arms.

"Put your arms down," said his mother firmly. "You've still got some of Wednesday's chocolate ice cream up by your hairline. Now let me see your ears."

"Oh, gosh, not my ears! You scrub them so hard you make 'em ache."

"If they ache too much let me know and I'll give you an aspirin," said his mother briskly.

When she had him all scrubbed Mrs. Quadrangle rammed Harbin's feet into his socks and shoes and then scooted him down the stairs ahead of her.

When he came into the dining room his father said, "Well, if it isn't the fireman. One ring of the bell and he's in his clothes and down the pole."

Sylvia his sister who was eleven said, "Do all of our meals have to be ruined by that little slowpoke?"

Janey said, "I'm going to tell the kids at school that Mother has to dress you."

"You do and I'll . . ."

"You'll sit down and eat your waffles," said his mother. "Sylvia, run upstairs and get me an elastic band out of my desk. Janey, come here and I'll finish you—oh, quick, Donald, the baby's putting his dish on his head."

The baby, whom they called "Old-Timer," had indeed put his dish of oatmeal on his head. Little rivulets of milk and cereal ran down his forehead and into his eyes. He blinked and smiled happily. The children laughed uproariously. So did Mr. Quadrangle. Mrs. Quadrangle sighed and sent Harbin upstairs for a washrag. As he got slowly up from his chair, his mother shouted at him "Hurry! H-U-R-R-Y!" She spelled it out.

Harbin said, "I *am* hurrying," and shuffled from the room. He was all right, or rather he kept moving until he got to the stairs. In fact, to the first step, then suddenly the stairs turned into a rope ladder up the side of a ship. The ship was a pirate ship and Harbin who had swum under water clear across the ocean, was boarding her secretly, carefully, bravely. Hand over hand up the rope ladder.

When Mrs. Quadrangle finally sent Janey to see what in the world was the matter with Harbin, why he hadn't brought the washrag, Janey found him lying on the stairs pulling himself up by the balustrade, hand over hand, very slowly. When Janey saw him she yelled to her mother, "Mom, he hasn't even gone upstairs at all. He's just lying here in the hall."

Mrs. Quadrangle sighed and mopped Old-Timer off with the dishcloth. Mr. Quadrangle walked sternly out to the hall and said to Harbin who was halfway up the side of the pirate ship and so tired he didn't think he could go any farther, "What's going on out here? Why are you draped on the staircase like an old Spanish shawl?"

Then Harbin did a strange thing. He turned to his father and said, "Shhhh. They'll hear you."

Mr. Quadrangle looked at his son for a minute then went back into the dining room and said to his wife, "Call Dr. Watkins. The boy's hit his head and he's delirious."

"Oh, good heavens," said Mrs. Quadrangle dropping Old-Timer into his play pen with a thump. She ran into the front hall and sure enough there was Harbin clinging to the balustrade and breathing heavily. Mrs. Quadrangle rushed up and knelt beside him. "Son,

son are you all right?" she said laying her hand on his forehead.

"Of course I'm all right," said Harbin looking around at his assembled family. "What's the matter? Why are you all looking so funny?"

"Did you fall, son?" asked Mr. Quadrangle.

"Of course he did," said Mrs. Quadrangle impatiently. "But how far? Did you fall from the first or the third floor, sonny? And where do you hurt the most? Is it your back or your legs?"

"It's his back. He's broken it and he's completely paralyzed," announced Sylvia importantly. "I saw a movie once where a man broke his back and he acted just like Harbin."

"His arms look funny to me," said Janey. "See how funny the bones stick out?"

"There's nothin' wrong with my arms or my back," said Harbin sitting up. "I was just tryin' to go upstairs hand over hand the way sailors go up a rope."

His mother heaved a vast sigh of relief then said briskly, "All right everybody, into your coats, it's after 8:30. Janey get me Old-Timer's ski suit, it's in the hall closet."

Everybody was in the car, the engine was running and Mr. Quadrangle was saying impatiently, "If we don't leave right this instant I'll miss my train," when Janey suddenly remembered she had to bring two potatoes to school.

As Harbin was closest to the door Mrs. Quadrangle sent him to get the potatoes. "Now RUN FAST!" she told him. And he did—at least as far as the back porch where the potatoes were kept. Then he saw the old piece of fish net he had found on the beach the summer before. It was hanging on a nail right by the mop. Harbin stopped dead in his tracks. What was his fish net doin' here on the back porch? Ready for the garbage man?

Harbin jerked it off the nail intending to take it upstairs to his room. But somehow or another the feel of the net in his hands, the faint smell of seaweed that still clung to it made him think of the sea and oysters and pearls and pearl divers and giant clams. He had on his aqualung and was at the bottom of the ocean searching, searching for the famous pink pearl that would make him the richest man in all the world. It was dark and scary at the bottom of the ocean. And there were sharks and octopuses and baracuda and enormous snapping turtles and worst of all giant clams that could catch your leg in their giant shells and hold you there until you drowned, unless you were brave enough to cut off your own leg with your deep sea diving knife. "Ow, ow, the pain is awful!" Harbin said to himself as he looked down and saw his leg caught clear to the thigh in the shell of a giant clam. "I will have to cut off my leg but it is worth it because I have found the famous pink pearl and . . ."

"Harbin Quadrangle!" Sylvia yelled right in his ear. "You've probably made Daddy miss his train. What are you doing with that smelly old fish net and where are Janey's potatoes?"

"Uh, uh . . ." Harbin said looking in bewilderment at the fish net.

Pulling open the cooler door Sylvia grabbed two potatoes. "Come on," she said jerking Harbin by the arm. "Daddy's just furious."

Mr. Quadrangle missed his train all right and would have to take the 9:15. Also the first bell had already rung when the children got to school. Sylvia and Janey were panicky and hurled themselves out of the car and into the building. Not Harbin. He carefully collected his books, kissed his mother and Old-Timer, then ambled slowly across the schoolyard.

"Just look at that," said Mr. Quadrangle to Mrs. Quadrangle. "Not a care in the world. Plenty of time to look at the view. The second bell has probably rung but it means less than nothing to Hairbreadth Harbin the Human Rocket."

"You know, Don, I think maybe he needs thyroid pills," said Mrs. Quadrangle. "I *am* going to call Dr. Watkins. Just as soon as I get home."

"Go ahead," said Mr. Quadrangle. "But I'll bet he'll tell you there's nothing wrong with him that a little spanking won't cure. Anyway it's time for the train. Good-bye Old-Timer. Good-bye, honey, see you at 6:30."

As soon as she got home Mrs. Quadrangle called Dr. Watkins but he had gone to Oak Beach. Mrs. Quadrangle left word for him to call her when he got in and set to work to make an applesauce cake. Harbin loved applesauce cake and it was full of raisins and nuts and butter and sugar—all very nourishing and undoubtedly just the thing for a pitiful little boy with a very low thyroid.

As soon as she had the cake in the oven she called the butcher and ordered two soup bones with lots of marrow because she had heard that marrow was excellent for rundown people. She also made an enormous bowl of cherry jello—gelatine contains lots of protein—and whipped a full pint of cream. She was looking in her cookbook under the section "Feeding the Invalid" and wondering what else to fix for poor little Harbin, when Old-Timer announced via loud howls that it was time for his bath and morning nap.

After she had him bathed and settled in his crib with a bottle, she called Mr. Quadrangle at work and asked him to bring home a giant-sized bottle of cod-liver oil.

"What for?" asked Mr. Quadrangle. "Don't those vitamin pills we all take contain everything we need?"

"They're supposed to," said Mrs. Quadrangle, "but I don't want to take any chances with Harbin. He's so weak and rundown!"

"He's what?" asked Mr. Quadrangle.

"Weak and rundown," said Mrs. Quadrangle. "You certainly haven't forgotten how he lay on the stairs this morning, too feeble to go up or down."

Mr. Quadrangle sighed. "Any particular brand of cod-liver oil?" he said.

"Just get the strongest," said Mrs. Quadrangle. "The kind they use for invalids."

"How about a wheel chair, too?" said Mr. Quadrangle.

"Don't joke about it," said Mrs. Quadrangle. "It's serious."

"The way you're going on about this," Mr. Quadrangle said, "maybe I'd better exchange that wheel chair for a stretcher. By the way what did Dr. Watkins say?"

"He wasn't in," said Mrs. Quadrangle crossly. "He's going to call me."

"Fine," said Mr. Quadrangle. "Let me know what he says."

Then it was time for the children to come home from school. First Sylvia and her best friend Annabell came giggling in, fixed themselves two peanut butter and pickle sandwiches, two huge pieces of applesauce cake, and two enormous dishes of jello heaped with whipped cream. Loading their food on a tray they staggered up to Sylvia's room with it and spent the rest of the afternoon eating and giggling and telephoning.

Then Janey and her best friends, Mona and Kathy, came giggling in, grabbed some sandwiches and cake, Janey's, Harbin's, and Sylvia's rollerskates and left. There was no sign of Harbin.

She fed Old-Timer his applesauce and cookies, put on his ski suit and put him out in the yard in his pen. "You watch for your brother," she told him. "Let me know as soon as you see him coming and I'll walk down and help him."

Old-Timer intent on throwing all of his toys out of the pen as fast as he could, said, "Gogglewopshinogrit."

"All right," said his mother, "I trust you."

She went in the house and began fixing an enormous, really overpowering after-school snack for Harbin. Three thick peanut butter and pickle sandwiches, a chunk of cake big enough for Man Mountain Dean, and a soup bowl full of jello slogged over with whipped cream. When she had everything ready and laid out on the kitchen table she went to the window and looked anxiously down the street for Harbin.

He was there all right. Clear down by Mrs. Axle's and moving so slowly he looked almost like a statue. "Oh, the poor, poor little thing," said his mother grabbing her sweater off the kitchen chair and running out the back door. "Harbin, Harbin, wait for me," she called out, as she hurried down the street.

Harbin who was escaping from a dungeon and with terribly heavy leg chains on, was trying to feel his way along pitch black dank passageways that ran under the castle of the wicked bandit who had captured him, paid absolutely no attention to his mother.

Then he was being crushed in a rather hysterical embrace and his mother was saying, "Do you want Mother to carry you, sweetheart?"

"Carry me? You?" Harbin looked at his mother as if she had suddenly gone crazy.

"Of course, dear," she said crouching down and peering into his face. "Mother knows how tired and weak and sick you are."

"I'm not weak and sick," Harbin said irritably. "I feel fine."

"But you were moving so slowly," said his mother.

"Oh, I was just, well uh, . . . well, oh, lemme alone," Harbin finished in disgust.

But his mother put her arm around him and tried to lift him. Harbin struggled wildly and finally his mother dropped him. "Whatsa matter with you?" Harbin said angrily.

"Well if you won't let me carry you," said his mother, "I'll walk along with you in case you should feel faint. I made an applesauce cake today."

"Hot dog!" said Harbin. "That's my favorite."

"I know," said his mother with a catch in her voice.

"Can I have two pieces?" Harbin asked.

"Certainly," said his mother. "As many as you like."

"Oh, boy," said Harbin beginning to run.

"Harbin, Harbin, darling," called his mother anxiously. "Be careful. You'll wear yourself out."

She needn't have worried. Harbin ran as far as the Wilcox's hedge then suddenly he saw the Wilcox's yellow cat, Dandelion, hiding behind the hedge. Harbin stopped short. "A lion. A full-grown vicious lion with a bullet in its shoulder and a little native child between its paws." The natives in the village had sent Harbin, armed only with a bow and arrow, out to save the chief's little son. Slowly carefully he crouched down. Then just as slowly and carefully he took an arrow out of his quiver, put it in his bow and began to pull back the string. He was just getting ready to let it snap when an arm grabbed him around the waist and his mother's voice said, "Son, son, what is the matter? Have you got a cramp in your stomach?"

"Oh, Mom," said Harbin disgustedly. "Why can't you lemme alone?"

"But your face was contorted with pain," his mother said.

"It was not," Harbin said. "I was just, well I was just, I mean I was practisin' shootin' a bow and arrow."

"Well, come along and get your cake," said his mother. "I have everything laid out on the kitchen table."

"Keen," said Harbin actually hurrying the rest of the way home.

When they got to the house Old-Timer who had thrown all his toys out and had nothing to play with held out his arms and whimpered to be picked up. Mrs. Quadrangle decided to take him out and let him run around while Harbin ate his little lunch. She put the baby on the grass and sat on the steps to watch him.

When Harbin walked into the kitchen and saw the enormous feast his mother had laid out for him he said, "At last, at last," and fell into the chair and began shoveling in the food because all afternoon he had been on a desert island without anything to eat but a few raw fish he caught with his hands and then just by chance when he was so weak he could hardly drag himself along the beach, he sighted this boat and they took him aboard and the cook fixed all this wonderful food and as he had eaten and gotten back his strength he was going to tell them about the uranium mine he had found. Harbin closed his eyes. The room began to go round and round. He felt terrible. Like a steer that had been roped around the stomach. He loosened his belt. That made him feel a little better but the kitchen seemed awfully hot. Slowly wearily he got up and went outdoors.

His mother still sitting on the steps, looked at him and said, "Harbin, honey, you look awful. Are you sick?"

"Well, I guess I am," Harbin said, slumping down beside her.

"Stick out your tongue," his mother demanded.

He did. She said, "Just as I thought. Your tongue is coated and your throat is red. You go right upstairs and get into bed. I'm going to ask Dr. Watkins to drop by."

Taking his belt off altogether made Harbin feel much better—so did his cool bed. He went to sleep. It was after supper when he woke up. He could tell because the house smelled faintly of lamb stew, he could hear Janey and Sylvia and the neigborhood kids quarreling over whose turn it was to be *it* in hide-and-go-seek. He turned over and closed his eyes again. There were steps on the stairs and Dr. Watkins boomed out, "Hi, there, sonny, what's the trouble?"

"Nothing," said Harbin. "I guess I just ate too much."

After Dr. Watkins had peered in his ears, nose and throat, poked and thumped him all over and pronounced him "sound as a nut," Mrs. Quadrangle who had been hovering anxiously in the background, said, "Dr. Watkins I want to talk to you." She took him downstairs and told him in full detail about Harbin's spells of weakness.

He said, "Nothing physically wrong with the boy. Let's see, he's going on nine isn't he?"

"Yes, he'll be nine next September," Mrs. Quadrangle said sadly as though Harbin would never live to see his birthday cake.

"Well, then," said Dr. Watkins fishing in his pocket for a prescription blank, "I would diagnose his trouble as extra acute daydreaming. Now, I'll write out this prescription and I'm pretty sure if you follow it, he'll be back to normal in no time." He wrote rapidly on a prescription blank, folded it and handed it to Mrs. Quadrangle. Then he was gone.

Taking the slip of paper Mrs. Quadrangle went into Mr. Quadrangle's study and said, "It's just as I thought, Donald. Harbin is sick. Dr. Watkins gave me a prescription for him."

"Let's see it," said Mr. Quadrangle.

Mrs. Quadrangle handed it to him. He unfolded it and read, "Call Mrs. Piggle-Wiggle. Vinemaple 1-2345."

"Mrs. Piggle-Wiggle!" exclaimed Mrs. Quadrangle.

"Certainly," said Mr. Quadrangle. "She's earned a pretty fine reputation for curing children of irritating faults. Let's give it a try."

"Well, you call her then," said Mrs. Quadrangle. "I wouldn't know what to say."

"Very well," said Mr. Quadrangle picking up the phone and dialing the number. "Hello, Mrs. Piggle-Wiggle, this is Harbin Quadrangle's father. I just wondered if you knew of anything that would help cure a slowpoke?"

Apparently Mrs. Piggle-Wiggle did know because

there was a silence on Mr. Quadrangle's end of the phone for quite a while, then he said, "Thank you very much, I'll be right over."

"What did she say? Where are you going? Can she cure Harbin?" asked Mrs. Quadrangle.

Mr. Quadrangle stood up, gave her a kiss and said, "It's in the bag." He was whistling as he went out the front door.

When he came back about half an hour later he was carrying a small bottle of clear fluid and a little sprayer.

"What is that?" asked Mrs. Quadrangle who was in the living room reading a book on child psychology.

"Mrs. Piggle-Wiggle said to spray his clothes with it. She said to lay out the clothes he will wear to school tomorrow and then spray them thoroughly, especially the shoes."

"But what will the spray do, what is it for?" asked Mrs. Quadrangle anxiously.

"Dunno," said Mr. Quadrangle humming "Yankee Doodle." "But let's get started." He uncorked the bottle and filled the little sprayer.

When they went into his room they found Harbin deeply asleep. His mother quickly felt his forehead but it was cool and moist. He appeared very relaxed and he was smiling. Apparently his dream was a happy one.

Tiptoeing over to the bureau Mrs. Quadrangle opened drawers and took out clean underclothes, socks, jeans, tee shirt and a sweater. She laid them out on the foot of Harbin's bed and Mr. Quadrangle sprayed them thoroughly. They were tiptoeing out when Mr. Quadrangle remembered the shoes and went back and sprayed them.

Mrs. Quadrangle didn't sleep very well that night. The minute she got out of bed the next morning she rushed into Harbin's room to see if he was all right. He was still fast asleep. She tiptoed out, went downstairs and put on the coffee.

Mr. Pierce scratched on the cellar door. She opened it and he wagged his tail and she patted him on the head and then she put him out. It was raining. A thin misty cold drizzle. Mr. Pierce looked at her reproachfully and tried to squeeze past her back into the house.

She said firmly, "Oh, no you don't, sir. You've been in the house all night and now I want you to take a little run." She tried to push him with her foot but he sat down heavily on it. She had just about decided to give up when suddenly the back door was flung open and Harbin fully dressed, and combed and washed, said briskly, "Whatsa matter, Mom? What are you tryin' to do?"

"It's Mr. Pierce," said Mrs. Quadrangle giving him another yank. "He won't go out and take his morning run, because it's raining and he hates the rain."

"Whatsa matter old boy," said Harbin kneeling beside him, "don't you like the rain?"

Mr. Pierce thumped his tail on the porch and licked Harbin's face.

Standing up Harbin said, "I'll go with him, Mom. We'll take a run around the block."

"But the rain," said Mrs. Quadrangle. "You'll get all wet."

"Not me," said Harbin. "I'll run too fast. You just watch."

He jumped off the porch skipping the steps entirely and raced down the driveway. Yelping happily Mr. Pierce followed. Mrs. Quadrangle went into the kitchen, put the milk on for the cocoa and poured herself a cup of coffee.

She had only taken two sips when the back door flew open and in came Harbin and Mr. Pierce. Harbin's cheeks were bright pink, his eyes sparkled and neither he nor Mr. Pierce seemed to be at all wet.

"My goodness," his mother said, "you must have run faster than the wind."

"Faster than the rain, you mean," said Harbin laughing. "Boy, I've never run so fast. Even Mr. Pierce couldn't keep up with me. What are we having for breakfast, I'm starved."

Mrs. Quadrangle, who didn't really wake up all the way until after she had had her coffee, said, "Well, uh, uh . . ."

"I know," said Harbin briskly. "We'll have French toast."

"Good idea," said his mother. "I'll get at it just as soon as I finish this cup of coffee."

"I'll make it," said Harbin. "You just tell me what to do." He flung open a cupboard and began rattling the pots and pans.

"Get out a bowl," said his mother, "and the eggs and some milk and . . ."

There was a sharp rapping at the back door.

It was Georgie Wilcox, the paper boy. He said he was sorry he was so late—but he had a flat tire on his bicycle, and here was the paper he hoped it hadn't gotten too wet while he was fixing his bike.

Harbin put down the mixing bowl he had taken out of the pan cupboard and said, "Hey, Georgie, want me to come along and help you deliver? I can take one side of the street and you take the other."

Georgie, who remembered Harbin as something of a human snail, said quickly, "Oh, that's all right, Harbin, I'll make it I guess."

Harbin said, "You can't. It's almost six-thirty."

Mrs. Quadrangle looked up at the kitchen clock, then wiped her eyes on her apron and looked again. It *was* only 6:25—heavens she and Harbin must have gotten up about 5:45. She looked at Harbin in astonishment. Could this bright-eyed eager little boy be the same one who always was the last to breakfast—in fact the last for everything?

Harbin said, "Wait a sec till I get my jacket, Georgie."

Georgie who looked sleepy and as messy as if he had dressed in a wind tunnel said, "Well, okay, but hurry."

In two seconds Harbin was back with the jacket. As he went out the door he said to his mother, "Better make a huge batch of French toast, Mom. Come on, Mr. Pierce. We got work to do."

When Mr. Quadrangle came downstairs a little after seven-thirty his first words were "What about the magic spray? Did it work?"

"I got up so early and have been so busy I forgot all about it," said Mrs. Quadrangle. "Now sit down and eat this French toast while it's hot. Did you waken the girls?"

"I think they're both up," said Mr. Quadrangle. "But what about Harbin? Have you called him yet?"

"Called him?" said Mrs. Quadrangle. "He was downstairs before six o'clock."

"Where is he now?" asked Mr. Quadrangle. "Dawdling some place I'll bet."

"He is not," said Mrs. Quadrangle. "Look out, that plate's hot as the dickens."

"Well then where is he?" asked his father impatiently.

"He's gone with Georgie Wilcox on his paper route. Georgie had a flat tire on his bicycle and was late and Harbin offered to help him."

"Hope Georgie's customers won't mind a morning paper being delivered in the afternoon," said Mr. Quadrangle through a bite of French toast.

Just then the back door burst open and Harbin called out, "Sure hope breakfast is ready. I'm starvinger than a lion." Seeing his father he said, "Hi, Dad. Say, know what? Georgie Wilcox said I'm the fastest helper he's ever had on his paper route and he said if his mom and dad let him go to California to visit his grandmother this summer he'll let me take over his paper route and he makes almost *forty dollars a month*. Zowie."

"But you'd have to get up so *early*," said his mother.

"Who cares?" said Harbin. "I'd make almost *forty dollars a month!*"

"You make forty dollars a month?" sneered Sylvia who had just come to the table. "Don't be fantastic. A slowpoke like you wouldn't be worth forty cents."

"Sylvia," said Mr. Quadrangle sternly, "be quiet. Now, son, what about this paper route? Do you think you could handle it?"

"Of course I could," Harbin said. "Gosh, this morning I delivered three papers to Georgie's one."

Mrs. Quadrangle said, "Where's Janey? Was she up when you came downstairs, Sylvia?"

"I don't know," said Sylvia. "I called her about thirty thousand times but when I went into her room to get my blue sweater she sneaked and wore and spilled Coke all down the front of, she was still in bed reading."

"I'd better call again," said Mrs. Quadrangle. She went to the foot of the stairs and called "Janey. Jaaaaaeeeeeee!"

After a while a muffled voice answered, "Be down in a sec."

Mrs. Quadrangle listened for a minute, then hearing no signs of activity from Janey's room she went up. She found Janey still in her nightgown leaning on the window sill and looking out at the rain. Her mother said quite sharply, "Janey Quadrangle, it is almost time to leave for school. Why aren't you dressed?"

Janey turned, gave her mother a dreamy faraway look and said, "Rain running down the window pane reminds me of tears. Do you think that rain could be the tear drops of all the poor people who have died?"

"My goodness what a morbid idea," said Mrs. Quadrangle pulling Janey's skirt and sweater out of the jumble of bedclothes. "Here put these on quickly then I'll start on your hair while you put on your shoes and socks."

Slowly Janey straightened up, took the skirt and sweater from her mother and then said, "Mother, if I should die would you and Daddy cry?"

"Don't talk that way," said her mother crossly. "In fact don't talk at all. Just hurry."

"But Mother," said Janey, "what if I did die tomorrow? What if I got run over by a truck?"

With an exasperated sigh Mrs. Quadrangle grabbed the skirt and sweater from Janey. "Come here," she said. "I'll dress you. Although I think it is perfectly ridiculous for a great big girl to have to be dressed by her mother." She had just begun to pull the skirt down over Janey's head when suddenly she remembered the little blower filled with Mrs. Piggle-Wiggle's magic liquid for slowpokes. She pulled the skirt off Janey's head, picked up her sweater, shoes and socks and said, "You go start getting washed, I'll be right back."

The little blower was in the drawer of Mr. Quadrangle's bedside stand. She took it out and carefully sprayed Janey's clothes. Then she went back to Janey's room where Janey instead of washing her face was lying across the bed singing "My country 'tis of thee." When she saw her mother she said, "I know all the verses to 'The Star Spangled Banner,' want to hear them?"

"No!" said her mother firmly. "Stand up so I can dress you."

She jammed the skirt and sweater down over Janey's

head. Stuffed her feet into her socks and shoes, then pushed her into the bathroom, washed her face and hands and was just braiding her hair when Mr. Quadrangle called, "Molly, I'll have to leave for the station in five minutes."

"All right, dear," said Mrs. Quadrangle snapping an elastic around the end of one of Janey's braids. To Janey she said, "You'll just have to eat some toast and peanut butter on the way to the station, now scoot and fix it while I get Old-Timer up."

"But he hasn't had his mush," said Janey who suddenly seemed very wide awake and bright.

"I know," said Mrs. Quadrangle, "but we're late so he'll just have to wait."

"I'll fix him some mush in a bottle," said Janey. "You change him and put on his ski suit and I'll fix the bottle and we'll give it to him in the car."

When they were all settled in the car complete with Sylvia's note for an early dismissal to go to the dentist, with Uncle Joe's elephant tooth for Harbin to show during natural history period, Janey with Old-Timer and the bottle, Mr. Quadrangle said, "Okay everybody?"

"Okay," they all said.

"All aboard then," he shouted stepping on the gas. "Next stop the station."

Then he turned to Mrs. Quadrangle and said, "Say did you by any chance spray any of that magic stuff on my clothes, I feel awfully quick and alert for this early in the morning."

Smiling a little sheepishly Mrs. Quadrangle said, "Only a little bit on your shoes."

"Then we're even," laughed Mr. Quadrangle. "I sprayed some on your hair when you were asleep."

"No wonder I woke up so early," laughed Mrs. Quadrangle.

"Let's all sing 'God Bless America,' " said Harbin, from the back seat.

"Let's all sing 'God Bless Mrs. Piggle-Wiggle,' " said Mr. Quadrangle, honking the horn at a fat gray pigeon.

MRS. PIGGLE-WIGGLE'S MAGIC

Mrs. Piggle-Wiggle's Magic

Betty MacDonald

Pictures by HILARY KNIGHT

HarperCollins*Publishers*

Dedication

To my mother, Sydney Bard, the one most often interrupted, the faithful laugher at "thought you saids," the patient corrector of bad table manners, the rapt listener to long, dull dreams and movie plots, the fairest receiver of tattle tales and eager participant in all timeworn riddles and tricks, I humbly dedicate this book.

Contents

MRS. PIGGLE-WIGGLE'S MAGIC

Of course the reason that all the children in our town like Mrs. Piggle-Wiggle is because Mrs. Piggle-Wiggle likes them. Mrs. Piggle-Wiggle likes children, she enjoys talking to them and best of all they do not irritate her.

When Molly O'Toole was looking at the colored pictures in Mrs. Piggle-Wiggle's big dictionary and just happened to be eating a candy cane at the same time and drooled candy cane juice on the colored pictures of gems and then forgot and shut the book so the pages all stuck together, Mrs. Piggle-Wiggle didn't say, "Such a careless little girl can never ever look at the colored pictures in my big dictionary again." Nor did she say, "You must never look at books when you are eating." She said, "Let's see, I think we can steam those pages apart, and then we can

1

wipe the stickiness off with a little soap and water, like this—now see, it's just as good as new. There's nothing as cozy as a piece of candy and a book. Don't look so embarrassed, Molly, I almost drool every time I look at those gems—which one is your favorite?—I think mine is the Lapis Lazuli."

When Dicky Williams, who was showing off for Patsy by riding in his wagon with his eyes shut, crashed through Mrs. Piggle-Wiggle's basement window and landed in the coal bin, Mrs. Piggle-Wiggle laughed so much she had to sit down on the front steps and wipe her eyes with her apron. Dicky was awfully scared and was going to sneak out the basement door and go home, but Mrs. Piggle-Wiggle, still laughing, leaned through the broken window and said, "Hand me the putty knife and that can of putty off the shelf and then go get me that pane of glass leaning against the wall over there by the furnace. Thank you very much. Now watch carefully, Dicky, because putting in window glass is something that every boy should know how to do. Especially boys who ride wagons with their eyes closed."

When Marilyn Matson who was helping Mrs. Piggle-Wiggle serve tea dropped and broke her brown teapot she said, "Well, that's the luckiest thing I've ever known—you didn't get a drop of hot tea on you and you broke that nasty teapot with the leaky spout that I've hated for fifteen years. Tomorrow I'll go to town and buy a new one—I think I'll get pink and I'm going to test the spout before I buy it." "But what about the tea?" said Marilyn, wiping her tears on her sleeve. "Make it in the coffee pot," said Mrs. Piggle-Wiggle, "and we'll call it toffee."

Another nice thing about Mrs. Piggle-Wiggle, when a child makes her a present no matter how splotchy or crooked it might be, she uses it and keeps it where everyone can see it.

Johnny Wilfred made her a vase out of a meat sauce bottle with such a little neck that only flowers with stems like hairs would fit in it. Not only that but he painted it a sort of bilious green and the paint was too thick and ran down the sides in warty lumps. But Mrs. Piggle-Wiggle loves Johnny and she loves the warty vase because Johnny made it for her, and she keeps it on the window sill above the sink with at least one flower, gasping for breath, jammed through its little neck. Every time Johnny comes into her kitchen he points proudly to the vase and says, "Do you see that pretty vase over there on the window sill. Well, I made it for Mrs. Piggle-Wiggle, didn't I, Mrs. Piggle-Wiggle?"

When Susan Gray came staggering over with a plate of the first cookies she had ever made for Mrs. Piggle-Wiggle, Mrs. Piggle-Wiggle didn't take one look at the tannish gray lumps and say, "No Thank You!" She said, "Why, Susan Gray, you smart girl. Eight years old and already making cookies! You're going to make somebody a very fine wife." "Yeah, somebody with good teeth," said Hubert Prentiss who had taken one of the gray lumps and had found that trying to eat it was like biting on a stone. Mrs. Piggle-Wiggle took the cookie away from him and said, "Oh, Hubert, these are special cookies, you dip them in hot tea and then take a bite."

She hurried to the kitchen and made some tea and then

she and Molly and Hubert and Susan sat at the kitchen table and drank tea and gnawed at the stony cookies, which in addition to being hard as rocks, tasted like glue because Susan had put in gravy coloring instead of vanilla. When Molly and Hubert made gagging motions at each other Mrs. Piggle-Wiggle slipped them some ginger cookies under the table and Susan was so proud that she didn't even notice.

Julie Ward knitted Mrs. Piggle-Wiggle a scarf that was about ten yards long and two inches wide and when Mrs. Piggle-Wiggle opened the box she didn't say, "My, Julie, you must have had a giraffe in mind when you made this scarf." Instead she said, "You know Julie, this is much too pretty to wear as a scarf and keep tucked inside my coat. I'm going to wear it as a sash." She took the long, dirty blue, wormy looking scarf and wrapped it around and around her waist and looped the ends over and it did look nice, from a distance. Julie was so proud. She said, "You know, Mrs. Piggle-Wiggle, when I was making that scarf I just thought to myself, 'Now I'll make this longer and then Mrs. Piggle-Wiggle can wear it as a belt too.'" Of course she hadn't really. What actually happened was that she knitted on the scarf every afternoon when she listened to the radio and she just forgot to stop.

Another wonderful trait of Mrs. Piggle-Wiggle's is the interested way she listens to dreams. Now every child in the world loves to tell what he dreams and if the dream doesn't seem to be quite long enough or interesting enough, sometimes some children work in old movies they have seen or stories their Daddies have read to them the night before.

Dream telling is an innocent pastime and very good for the imagination but unfortunately dream telling usually occurs at breakfast, a time when daddies and mothers are slightly irritable and always in a hurry and in no mood for long-drawn-out stories of "and then I was riding on this elephant and two Indians came up and tried to shoot me but then er, uh, uh, uh, I turned into a walnut and dropped on the ground and uh, uh, uh, this—" About this time Mothers say, "Just let the dream go and finish your cereal!" or Brother or Sister will say, "Oh, you're just making that up and anyway it's my turn. Now I dreamed . . ."

Mrs. Piggle-Wiggle not only listens to dreams, she asks about them. Right after school when the children come over to dig for treasure in her back yard (Mr. Piggle-Wiggle was a pirate and when he died he buried his treasure in his back yard) or to have tea or to play dolls, she'll say, "Anybody have any good dreams last night?" and they'll be off.

Once Molly O'Toole dreamed she was a raisin and was eaten by a rat. Johnny Green dreamed that he was a pirate and lived in a whale. Hubert Prentiss dreamed that he was an icicle and could freeze anyone he touched. Susan Gray dreamed that her dolls all came alive. Larry Grav dreamed he was a cowboy and had a white horse. Mary Lou Robertson dreamed that her covers were frosting and woke up with her mouth full of blanket. Kitty Wheeling dreamed that she was a movie star and had a real fur coat. Patsy said that she dreamed that she was an electric toaster and everybody said she was making it up and Patsy cried and Mrs. Piggle-Wiggle said she would help Patsy with her dreams. Some of the children's dreams are so long and dull and full of er—ra and uh—ruh's that Mrs. Piggle-Wiggle finishes them off for them and says, "That was the way it was, wasn't it, Bobby," much to their evident relief.

So you can see that loving children the way she does, Mrs. Piggle-Wiggle just naturally understands them even when they are being very difficult, which is of course why all the mothers in our town call Mrs. Piggle-Wiggle whenever they are having trouble with their children. Mrs. Piggle-Wiggle always knows what to do and then of course she has a big cupboard full of magic powders and pills and appliances to help cure children's bad habits.

THE THOUGHT-YOU-SAIDERS CURE

$\mathcal{M}$r. Burbank absently reached from behind his newspaper for the sugar bowl. His groping fingers hit the toast, the honey comb, the salt cellar and finally found the sugar bowl. His children Darsie, Alison and Bard nudged each other and laughed. Every morning Daddy felt around on the table for the sugar while he read bad news in the newspaper.

One morning the news was so bad and he was so absent-minded he put currant jelly in his coffee. The children were anxious for a repeat performance and hopefully pushed everything but the sugar in the path of his searching hand. This morning as soon as Mr. Burbank had found the sugar he let the paper down with a bang. "The sugar bowl's empty," he said in an aggrieved, hurt way.

Mrs. Burbank, who was buttering toast said, "Darsie, run out to the kitchen and fill the sugar bowl, dear. The sugar's in the big red can."

Darsie obediently got up, took the sugar bowl and went out to the kitchen. After a long long time he came back to the breakfast table with a plate of cinnamon rolls.

"What are these for?" his father said. "And where is the sugar?"

"Sugar?" said Darsie. "What about sugar?"

"I told you to fill the sugar bowl," said Mrs. Burbank.

"Oh," said Darsie, "I thought you said, 'Get the cinnamon roll.'"

All three children looked at each other and laughed loudly. Finally Mr. and Mrs. Burbank laughed too. Darsie went out and filled the sugar bowl and Mr. Burbank, after three cups of coffee, missed his bus and decided to walk as far as the school with the children.

Just as they were going out the front door, Alison remembered her arithmetic book and dashed upstairs for it. In a minute she leaned over the bannister and called, "Mother, did you see my arithmetic book?"

Mrs. Burbank said, "What does it look like?"

Alison said, "It's blue and not very thick."

Mrs. Burbank said, "I think it's on the table in the hall."

Alison said, "How did it get out there?"

Mrs. Burbank said, "Out where? I said it's on the table in the hall."

Alison said, "Oh, I thought you said it's out in the stable in a stall." All three children roared with laughter.

Alison found her arithmetic book and they all left the

house laughing and repeating, "Out in the stable in a stall."

Mr. Burbank said, "Come on, come on, we haven't all day." He walked briskly along the street, his footsteps ringing loudly and purposefully in the thin autumn air. The children giggled and jostled along behind him, their progress so uneven and broken by "thought you said" and shrieks of laughter that Mr. Burbank reached the corner first, in fact almost before they had left the yard. He stopped to wait for them and to survey the city spread out below him in the morning sunshine. He was glad he lived on a hill, he was glad he was alive and he was glad he had a little boy nine, a little girl seven and a little boy six.

When the children had caught up with him he said, "Look, children. See how beautiful the city looks from up here. Watch the fog rise over there."

"Where's the dog?" said Bard.

"What dog?" asked Darsie.

"What color are the dog's eyes?" asked Alison.

"What on earth are you talking about?" said Mr. Burbank. "I said, 'Watch the fog rise over there.' "

"Oh," Bard said, "I thought you said, 'Watch the dog's eyes glare.' " All the children laughed and laughed. Mr. Burbank said, "What nonsense," but it was a beautiful morning so he laughed with his lighthearted children.

When they were half way down the next block, the children suddenly stopped stock still in front of a pretty white house and yelled in unison, "Marilyn! Mar-ee-lun! Come on, we'll be late!"

Mr. Burbank said, "That's no way to do. If you want Marilyn, go to the door and ask for her."

The children looked surprised but went obediently up to the door and rang the bell. Marilyn's mother opened the door and said something to the children which seemed to send them into convulsions of mirth. Doubled over with laughter and holding their sides they came down the walk to their father.

"Now what's so funny?" Mr. Burbank asked.

Darsie said, "Marilyn's mother said Marilyn fell in the toaster and is burnt up dead."

Mr. Burbank said, "What did Marilyn's mother really say and why isn't Marilyn going to school."

Alison said, "She said Marilyn fell in her coaster and hurt her head and Darsie thought she said Marilyn fell in the toaster and is burnt up dead." She went into another paroxysm of laughter.

Mr. Burbank didn't laugh. Instead he bent down and examined Darsie's ears which were large and pink and soft and quite clean.

"They *should* work," said Mr. Burbank, looking at the other children's ears. They all seemed quite normal. The children wanted to know what he was doing.

Bard said, "What are you doing that for, Daddy?"

Mr. Burbank said, "I'm trying to decide whether I should get you an ear trumpet."

"Beer crumpet? What's that?" Bard said.

The other children repeated after him, "Beer crumpet? Beer crumpet?" They all laughed but Mr. Burbank, who had had enough. He said, "Come on. I'll supervise a race to school. On your marks, get set, go!"

When Mr. Burbank reached his office the very first thing

he did was to call Mrs. Burbank. He said, "Mary, have our children ever had scarlet fever?"

She said, "Now you know they haven't, Bernard."

"Well," he said, "have they ever had ear infections?"

"Goodness, no," said Mrs. Burbank. "They've never had anything. They are the healthiest children in the neighborhood. What's the matter?"

Mr. Burbank said, "Plenty. They can't any of them hear well. I told them to look at the fog rise and they thought I was talking about dog's eyes. Marilyn's mother said that Marilyn fell off her coaster and hurt her head and they thought she said Marilyn fell in the toaster and was . . ."

". . . Burnt up dead," Mrs. Burbank finished for him. "Bernard, did you ever hear of anyone falling in a toaster? Of course not. There is nothing wrong with our children's ears. It is just that they are going through that awful Thought-You-Said phase."

"Well let's get them out of it," said Mr. Burbank. "They sound like dopes. Dog's eyes, indeed."

Mrs. Burbank said, "Don't worry, dear, I'll take care of it."

As soon as she finished talking to Mr. Burbank, Mrs. Burbank called Marilyn's mother to find out about Marilyn, if she was badly hurt and if there was anything she could do. Marilyn's mother said Marilyn was just fine but the doctor thought she should be quiet for a day or two.

When Mrs. Burbank asked Marilyn's mother if she had ever had any trouble with Thought-You-Said, and told

about the sugar bowl and the cinnamon rolls, the arithmetic book in the stable in the stall, about Marilyn's fall
in the toaster and the dog's eyes, Marilyn's mother said,
"Oh, Mrs. Burbank, I'm so glad you called and told me
all this. You see Marilyn has been doing the same thing all
morning and I was terribly afraid that the blow on her
head had affected her mind. When I asked her if she
wanted crumpets or toast she said, 'Bumped on the nose,
who?' When I asked her if her head pained her she said,
'I thought you said, Is the bed painted yet?'"

Mrs. Burbank said, "I'm going to call up Mrs. Teagle
and see if Terry or Theresa are Thought-You-Saids. She is
such a good manager that if they have Thought-You-Saiditis she's probably thought of a cure." Marilyn's mother
asked Mrs. Burbank to call her back if she got any useful
information and they said goodbye.

Then Mrs. Burbank called Mrs. Teagle. She told her all
about the Thought-You-Saiditis and asked if she had had
any similar experience with Terry or Theresa. Mrs. Teagle
said, "Ohwa, nowa, Mrs. Burrrrbank. Youwa see we have
allaways studied korrect speeeeeech and wea all speak
korrectly. Thee cheeldren alaways pronounce all theirrrr
vowels and all theirrr consonants and therefore we neverrrr
have any trouble understanding each otherrrr. Perhaps
the trouble lies with you and Mr. Burbank—perrrhaps
you do not speak deestincktly. Perhaps the poor leetle
cheeldrun cannot underrrrstahnd you. I am holding lit-tul
speeeeech clahsses everrrry ahfternoon and eef you and
Mrrrr. Burrrbank are interrrest-ed I would be glad to
hahve you attend. I wouldn't carrrrre to hahve the cheel-

drun becawse I am afrrrraid they might corrupt my cheel-drun's perrrrfect speeeeeech."

Mrs. Burbank thanked Mrs. Teagle for her kind offer and told her that perhaps she was right. That she and Mr. Burbank would try to speak more distinctly and if things didn't improve within the week they might join the speech classes. Mrs. Teagle said, "Glahd to bee of help annnny tihum, Mrs. Burrbank," and hung up.

That night when Mr. Burbank came home she told him about calling Mrs. Teagle, and told him that she thought that from now on they should both try to speak more carefully so that their poor little children could understand them.

That night at dinner Mr. Burbank announced in a very loud voice, "Pleeeeeese pahssssss the butterrrrrr!" The children all exchanged glances and whispers, then laughed. The butter remained cool and comfortable on its little plate in front of Darsie.

Mr. Burbank looked accusingly at Mrs. Burbank. She said in a high unnatural voice, "Cheeeldrun, leesten to meee. Pleeeeese pahssss youh fahtherrr the butterrrrrr!"

"Oh," said Darsie, "did you say pass the butter. I thought you said, 'Fleas gasp and mutter.' "

Alison said, "I thought you said, 'He's pa's mother.' "

Bard said, "I thought you said, 'Freeze Pat's brother.' "

Mr. Burbank said in a low grim voice, "I said 'Please pass the butter.' " Darsie passed it to him with a beaming smile.

The next morning after breakfast, Mr. Burbank called from upstairs, "Where's my briefcase, anybody seen my briefcase?"

Alison said, "Whose got a thief's face?"

Darsie said, "Beef paste, what do you want that for?"

Bard said, "Leaf race, I thought he said leaf race." They all laughed loudly and did not look for the briefcase.

They could hear their mother and father banging doors and scuffling around upstairs but they were so busy Thought-You-Saiding they didn't even notice that Bard was standing in front of the briefcase, which was leaning against the radiator in the front hall.

Finally Mr. Burbank came running downstairs, wild-eyed and almost too late for his bus. He called to Mrs. Burbank, "If you find it, dear, bring it right down to the office. I must have it this morning." He slammed the front door and ran like the wind for his bus.

Mrs. Burbank was giving the children their final inspection before school when she saw the briefcase leaning against the wall right behind Bard's fat little legs. She said, "Why children, why didn't you tell Daddy his briefcase was down here. You must have seen it! Now I'll have to make a special trip all the way down to take it to him. Why didn't you tell him?" She looked sternly at her three children.

Alison said, "Briefcase! I didn't know that's what he wanted, I thought he said, 'Thief's face.'"

Darsie said, "I didn't know he wanted his briefcase, I thought he said, 'Beef paste.'"

Bard said, "I thought he said 'leaf race.'"

Mrs. Burbank said, "You know perfectly well that Daddy wouldn't talk about a thief's face, beef paste or leaf races. That's just nonsense and I'm getting good and tired of all this Thought-You-Said business." She sent them off to school with a little push and without a kiss.

But the Thought-You-Saiditis continued all the rest of
that week. By Friday morning Mr. and Mrs. Burbank were
so irritable they didn't even want to come downstairs and
eat breakfast with the Thought-You-Saiders. They tried
to solve the problem by not speaking to the children but
of course the telephone rang and Mrs. Burbank said to
Alison, "Answer the phone" and Alison didn't move and
her father said, "ANSWER THE PHONE!" and Alison
said, "Oh, answer the phone, I thought you said, 'This
ham's got a bone' " and Darsie said, "I thought you said,
'The dancers are home' " and Bard said, "I thought you
said, uh, uh, uh, 'The jam's all alone.' " It was the last
straw. Mr. Burbank said, "This nonsense has got to stop,
now. I'm not going to eat another meal with the Thought-
You-Saids."

As soon as the children had left for school and even
before she washed the breakfast dishes, Mrs. Burbank decided that she must do something about the Thought-You-
Saiders. She poured herself another cup of coffee and sat
down at the breakfast table and thought and thought. Ole
Boy, the dog, came and sat beside her and she gave him a
small piece of ham and stroked his head and wondered and
wondered what to do.

She was just going to call Mr. Burbank's mother when
the telephone rang again. Mrs. Burbank answered it. It
was Mrs. Piggle-Wiggle and she wanted the children to
come for tea. Mrs. Burbank said, "Oh, Mrs. Piggle-Wiggle
I am so delighted that you called. I was just sitting here at
the breakfast table wondering what in the world to do."

And so she told Mrs. Piggle-Wiggle about the Thought-You-Saiders.

Mrs. Piggle-Wiggle said, "There is a regular epidemic of Thought-You-Saiditis all over town. It really is a very harmless disease but can be most annoying to parents, especially when they are trying to hurry. I have suffered with it myself this past week. Put on your shoes is Thought-You-Said sat on a fuse—Get me a tack is Thought-You-Said butter a cracker, and on and on. Fortunately the cure is very simple. I have a magic powder which you sprinkle in the children's ears tonight. It will make their hearing so keen that they'll be able to hear spiders stamping across the floor, leaves crashing to the ground, flowers snapping open their petals and fireflies striking the matches that light their lanterns. I must warn you that tomorrow when the children are wearing the magic hearing powder, you mustn't pop corn, run the vacuum cleaner or serve dry crunchy breakfast foods. The noise would be too painful to them. I'll send the powder over when the children stop by after school. You might lend a little to Marilyn's mother. Goodbye and good luck." Mrs. Piggle-Wiggle hung up the phone.

After school the children came rushing in to deliver the package from Mrs. Piggle-Wiggle and to change their clothes. Mrs. Piggle-Wiggle's package contained a tiny little box of white powder. Mrs. Burbank felt the powder and smelled it—it felt like talcum powder and it smelled like ginger. She put it under the pile of clean handkerchiefs in her handkerchief box. That evening after the children were in bed, she told Mr. Burbank about it. He thought the magic powder sounded wonderful and decided to try a little in his own ears.

Mrs. Burbank went up and got the bottle and Mr. Burbank put a pinch in his left ear. Immediately he shouted, "TURN OFF THAT TERRIBLE RADIO. IT'S KILLING ME." Mrs. Burbank rushed and turned the radio off. Mr. Burbank said, "It's thundering, we must be going to have a storm." Mrs. Burbank listened. She couldn't hear any thunder. She opened the front door and went out and looked at the sky. It was a clear dark blue and spangled with stars. The night was as still and quiet as a picture. Mr. Burbank shouted, "The storm's getting closer. Almost overhead now!"

Mrs. Burbank came in and closed the door. She said, "Bernard Burbank, it's a cold, clear, perfectly peaceful night. There is no thunder."

Mr. Burbank said, "Listen. Don't you hear it. Deafening—that's what it is. Deafening!" Mrs. Burbank listened very carefully. Then she heard from the kitchen a soft very faint thumping noise. She went out to investigate and found Ole Boy the dog, lying under the kitchen table scratching and bumping his elbow on the floor. She gave Ole Boy a dog biscuit and put him out, then she went back to the living-room and asked Mr. Burbank if the storm had passed over.

He said, "Do you have to stamp your feet like that? You certainly must be getting fat, you sound like a coal truck when you walk."

Mrs. Burbank, who was very slight, looked down at her soft red house slippers and said, "Bernard, I think you had better wash that magic powder out of your ear because I'm going to go out right now and get some graham crackers and think of the torture you'll go through if I drop a crumb."

Mr. Burbank said, "Stop shouting!"

Mrs. Burbank said, "I'm whispering, dear," so Mr. Burbank went upstairs to wash out his ear. When he snapped on the light in the bathroom he flinched because it sounded like a pistol shot. When he turned on the faucet it sounded like Niagara Falls and when he accidentally brushed a hairpin off the window sill it sounded like a huge iron chain crashing to the tiled floor.

Mr. Burbank filled the bathroom glass with warm water. He had decided that that would be the best way to wash out the magic powder, and was just about to pour some in his ear when from behind the bathtub he heard the most awful screaming, screeching, whining noise. He straightened up, put down the glass and peered over by the bathtub. He didn't see anything. He bent down over the basin again and picked up the glass. He was just about to pour the warm water in his ear when the horrible, screaming, squealing noise came again, this time right by his head. Mr. Burbank was so scared he dropped the glass, spilled the water and banged his head on the faucet. He looked all around but he couldn't see anything. The noise came again. This time a little fainter and from behind the Venetian blind. He raised the blind and looked carefully. He couldn't see a thing. The terrible noise came again, this time by the mirror; then Mr. Burbank saw what it was. A big mosquito. He grabbed a washcloth and without thinking of his magic hearing, swatted the mosquito. The screams of agony that immediately filled the bathroom were horrible. Mr. Burbank hurriedly turned on the warm water and stuck his ear right under the faucet. Whew, what a relief!

He picked the dead mosquito up by one leg and put it in the wastebasket, then he called to Mrs. Burbank. "Hey, Mary, I'm all right now but I think we'd better go easy with that magic powder in the children's ears. It's awfully strong."

Mrs. Burbank said, "Perhaps you used too much. Here, I'll measure it out. I'll use a toothpick and I'll just put a grain or so in the right ear of each child. Come on now, help me."

They tiptoed into the children's rooms and put a toothpick full of the magic powder in each one's right ear. Even in his sleep Darsie was saying, "Miss Anderson, I didn't hear you say, 'Hand me that ruler'—I thought you said, 'Bananas are cooler.' "

Mr. and Mrs. Burbank looked at their sleeping son and then at each other. "Just wait until tomorrow, Darsie old boy," said Mr. Burbank.

The next morning at seven o'clock, Bard came running into his parents' room and said, "Mother, Daddy, there is a terrible noise in our room. It sounds like sawing." Mr. and Mrs. Burbank got out of bed, put on their robes and went in to investigate. They couldn't hear a thing. Darsie said, "Isn't that a nawful noise, Daddy? Do you think it's a buzz bomb?" Mr. and Mrs. Burbank looked and looked but they couldn't see or hear anything.

Mr. Burbank told the children to get dressed and come down to breakfast. Bard began to cry. He said, "We'll

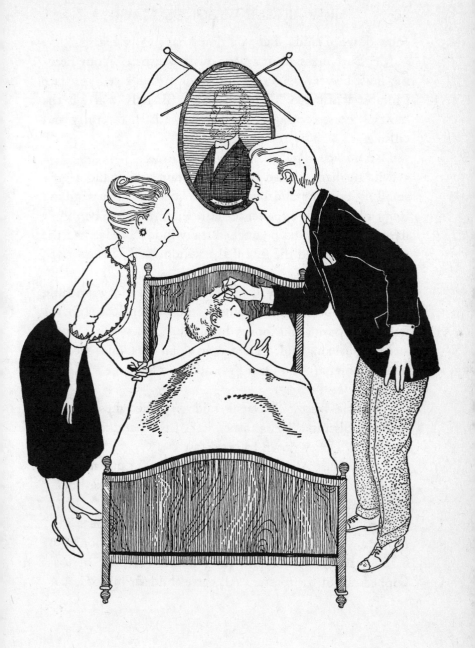

come down, Daddy, but you don't have to yell at us."

Mr. Burbank said in a very quiet whisper, "Your hearing must be very good this morning. I didn't yell—in fact I almost whispered." Then he said, "Exactly where is the buzzing noise coming from, Darsie? Listen carefully and tell me."

Darsie said, "Right there by the curtain."

Mr. Burbank pulled back the curtain and found a very small fly buzzing and buzzing in a corner of the window. Remembering his experience with the mosquito, he didn't dare swat the fly, so he opened the window, unlatched the screen and pushed the fly off the window sill. It flew happily away.

Darsie said, "Daddy, I can't stand this awful crunching noise my shoelaces make when I push them through the holes. It sounds like bones breaking."

Mr. Burbank said, "Here, I have an idea." He tied his handkerchief around Darsie's head like a bandage. "This'll fix it," he said softly.

"Whistle biscuit!" Darsie said. "I thought you said 'Whistle biscuit.'" His father jerked the handkerchief off and said, "Hurry down to breakfast."

At breakfast Alison said, "Oh, Mother, I can't stand the sound of you buttering that toast. It sounds like hoeing on cement."

Bard said, "Hoeing on cement! I thought you said, I thought you said, uh, er ah . . ." He took a spoonful of oatmeal and never finished the sentence. A piece of toast popped out of the toaster. All three children jumped.

Darsie said, "Mother, you should warn us when you're going to make so much noise."

Mrs. Burbank said, "I'm sorry but it didn't seem loud to me. I guess my ears aren't very good."

Alison said, "Come on, boys, let's go to school."

Darsie said, "I thought you said Poison, I mean I thought you said, Poison, I mean . . . Oh, I don't know what I meant."

Alison said, "Ole Boy's breathing so loud I can't hear a thing. And does he have to splash his tongue around in his mouth like that, Mother?"

Mrs. Burbank called Ole Boy and gave him a piece of bacon. He snapped and gulped and all three children jumped and shuddered.

"What a noise," said Alison glaring balefully at poor Ole Boy. "He's just like some terrible kind of a jungle beast."

Mrs. Burbank said, "Come, children, put on your coats and go to school."

Alison said, "Spit on your coats. I thought you said spit on your coats." Nobody laughed.

Darsie said, "Don't talk so loud, Alison, it hurts my ears."

Bard said, "Didn't you hear what Mother said. She didn't say, 'Spit on your coats.' She said, 'Put on your coats.' "

Alison said, "I know it. I can hear. Let's go."

The front door closed quietly and Mrs. Burbank said to her husband, who was groping for the sugar, "That's the first time in five years they haven't banged the front door.

Here's the sugar, dear, and you have four minutes before the next bus."

Just then the front door opened and the three children came crying into the house.

Alison said, "Mother, we just can't stand it. The sidewalk is covered with leaves and when we walk through them the noise is so dreadful we just can't bear it. It sounds like hundreds of giants chopping wood."

Bard said, "It sounds like millions of paper bags."

Darsie said, "It sounds like thousands of houses burning up. Crackle, crackle, crash."

Mrs. Burbank said, "Well, Bernard, I think we'd better wash out their ears and we'll give Mrs. Piggle-Wiggle our heartiest thanks."

Mr. Burbank said, "What's she done wrong?"

"Who?" said Mrs. Burbank.

"Mrs. Piggle-Wiggle," said Mr. Burbank.

"What are you talking about?" said Mrs. Burbank. "I said that we should give Mrs. Piggle-Wiggle our heartiest thanks."

"Oh," said Mr. Burbank. "I thought you said 'Go give Mrs. Piggle-Wiggle your hardest spanks.'"

The children looked disgusted.

THE TATTLETALE CURE

It was a cold snowy day. Mrs. Hamilton gave the hot cocoa a little stir and then went to the kitchen window to see if the children were coming. It was ten minutes past three and almost time for them. Mrs. Hamilton fixed a plate of sugar cookies and got out two big shiny red apples. Then just as the children rounded the corner she poured the hot, fragrant cocoa.

Wendy and Timmy came stamping up on the back porch and Mrs. Hamilton helped them off with their galoshes, brushed off some of the snow and hurried them into the nice warm kitchen.

"And how was school?" she asked Wendy as she helped her off with her coat and leggings.

Wendy said, "Well, I hate everybody at school and everybody at school hates me."

25

Mrs. Hamilton was shocked. Wendy was nine years old. She had nice fat pigtails, shiny brown bangs, sparkling brown eyes and pink cheeks. Mrs. Hamilton didn't see how anyone could hate her. She said, "Why Wendy, that's dreadful, dear. Why does everyone hate you?"

Wendy said, "I don't know. They just do. And I don't care because I hate everybody." She sat down at the kitchen table and took a bite of sugar cookie.

Timmy, who was seven, was sitting on the floor taking off his leggings. His mother said, "Here, Timmy, let me help you."

Timmy said, "No thanks. I can do it myself. You want to know why everybody hates Wendy—it's because she's such an old tattletale. She tells the teacher on everybody. I hate her too."

Mrs. Hamilton said, "Why, Wendy Hamilton. Do you tell on people?"

Wendy said with evident pride, "Uh, huh. I tell Miss Worthington every time anybody whispers or cheats or writes notes. I even told her when Jimmy Murton sucked his paintbrush today. We're not supposed to suck our paintbrushes; we're supposed to use our fingers to make points." She took a little sip of her cocoa and wiped her lips daintily. Wendy was very pleased with herself.

Mrs. Hamilton wasn't pleased with her. She said, "Wendy Hamilton, I think that's horrid. Telling the teacher about a little thing like sucking a paintbrush."

Timmy said, "Oh, she's always in there tattling. She's so busy spying and tattling she doesn't even have time to play."

Wendy said, "You better be careful, Mr. Timothy

Hamilton, or I'll tell Mother that you haven't brushed
your teeth for five nights and you gave your liver to Spot
last Wednesday and you spent some of your Sunday School
money on candy and last night you read in bed with a
flashlight."

Timmy said, "Yeah, and this morning you put the rest
of your toast in the silverware drawer, you spilled Spot's
water and didn't wipe it up, and you ate half the candy I
bought with my Sunday School money."

Wendy, quite red in the face, said, "Oh, bah, bah, bah,
to you, you old crumpet."

"Bah, bah, bah, yourself, old dog eyes," Timmy said.

Wendy said, "Motherrrrrrrr, he calls me dog eyes all the
time. He says that only dogs have brown eyes."

Mrs. Hamilton said, "Wendy, change your school clothes
and then go in and start your practising. Timmy, change
your school clothes and then go down in the basement and
put away all of Daddy's tools that you got out last night.
I must say, you're both so disagreeable I'm sorry you came
home from school and spoiled my nice peaceful afternoon."

Mrs. Hamilton went up to her sewing-room and closed
the door. There was a nice little fire in the grate and it was
very cozy in there with the radio playing softly, big snow-
flakes drifting down past the window and no sounds of
quarreling from downstairs. Mrs. Hamilton was letting
down the hems of Wendy's summer dresses and as she
sewed she thought about the tattling and wondered why
Wendy had turned into such a horrible little prig. Tattling
was a loathsome disease and she was afraid that Timmy
was catching it too.

While Mrs. Hamilton sewed and worried, the snow piled

up in fluffy white heaps on the window sills, the coals hummed and blazed in the grate and from downstairs came "da, daa, duh, duh, da, daa, duh, duh, daa, daa, daa, daa, daa, daaaa, duh, duh . . ." as Wendy practised *The Happy Farmer*.

Mrs. Hamilton had just reached the stage where she was thinking, "Oh, well, it will all straighten out. Wendy is just going through a phase," when the practising suddenly stopped, the sewing-room door was thrown dramatically open and Wendy announced, "I think you should know that Timmy is just sitting on the basement stairs looking at a book and when I told him to do his work he said, 'Oh, go bang on the piano, Dog Eyes.' "

Mrs. Hamilton said, "I didn't tell you to check up on Timmy. I told you to do your practising."

Wendy said, "If I don't see that Timmy does his work, who's going to? You just sit up here and sew with the door closed."

Mrs. Hamilton said, "When I need your help, Wendy, I'll ask for it. Now go downstairs and finish your practising." Wendy turned and flounced down the stairs.

Mrs. Hamilton got up and closed the sewing-room door. Again everything was peaceful. *The Happy Farmer* was thumped out indignantly on the piano and from the basement there was silence. This lasted exactly ten minutes. Then the sewing-room door was again thrown open to reveal both Wendy and Timmy jostling for position and tattling at the top of their lungs. "She's just an old spy . . . He's not doing a thing but reading . . . Nobody likes her and that includes me . . . He's the one that ate all those ginger snaps last winter . . . If you want to know what happened to that old fountain pen that Mrs. Wentworth left here three years ago, Wendy took it to school and Marty Phillips stepped on it and . . . Timmy owes thirteen cents on his library books and he can't find his card . . . He called me Dog Eyes right in front of everybody at recess . . . She broke my kaleidoscope . . . He spilled ink in my desk drawer . . . She hit me . . . He teases me . . .''

Mrs. Hamilton marched them to their rooms and closed the doors. ''You're to be perfectly quiet and stay in your rooms until dinner time.'' With a sigh she went downstairs to start dinner. She had just put the teakettle on when the telephone rang. ''Hello,'' said Mrs. Hamilton.

''Hello,'' said Mrs. Piggle-Wiggle. ''I've just baked gingerbread and I wondered if Timmy and Wendy wouldn't like some. Molly O'Toole is making the tea and Kitty Wheeling is setting the table.''

Mrs. Hamilton said, ''Oh, that's very kind of you, Mrs. Piggle-Wiggle, but Wendy and Timmy are being so naughty I have sent them to their rooms to stay until dinner time.''

Mrs. Piggle-Wiggle said, ''Oh, I'm sorry to hear that. What seems to be the trouble?''

''Tattling,'' said Mrs. Hamilton. ''Wendy came home this afternoon and told me that she tells the teacher on everyone in school. She also tattles on Timmy and Timmy tattles on her. I'm really terribly distressed. I simply despise tattletales.''

''Oh, so do I,'' said Mrs. Piggle-Wiggle, ''but Tattletale-itis is certainly a common ailment among children. 'Johnny said Bah, bah, bah, and I said Boo, boo, boo and Johnny said You're an old ugh and I said Is that so then you are too and he said Hah, hah, aha . . ." Mrs. Piggle-Wiggle laughed. She said, "I have listened to every kind of tattling there is. I have heard the sneaks, the teacher's pets, the cry-babies, the mama's boys, the bosses, the little prissies, the whiners, every variety of tattletale and I know that tattle-tales are really unhappy children."

Mrs. Hamilton said, "Wendy told me this afternoon that everybody at school hates her but she doesn't care be-cause she hates everybody at school."

"At present that is only temporary," said Mrs. Piggle-Wiggle. "But I do think we should start the tattletale cure right away. I have some marvellous medicine which I'll send over with Molly O'Toole on her way home. The pills look and taste just like licorice drops but the effect is quite remarkable. Let me see, today is Thursday. Better not give the medicine to Wendy and Timmy until Friday night. Give them each a pill Friday night and another one on Saturday. Call me Sunday night and let me know how things are. Oh, by the way, I wouldn't plan on having any company over the week-end—the tattletaleitis cure is rather startling. Goodbye. Give my love to Wendy and Timmy."

There was a little click as Mrs. Piggle-Wiggle hung up the phone.

Mrs. Hamilton sat and looked at the telephone for a few minutes. "Little Black pills—remarkable effect. I wonder what they are? I wonder what they do?"

About five-thirty, Molly O'Toole, all frosted with snow and starry-eyed from eating hot gingerbread, rang the doorbell and handed Mrs. Hamilton a small package.

"A present from Mrs. Piggle-Wiggle," Molly said.

"Mrs. Piggle-Wiggle said to tell Wendy and Timmy that she's baking gingerbread next Thursday and for them to be sure and be there."

Mrs. Hamilton asked her to come in but she said no she had to go home and set the table and she turned and skipped off into the snowy winter evening.

Mrs. Hamilton went into the kitchen and undid Mrs. Piggle-Wiggle's package. There was a small black box marked CURE FOR TATTLETALEITIS. Inside the box was a small black bottle. Inside the bottle were four black pills. Mrs. Hamilton examined the pills very carefully. They looked and smelled just like licorice drops but she was sure they weren't licorice drops because Mrs. Piggle-Wiggle had said they were magic and they undoubtedly were. She put the pills back in the bottle, put the bottle back in the box and put the box on the top shelf of the spice cupboard by the stove. Somehow or other just seeing that box marked CURE FOR TATTLETALEITIS made her feel better. She hummed as she got dinner and set the table and when Mr. Hamilton came home he looked so tired that she didn't mention her trouble of the afternoon. Instead she waited until dinner was on the table before calling the children and then she pretended not to notice their tight little buttonhole mouths and flashing eyes.

When Timmy put almost a half a baked potato in his mouth and Wendy started to tattle about it, Mrs. Hamilton quickly sent her to the kitchen for the pepper grinder. When Wendy gulped her milk and Timmy opened his mouth to tattle, Mrs. Hamilton said, "Oh, look at poor Spotty, he's so hungry he has tears in his eyes." By constant maneuvering, dinner was kept tattle free.

But the next morning and afternoon were horrible. The children quarreled and tattled from the moment they got up until they went to bed. Mrs. Hamilton closed her ears and thought of the little black pills. But Mr. Hamilton finally gave Wendy and Timmy each a spanking and told them that they could tattle to each other about him. Just before they went to sleep and when they had stopped crying sufficiently so that she was sure they wouldn't choke, Mrs. Hamilton gave them each one of the licorice drops. She could hardly wait until morning to see what the magic medicine would do.

The next morning it was still snowing and the children slept late. Wendy was the first downstairs. She came shuffling into the kitchen looking like a cross between a scarecrow and a windmill. She had put on an old faded very small pair of summer shorts, a thin raggedy T-shirt and some old white sandals of her mother's. She hadn't washed her face and she had slept wrong on her braids so that one pointed north and one pointed south. Her eyes were all squinty and sleepy.

Mrs. Hamilton said, "Wendy Hamilton, there is a blizzard blizzing outside and here you come downstairs in all your old summer clothes. Go up and put on your blue jeans and a sweater, wash your face and brush your teeth and bring me the hairbrush." Wendy gave her mother a baleful look and went shuffling back upstairs.

Then Timmy came down. He had on his jeans and a sweater but when his mother went to roll up his sleeves to see if he had washed, she found that he had on his pajamas and not only that but under his pajamas he had on his underwear. As Mrs. Hamilton sent him back upstairs to change, she wondered fearfully if the strange outfits her children had put on had anything to do with the magic pills. She certainly hoped not. It was bad enough to have two little tattletales but to have tattletales who slept in their underwear and wore their pajamas in the daytime and wore summer clothes in the middle of winter, was well-nigh unbearable.

As Mrs. Hamilton took up the children's oatmeal and poured their milk, she glanced fearfully toward the back stairs. How would they look this time and what had the magic pills done to them. In no time at all she had her answer. First she heard shrill fighting voices, quick chasing footsteps, slaps and yelps and then racing down the stairs came the tattlers, each redfaced and anxious to tell first.

"Motherrrrrrrrrrrr," said Wendy as she slid through the kitchen door. "Motherrrrrr, Timmy—" but instead of the long tattletale she intended, out of Wendy's mouth came a big puff of black smoke. The puff of smoke was shaped like a little black cloud except that hanging fom the bottom of it were four little black tails. Little black tattletales. The black cloud rose to the ceiling and stuck—the four little tails swayed gently back and forth.

Timmy said, "My Gosh, did you see that. Smoke came out of Wendy's mouth. Say, Mother, I bet ole Wendy's been—" but instead of saying "smoking" as he intended, a big puff of black smoke came out of his mouth. It too was a little black cloud but it had only one tail hanging from it because he had only intended to tattle about one thing. Timmy and Wendy stood with their mouths open staring at the ceiling.

Mrs. Hamilton said, "Well, I've always wondered what

a tattletale looks like, now I know. Ugh, what ugly things!" Wendy and Timmy didn't say anything. They looked at the ceiling, then at each other and then back at the ceiling. Finally they sat down to breakfast.

After breakfast it was still snowing hard but Wendy and Timmy said they were going out to shovel the walks. They put on their leggings, coats, caps and mittens without a word but they couldn't decide whose galoshes were whose and they began jerking them back and forth and pushing and shoving and finally were just going to yell for Mrs. Hamilton to tattle when out of their open mouths came two huge rolls of black smoke each with a long black tattle-tale suspended from it. The two new tattletales soared slowly upwards and stuck to the ceiling not far from the first two.

Wendy said, "What if that happened in school?"

Timmy said, "Boy, the kids would sure be surprised. I can just hear ole Miss Harkness. She'd say, 'Timothy Hamilton, you have been SMOKING!'"

Wendy said, "I don't think I'd like to have that happen in school. All the children would laugh at me. Hey, these are your galoshes. I can tell because they are a teensy bit littler than mine."

They put on their galoshes and went quietly out to shovel the walks.

Every once in a while Mrs. Hamilton peered out at them. She wondered what would happen to the black tattletales outside. Would they float clear up to the sky or would they hang just above the head of the tattler. About noon Mrs. Hamilton found out. The children had finished the walks and were building a snowman. Wendy, who was the

tallest, was putting on the head when she slipped and fell against the snowman and knocked him over. Timmy was furious. He thought Wendy had deliberately knocked over the snowman and he ran and pounded on the front door and yelled for his mother—to tattle.

When Mrs. Hamilton opened the front door Timmy opened his mouth and out came a big black puff of smoke with a tattletale hanging from it. The smoke rose slowly until it was about four feet above Timmy's head. There it stayed. When he walked it moved with him. Timmy took his shovel and tried to bat the tattletale but the shovel went right through it and all it did was to make the tail swing a little.

Wendy thought it was very funny. She said, "I'm going to get Molly and Dick and Hubert and Patsy so they can all see what an old tattletale you are."

Timmy said, "You do and I'll wash your face with soap, ole Dog Eyes."

Wendy said, "You just try it, and Mother said you weren't to call me Dog Eyes. I'm going to tell Mother. She said she'd punish you if you called me Dog Eyes. Motherrrrrrr!"

Out of Wendy's mouth came a big puff of black smoke with a big black tail hanging from it. It floated up until it was about four feet over Wendy's head and there it stayed. Wendy said, "Come on, Timmy, let's go in the house. What if the postman should see those old black things." They put away their shovels and went in the house. The black tattletales followed them in and floated up to the kitchen ceiling to join the other tattletales.

Once during the afternoon a strange thing happened.

Wendy and Timmy were coloring at the kitchen table and Timmy joggled Wendy's elbow and Wendy was just going to tattle on Timmy when suddenly remembering the ugly black tattletales, she looked up at the ceiling and swallowed her tattling. As the tattletale went back down her throat Wendy noticed that one of the ugly black clouds shriveled up and disappeared.

A few minutes later Wendy broke Timmy's red crayon and he started to get up to tattle when he happened to look up at the ceiling. Seeing all the ugly black tattletales made him decide that perhaps Wendy didn't mean to break his red crayon so he swallowed his tattletale and sat down again. Immediately another black cloud shriveled up and disappeared from the ceiling.

By the time Mr. Hamilton came home there were only two left. The one with the four tails and the biggest one with one tail. Mr. Hamilton took one look at the ceiling and said, "Good Heavens, did the oil burner blow up?"

Mrs. Hamilton said, "Come in the living-room a minute, Charles, I want to talk to you."

In a few minutes Mr. Hamilton came out to the kitchen with a golf club with which he poked and poked at the tattletales. It didn't do any good. The golf club went right through them but they didn't move or change shape.

During dinner the children were surprisingly quiet and surprisingly pleasant. In fact, there wasn't a cross word spoken the entire evening. When they went to bed Mrs. Hamilton gave them the last of the pills but she didn't really feel that it was necessary.

After the children were in bed, Mr. Hamilton got up on the kitchen stool and tried to pull down the tattletales.

It was like trying to pull down smoke. He finally gave up. He said, "That's the darnedest thing I've ever seen."

Mrs. Hamilton said, "I think they're beautiful."

On Sunday, Wendy made one more tattletale and Timmy shriveled his last old one. Sunday night Mrs. Hamilton called Mrs. Piggle-Wiggle. She told her everything that had happened and asked her if she thought the children were cured. Mrs. Piggle-Wiggle said that she was sure they were cured but that the important thing was for Mrs. Hamilton never to tell the children about the magic medicine in case she ever had to use it again.

Monday morning all the tattletales were gone from the kitchen ceiling, and if Wendy and Timmy had known it they could have tattled to their hearts' content and no smoke would have come out of their mouths because they hadn't taken any magic medicine the night before. But they didn't know it and every time they started to tattle they would gulp and look guiltily at the ceiling.

Monday afternoon Wendy came home from school and said that everyone in school liked her and she liked everybody. Timmy didn't say anything. He had a black eye and a skinned nose but he didn't say a word. He and Wendy laughed and talked as they drank their cocoa but they kept their eyes on the ceiling.

THE BAD-TABLE-MANNERS CURE

Slop, slurp, gulp, bang," Christopher Brown was through with his milk. His mother was in the pantry polishing silver but she didn't have to go into the kitchen to see that Christopher was through eating. She could tell because the loud noises had stopped. Mrs. Brown was terribly ashamed of Christopher's table manners and she talked and talked and talked and talked and talked and talked, but so far it hadn't done a speck of good.

Christopher was ten years old and a very nice little boy in other ways. He had red hair, he was a fine baseball player, he was a good sport, he got excellent grades in school and he kept his room reasonably neat, but he certainly had horrible table manners. No, that isn't right—he really had no table manners at all. He ate just like an animal. A starving, wild animal.

Mr. and Mrs. Brown had gradually become used to Christopher's table manners. Of course they made him eat in the kitchen, but what worried Mrs. Brown so terribly was that some day one of Christopher's friends would invite him to dinner. Not just a children's party. Chris had been to lots of those and he was so much fun and so good at the games that the children didn't care if he ate like a starving animal. No, Mrs. Brown was afraid he'd be asked to stay all night or to visit in another town or to go to the country with some of his friends' families. How dreadful it would be when Christopher took his first bite and began to chew!

Christopher chewed with his mouth open so that you could see all the food as he rinsed it around in his mouth. Also he smacked his lips so loud it sounded like someone slapping their hands on water; he gulped when he swallowed; he washed food down with milk; he made enormous piles of meat, potatoes, peas, carrots and gravy on his fork and then thrust the fork so far down his throat you could hardly see the handle; he used his thumb to assemble big fork loads; he propped his knife and fork against his plate with the handles on the table; he buttered whole slices of bread on his hand; he chopped and smashed and mixed his food until his dinner looked like dog food; he picked up his soup bowl and held it just under his chin while he slurped his soup; he talked while he was chewing; he gestured with a fork full of food so that bits of food shot around the room like stones from a slingshot. I could go on indefinitely about Christopher's table manners but I think I've told enough to show you that having Christopher sitting beside you at the table was almost exactly like eating next to a wolf. Watching him eat was certainly not a sight to whet the appetite.

Mrs. Brown rubbed polish on the silver and thought about Christopher's table manners and was sad. "There should be a school for table manners," she said to herself, "and attendance should be compulsory."

The telephone rang. It was Mrs. Thompson, Dick's mother. She said, "I'm having a few of Dick's friends over for dinner a week from Saturday. My brother Charles, the big game hunter, is going to visit us for a few days and I thought it would be so nice if some of Dick's friends could meet Charles and see his movies of hunting lions and tigers in Africa. I'm just asking Christopher, Hubert Prentiss and Larry Gray because there will be twelve grown-ups too."

Mrs. Brown thanked Mrs. Thompson, said that she knew Christopher would be delighted and then went out and made herself a big pot of black coffee. Her hands shook when she poured the first cup. Twelve grown-ups and Mrs. Thompson's famous brother Charles, all sitting at the table with Christopher. Mrs. Brown couldn't bear even to think about it. "Oh, what will I do? What will I do?" she said. She would give Christopher a good talking to and he would be very nice and pleasant and agree to everything she said and really try to have better manners for a meal or two. Then back he'd go, slurp, splash, smack, crunch, choke, gurgle, gulp, bang! Mrs. Brown shuddered.

She called her friend Mrs. Penzil. She said, "Mrs. Penzil, I'm not going to beat around the bush. My son Christopher has the worst table manners in the whole world, and I don't know how to cure them. Do Percy, Pamela and

Potter have nice table manners?"

Mrs. Penzil said, "Why I never noticed, Mrs. Brown. You see Percy, Pamela and Potter have always been allowed to make their own decisions about everything. As soon as they were born we gave them free rein and actually I haven't seen them eat for several years."

"What do they live on?" Mrs. Brown asked. "Oh, they eat," said Mrs. Penzil, "but only when the need for food occurs to them. Now Potter eats nothing but peanut butter and poppy seeds, and he always eats at night. He says that eating during the day is much too common a practice and should be stopped. Pamela eats nothing but weenies and bananas. She does her own shopping and peels the bananas herself which I think is very progressive for a child of seven years."

"I don't," said Mrs. Brown crossly. "I think it's dreadful to let a child live on weenies and bananas. What does Percy eat?"

"Percy? Now let me see," said Mrs. Penzil. "Oh, yes, Percy. Why Percy eats anything. He is most co-operative. Just give him cookies, candy, marshmallows, cake, ice cream and root beer and you don't have to worry about Percy. He's a fine boy."

Mrs. Brown said, "Well, Mrs. Penzil, I guess everyone has their problems. You have cheered me up a lot and I do hope you know a good doctor. You are going to need one."

Mrs. Penzil said, "Oh, I think not. Both Mr. Penzil and I were brought up the same way and we're both terribly happy. Mr. Penzil never eats anything but kippered salmon and Grapenuts and I never eat . . ."

Mrs. Brown hung up the phone. "Kippered salmon and Grapenuts—ugh."

She called Mrs. Piggle-Wiggle and told her the whole problem. She didn't leave out a thing when she described the way Christopher ate and when she told about the dinner party he had been invited to and how ashamed she was going to be, she got tears in her eyes.

Mrs. Piggle-Wiggle said, "Now, Mrs. Brown, don't worry so. Christopher is such a darling boy and I know how to cure him. It's going to take co-operation on your part and it may be a little inconvenient, but I have the cure. I'm going to lend you Lester."

"Lester?" said Mrs. Brown. "Who is he?"

"He is a pig," said Mrs. Piggle-Wiggle.

"Oh, no!" said Mrs. Brown. "Not a pig! I have no place to keep a pig and this is a restricted neighborhood."

"Just a minute," said Mrs. Piggle-Wiggle. "Lester is absolutely no trouble. He has beautiful manners, is very quiet and sleeps in the basement. So nobody in the neighborhood need know about him."

"But where shall I put his trough?" said Mrs. Brown.

"Oh, Lester doesn't use a trough," said Mrs. Piggle-Wiggle. "That's the whole point. Lester has the most beautiful table manners you have ever seen, and I want him to eat at the kitchen table with Christopher. You'll be very surprised. Lester will teach Christopher how to eat."

"But it sounds fantastic!" said Mrs. Brown.

"I know," said Mrs. Piggle-Wiggle. "Every mother I send Lester to has the same feeling. But let me tell you that once you have had Lester in your house, you won't want to let him come home to me. I always have that trouble. Everybody adores Lester and wants to keep him. Oh, by the way, he likes to sleep on a clean blanket on the basement floor. Also he likes to have the basement door left open so he can go out for his exercise after dark and when the neighbors are asleep. Have Christopher stop by after school and I'll send Lester over. Mrs. Martin just returned him this morning."

"But what does he eat?" said Mrs. Brown.

"Exactly what Christopher does, except much larger portions. Oh, yes, I almost forgot. Lester is very fond of coffee. He takes cream and sugar and he often drinks as many as five cups at a meal. Now don't worry, Mrs. Brown. Fix Lester a nice bed on a clean blanket by the furnace and I'm sure he'll solve all your problems. Goodbye."

Mrs. Brown went up and got a clean blue blanket out of the guest-room closet and with many misgivings unfolded it and put it on the floor beside the furnace in the basement. She looked at the clock. She had ten minutes before she could expect Christopher. She made some cocoa with whipped cream, fixed two plates of ginger cookies, one much larger than the other, and polished two large red apples. She got out spoons and napkins and then remembering what Mrs. Piggle-Wiggle had said about Lester's manners, she took two of her good linen doilies and put them on the kitchen table.

At exactly three-thirty there was a knock at the back door and there stood Christopher, who usually never knocked, and a large white pig. Christopher said, "Mother, this is Lester and we got to keep him. Oh, he's fun! He's so smart he knows everything, don't you, old boy?"

Mrs. Brown said, "Come in, Christopher and Lester, I have some cocoa for you."

Christopher said, "Oh, boy," dashed over to the table and began gulping his cocoa. Lester walked daintily into the kitchen, closed the door carefully behind him, climbed up and sat down across the table from Christopher. Christopher was jamming his mouth full of cookie and washing it down with cocoa. Lester looked at him, then took one cookie carefully between the split in his front hoof and ate it very slowly and with tiny bites. He picked his cocoa cup up with his hoof and after one small sip put it carefully down, while he patted his snout with his napkin.

Christopher stopped eating, or at least stopped chewing, to watch Lester eat. Christopher's mouth was open but full, he had whipped cream on his upper lip and crumbs on his chin. Lester reached across the table and gently closed Christopher's mouth. Then he wiped the whipped cream off his upper lip and the crumbs off his chin.

Christopher was delighted. He said, with his mouth full, "Gosh, you're smart, Lester."

Lester put his hoof across his lips and pointed to Christopher's full cheeks to indicate, "No talking with a full mouth."

Christopher looked up at his Mother. "Isn't he smart, Mother? Isn't Lester wonderful?"

Lester looked over at Mrs. Brown and she was sure he winked at her.

It usually took Christopher about three and a quarter minutes to gag down his cookies and cocoa. This day, either because of the excitement of having Lester with him or perhaps because of the good example set by Lester, Christopher was still eating at four o'clock. Mrs. Brown came downstairs to clear up the cocoa things and was most surprised to find that Christopher had only just finished and Lester was but half way through. Mrs. Brown asked Lester if he'd care for some more cocoa and he nodded his head and handed her his cocoa cup.

Christopher said that he didn't care for any more and began eating his apple—crash, crunch, smash, gulp. Lester reached across the table and took the apple away from him, got down off his chair, went over to a drawer in the kitchen, took a knife and cut Christopher's apple into small sections, cored each section, put them on the empty cookie plate and handed the plate to Christopher. Christopher put a whole section of apple in his mouth. Lester shook his head at him, reached over and took one of the sections and took one very small bite. Chris gulped down the first section and took another, but this time, instead of stuffing it all in his mouth, he took one small bite. Lester nodded approvingly at him.

At four-thirty both Lester and Christopher had finished their cocoa and apples and Christopher took Lester down to the basement to show him his bed. Lester looked carefully around the furnace room, straightened out several wrinkles in the blue guest-room blanket, then nodded at Christopher to show him the bed was all right. They went into the game room. There was a red tennis ball on the floor. Lester picked it up and threw it at Chris. Chris caught it and threw it back. Lester caught it neatly in his mouth, then took it out with his hoofs and threw it at Chris. They played ball until it was time for the mystery

cowboy radio programs that Christopher listened to every evening.

He said to Lester, "Gee, Lester, I hope you don't mind but I always listen to a bunch of keen radio programs at five o'clock. Of course, if you'd rather play ball, I don't have to."

Lester shook his head, turned and pointed to the fireplace, where a nice little fire was laid.

Christopher said, "Do you want me to light the fire, Lester, do you?"

Lester nodded. Christopher struck a match and lit the paper. Lester stretched out on the hearth rug and closed his eyes. Christopher crouched by the radio and listened to his programs. It was very peaceful.

When Mr. Brown came home from work, Mrs. Brown told him about the invitation to dinner to meet Mrs. Thompson's famous brother, Charles, about Mrs. Piggle-Wiggle and about Lester. Mr. Brown was most skeptical about Lester being able to teach Christopher table manners. "Talk about the blind leading the blind," he said and laughed loudly.

Mrs. Brown said, "Hush, Phillip, Lester's right down in the basement and really he has the most beautiful table manners I've ever seen."

Mr. Brown said, "Guess I'll go down and have a look at Lester."

He went down the basement stairs whistling, "Who's afraid of the big, bad wolf?"

Mrs. Brown groaned. Mr. Brown looked first in the woodroom; no Lester. Then he looked in the furnace room. He saw the blue guest-room blanket lying on the floor so he picked it up, shook it, took it into the laundry and stuffed it in the laundry chute. He went around the laundry peering under the washing machine, laundry tubs and ironing board saying, "Oink, oink, oink." He got no response. He noticed that the basement door was open a little so he closed and locked it, muttering about burglars and carelessness.

Then hearing the radio from the game room he decided to go in and ask Christopher where he kept his pig. He was certainly surprised to see Lester lying on the hearth rug in front of a crackling fire apparently listening to the radio. He said, "So this is Lester. Oink, oink, oink!"

Lester opened his eyes and gave him a cold look, then seeing that it was Mr. Brown he jumped to his feet and held out his hoof.

"Well, I'll be darned!" said Mr. Brown, shaking hands and beaming.

Christopher said, "Boy, isn't Lester smart, Daddy? Isn't he?"

Mr. Brown said, "I always said that you can teach a pig anything. Pigs are the smartest animals there are." Lester still looked coldly at him. He hadn't forgiven him for the Oink, oink, oink business. Mr. Brown bent over and began scratching Lester behind the ears. Lester gently but firmly pushed his hand away, then went over and lay down again by the fire. Mr. Brown, slightly red in the face, said, "Well, I guess I'd better see how dinner is coming along."

Christopher said, "Just a minute, Daddy, I want to show you how keen Lester plays ball. Come on, Lester old boy. Let's play a game." He picked up the red tennis ball and Lester rather unwillingly got to his feet. Christopher threw him the ball and he caught it in his mouth and threw it back. Christopher threw it again and Lester caught it but this time Lester threw it to Mr. Brown. Mr. Brown was so surprised he almost missed but you could tell he was pleased because he kept looking at Lester and smiling. They played three-cornered catch until Mrs. Brown called to say dinner was ready and to tell Christopher to wash his hands.

There was a small lavatory off the game room and Christopher rushed in and in his usual way, wet his hands, splashed a little water on his face and was going to wipe all the dirt off on the towel, when Lester, who had followed him in, took the towel away from him and put it back on the towel rack; put the stopper in the basin, filled it to the brim with hot water and began washing his own face and hoofs thoroughly and with lots of soap. When he had finished he let the water out of the basin and filled it up with fresh hot water for Christopher.

While Lester dried his nice clean face and hoofs, Christopher washed, thoroughly and with lots of soap. While he dried his face and hands, Lester took the hairbrush and dampened and smoothed the bristles on his neck and around his ears. Christopher watched him, then dampened and brushed his hair too. Then they went up to dinner.

Unfortunately Mrs. Brown, forgetting about Lester, had spareribs for dinner. They were crisp and brown and Mr. Brown gave Lester an extra large helping. Lester sat down at the table, smiled because everything looked and smelled so delicious, unfolded his napkin, took a sip of milk, then cut off a small piece of the sparerib. He put it in his mouth, began to chew, then turned terribly pale and pushed his plate away.

Christopher watched him anxiously. "Gosh, Lester, what's the matter? Don't you like spareribs?"

Lester took his spareribs and put them on Christopher's plate.

Christopher said, "Lester, I'll go tell Mother you don't like spareribs. She'll fry you some eggs or something. That's what she does for Daddy when he doesn't like something." He started to get down from his chair. Lester reached over and took hold of his shoulder. He shook his head sternly, pointed to Christopher's dinner, and by chewing motions indicated that Christopher was to continue with his dinner.

Lester had two helpings of dressing, sweet potatoes and string beans. He also ate his salad, two dishes of peaches, two pieces of applesauce cake and drank four cups of coffee. Christopher ate all his dinner and with much less noise than usual. He even asked Lester if it was all right to pick his sparerib bones up in his fingers.

After dinner he and Christopher and Mr. Brown played ball for a while. Then it was time for Chris to go to bed. He and Mr. Brown said goodnight to Lester and went upstairs.

Lester went in to his bed but it wasn't there. He looked all over the basement thinking perhaps Mrs. Brown had moved it. He couldn't find it any place. Then he checked to see if the back door had been left open and found it shut and locked. He looked again to see if he could find the blanket. It just wasn't anywhere so he decided to go upstairs and ask Mrs. Brown where it was. He went up the basement stairs, had quite a time with the basement door which stuck, trotted through the kitchen and dining-room and then stood politely at the living-room door.

Mr. and Mrs. Brown were playing cribbage and arguing so they didn't see Lester for a few minutes. When Mrs. Brown happened to look up, she said, "Why Lester, have you come up to visit us?" Lester shook his head. Mrs. Brown said, "What's the matter then, is it cold down in the basement?"

Lester shook his head.

"Oh, I know," Mr. Brown said, "you want me to play ball with you, don't you, old boy?" Lester shook his head. Then, deciding that would be a very good way to get them down to the basement, he nodded his head vigorously several times. Mr. Brown beamed. "Okay, old boy," he said. "Come on down Alice and watch." Mrs. Brown said she'd like to, so they went downstairs.

But Lester, in spite of his flawless manners, went first and instead of going into the game room, stood by the furnace-room door. Mrs. Brown looked in the furnace room. "But where is your blanket?" she said. Lester shook his head. Mrs. Brown said, "Why, that's the funniest thing. I put the blue guest-room blanket on the floor here this afternoon. I wonder what could have happened to it?"

Mr. Brown, looking very embarrassed, went and got it out of the laundry chute. He said, "I didn't know it was Lester's bed, I just thought it had fallen on the floor."

Mrs. Brown spread it out on the floor and Lester carefully smoothed out the wrinkles and turned one corner over like a little pillow. Mr. and Mrs. Brown watched him in amazement.

"I've never in my life seen such a smart animal," said Mrs. Brown. "He seems almost human." Lester looked up at her quizzically. "Now you're all ready to go to bed, so I guess we'll go upstairs," said Mr. Brown.

He started toward the stairway but Lester took his hoofs and gently pushed him toward the basement door.

"Now what's the matter, old boy?" said Mr. Brown. "The basement door's locked and there's not a thing to worry about."

Mrs. Brown said, "Well of course that's the trouble. Mrs. Piggle-Wiggle told me to be sure and leave the basement door open a crack so Lester can go out in the night and get his exercise." She unlatched the door and opened it one inch.

Lester nodded approval, waited politely while they preceded him through the doorway and started up the stairs. Then he went in, lay down on the blue blanket and went to sleep.

The next morning when Christopher came downstairs and found his mother frying bacon he was shocked. He said, "My gosh, Mother, don't you have any heart at all? Last night you had spareribs for dinner and Lester almost got sick, and now this morning you are cooking bacon."

Mrs. Brown said, "Why, Chris, I thought I had a delicious dinner last night. Spareribs have always been one of your favorite foods."

Chris said, "But, Mother, spareribs are *pork*. They come from *dead pigs!*"

Mrs. Brown clapped her hand over her mouth. She said, "Oh, Chris, I didn't think about that. I'm terribly sorry. Do you suppose Lester noticed?"

Chris said, "I should say he did notice. He took one bite and then turned pale and pushed his plate away. I was going to tell you but he wouldn't let me."

Mrs. Brown said, "Come hurry, before he comes upstairs. Take this bacon in to your father. I'll give you and Lester cereal and scrambled eggs and toast for breakfast. Hurry now, take the bacon to Daddy and I'll air out the kitchen." She opened the back door and shooed the bacon smoke out with her apron so that when Lester came upstairs a few minutes later the kitchen smelled only of oatmeal and buttered toast.

As a usual thing at breakfast, Chris dumped a pitcher of cream on his mush, put on four heaping spoons of sugar, then stirred and stirred as though he were mixing cement. When the mush was exactly the right consistency and the correct degree of coolness, he would lift the bowl up to just below his chin and shovel in the mush as fast as he could swallow.

This morning, forgetting about Lester, he began his usual gluttonous proceedings, dumped the entire pitcher of cream on his mush and was just reaching for the sugar when he looked up and saw Lester looking sadly into the empty cream pitcher. Instantly he was sorry.

He said, "Oh, gee, Lester, I didn't mean to be such a pig. I mean, I mean, I mean such a glutton." Lester just looked at him. Chris said, "I'll get some more cream. Wait a minute."

Lester shook his head. He reached over and picked up

Chris' bowl of oatmeal and then carefully poured half the cream on his own cereal.

Chris said, "That's right, we'll each have half. Would you like some sugar?"

Lester nodded and helped himself carefully to two level spoons of sugar. Chris, who had watched him, did the same.

When Chris started his cement-mixer stirring, Lester reached over and took his spoon away and showed Chris how cereal should be eaten. A spoonful at a time, lifted slowly and daintily from the bowl so that each spoonful contained hot cereal, cold cream and sweet sugar.

Chris tried it. He said, "Say, Lester, this tastes much better than the old way." Lester nodded and smiled.

When Chris began to scrape his dish, Lester shook his head and pointed to his spoon, placed on the plate beside his almost empty dish.

When Chris was eating his scrambled eggs, Lester reached over and closed his mouth three times; he showed him that he must break his toast into small pieces and that he must not hold the toast in the palm of his hand when putting on jam. He made him put down his milk glass and wipe the milk mustache from his upper lip between sips. Chris obviously didn't mind these criticisms because he hugged Lester goodbye when he left for school and promised to run all the way home for lunch.

It was a beautiful morning and Mrs. Brown did a large washing. When she went to hang it on the line, Lester helped her carry the clothesbasket of wet clothes from the basement, handed her clothes pins as she needed them and then when the washing was all up he lay down on the grass in the sun, well hidden from the neighbors by two sheets and a tablecloth.

Mrs. Brown knelt down and timidly stroked his back. She said, "Thanks so much for helping with the clothes, Lester, and thank you so much for helping me with Chris's manners. I can see a great improvement already." Lester grunted a little.

By the night of Dick Thompson's dinner party, Chris's table manners were absolutely perfect and the Brown family all loved Lester so much they couldn't even think about his ever leaving. Lester came upstairs with Chris while he bathed and got dressed. He washed Christopher's back and made him wash his ears twice. He made him polish his shoes and he sent him back to his room for a clean handkerchief.

After Chris had gone Lester went out to the kitchen to wait for dinner. Noticing immediately that there was no place set for him on the kitchen table and feeling lonely for Chris and quite sad, he started down to the basement to lie on his blanket.

Mrs. Brown called to him. She said, "Lester, I thought that as long as Chris wasn't here, you would like to eat in the dining-room with Mr. Brown and me." Lester nodded his head vigorously and trotted happily after her into the dining-room.

They had roast of lamb for dinner and though Lester ate three large helpings, his table manners were so beautiful that Mr. and Mrs. Brown just stared at him in admiration.

After dinner, Mr. Brown and Lester played catch while Mrs. Brown washed the dishes. Then they all sat in the living-room and listened to the radio and waited for Christopher. He came home at ten o'clock, bursting with excitement and filled with tales of Africa and lions. Everyone listened to his stories, heard what the Thompsons had to eat and what Uncle Charlie looked like and then went to bed.

The next morning Mrs. Brown had two telephone calls. The first one made her very proud. It was from Mrs. Thompson and she said that she just had to call Mrs. Brown and tell her that in all her life she had never seen such a beautifully behaved boy as Christopher. "His table manners are simply perfect," she said and Mrs. Brown smiled and smiled.

The second telephone call was from Mrs. Piggle-Wiggle and it made Mrs. Brown very sad. Mrs. Piggle-Wiggle asked Mrs. Brown how she liked Lester and Mrs. Brown said, "Oh, Mrs. Piggle-Wiggle, he has such perfectly beautiful manners; he is such a wonderful teacher and he is so charming that I feel just like crying when I think of all the times I've said that people are pigs, or ate like pigs or were selfish like pigs."

Mrs. Piggle-Wiggle said, "Well, of course all pigs aren't like Lester but he certainly is a dear and I hate to take him away from you so soon but I have just had an emergency call from Mrs. Burbank. Tell Christopher to bring Lester over on his way back to school this noon."

When Mrs. Brown said goodbye to Lester she had tears in her eyes and she thought he seemed a little sad at leaving.

THE INTERRUPTERS

𝒲hat do you suppose happened at the Garden Club today?" Mrs. Franklin asked her husband at dinner. Before Mr. Franklin could answer, Benji Franklin said, "Hey, Dad, I'm the pitcher of our team."

"Please don't interrupt, Benjamin," Mr. Franklin said. "Now, what happened at your garden club, Carol?"

"Well, John, I won the first prize for my arrangement of forsythia and driftwood," Mrs. Franklin said.

"The thing I don't understand about flower arrangements . . ." Mr. Franklin began when Stevie interrupted to say, "I caught a little green frog on my way home from school."

"Don't interrupt Daddy," Mrs. Franklin said. "Now what is it you don't understand about flower arrangements, John?"

"I don't see why you don't use flowers. Why you always have to use—" Sally Franklin interrupted. She said, "I need a pair of new roller skates. My roller skates are so slow I'm ashamed to skate on them and—"

"You had roller skates last spring and I need a new baseball—" Benji began, when Stevie interrupted to say, "This little frog was just sitting there—" Benji interrupted. "I can't pitch with that old ball—" Sally said, "Everybody in our block has new roller skates and I—"

As each child interrupted the talk became louder and louder until they were all shouting.

Mr. Franklin shouted louder than anyone, "BE QUIET ALL OF YOU. I desire to finish my thought. Now, the thing I don't understand about flower arrangements is why you don't use flowers. Why you always have to stuff sticks or old weeds or seedpods or broken flower pots in with the flowers."

Mrs. Franklin smiled indulgently at her husband and began explaining, "Flower arranging is an art—" when Sally interrupted, "If I try to make figure eights with a broken strap I'll probably kill myself. Ball bearings only cost—" Stevie interrupted her, "Would you like to see my little frog? I've got—" Benji interrupted him. "Doesn't anyone in this family care whether I'm captain of my baseball team? Doesn't anyone—"

"STOP INTERRUPTING!" Mr. Franklin shouted. There was quiet for a minute. Mrs. Franklin began again.

"Flower arranging is an art—" There she was interrupted by a loud scream from Sally. "Mother, Daddy, Stevie has a frog in his pocket! I heard it. I hearrrrrrrd it—eeeeeeeeeee!"

"Stevie," said Mrs. Franklin, "do you have a frog in your pocket?"

"Well, yes, I just happen to," said Stevie, reaching in and bringing out a very small green tree frog.

"Ohhhhhhhhh," squealed Sally. "Take it away."

"Hey, lemme see it," Benji said. "Boy, he's nifty! How did you catch him?"

"It wasn't hard," Stevie said. "I was just walking along and I heard him."

"Take the frog outside," Mr. Franklin said sternly.

"Oh, Daddy, not outside," Stevie said. "He'll get away."

"Outside," Mr. Franklin repeated.

Stevie started slowly to his feet, carefully holding the frog between his cupped hands. When he got to the kitchen door he turned to his mother, "Say, Mother," he said, "this frog would be just right for your flower arrangements."

"Why, Stevie, what a wonderful idea," said Mrs. Franklin excitedly. "But how would I get him to stay in the bowl?"

"Oh, Cheeper'd stay," said Stevie. "He's awful tame. He does just anything I want him to."

"If he's so tame and does what you want him to, put him outside and tell him to WAIT THERE FOR YOU," Mr. Franklin said.

Benji said, "Oh, gee, Daddy, can't we put him in the basement. He'll get lost outside."

Mr. Franklin said, "All right, put him in the basement but put him in a box or something. Now, Carol, dear, what were you telling me about flower arranging?"

Mrs. Franklin smiled and began again, "I said flower arranging is an art—"

"Hey, Daddy, is this box all right?" Stevie called from the kitchen where he was standing on a high stool rummaging around on a shelf.

Mr. Franklin said, "Don't interrupt, your mother is talking."

Mrs. Franklin began, "Flower arranging is—" Stevie came into the dining-room, poked at his father's arm and whispered, in a loud hoarse whisper, "Is this box all right, Daddy?"

Mr. Franklin put his hands up to his head. "I'm going crazy," he said. "Interrupt! Interrupt! Interrupt! That's all these children do. We haven't finished a sentence in this house for weeks. Now Stevie, you stand right here and wait until your mother finishes explaining that flower arranging is an art," and Stevie did although it took Mrs. Franklin almost fifteen minutes. It was very uninteresting to him and his frog kept cheeping loudly.

The very second Mrs. Franklin finished her explanation of flower arranging, Stevie said, "Hey, Daddy, is this box all right?"

"Yes, yes, yes," said Mr. Franklin. "Go put the frog in it. Carol, do you suppose that Mrs. Piggle-Wiggle knows a cure for interrupting?"

"I wouldn't be surprised," said Mrs. Franklin. "I'll call—"

Sally interrupted, "If I had new roller skates, I could do a double figure—"

"What do frogs eat?" called Benji from the basement stairs.

"—eight backwards," finished Sally.

"Are flies all right?" called Stevie.

Sally said, "I could help with the dishes every night—"

"I mean dead flies?" called Stevie.

"To pay for them and it wouldn't—" Sally began.

Benji yelled, "Stevie has the box half full of ole dead flies. Won't that kill this little frog?"

Sally said, "If you don't leave roller skates outside—"

"Hey, Mom, Benji's dumpin' flies all over the basement stairs," Stevie called.

"CALL MRS. PIGGLE-WIGGLE RIGHT NOW!" roared Mr. Franklin.

So Mrs. Franklin did.

Mrs. Piggle-Wiggle said, "I have some wonderful magic interrupter powder. It comes with two little blowers and I would suggest that you and Mr. Franklin each use one. At the dinner table when you start to talk, have Mr. Franklin blow the powder at the children. When he talks, you blow the powder on the children. There will be no interrupting, I'll guarantee. Why don't you send Benji and Stevie over for it now while it's still light outside?"

Mrs. Franklin said she would, thanked Mrs. Piggle-Wiggle and hung up.

Benji and Stevie were glad to go because they loved Mrs. Piggle-Wiggle and anyway they wanted to show her their frog, Cheeper. While they were gone Mrs. Franklin and Sally washed the dishes and Mr. Franklin smoked his pipe and read the paper.

When the boys came home they gave the package to their mother and then went right to the basement to fix their frog because Mrs. Piggle-Wiggle had given them a box of

frog food and they were anxious to see if Cheeper would eat it. They asked Sally to come to the basement with them but she had a map to draw so went up to her room.

When they were alone Mr. and Mrs. Franklin opened Mrs. Piggle-Wiggle's package. It contained a little can of white powder and two little blowers. The directions on the can said, "INTERRUPTER POWDER. Place a small amount of the powder in the bowl of the blower, then when you wish to stop an interrupter, blow a little of the powder in his face. The powder cannot be seen or felt but it is wiser to blow it when the interrupter is not looking."

Mr. and Mrs. Franklin were most anxious to try the magic powder but knew that it would be wiser to wait until breakfast time the next morning, so they sent the children to bed early and spent the rest of the evening in blissful uninterrupted quiet.

Just before they went to bed they filled their little magic blowers and put them on the table in the upper hall, where they wouldn't forget them. The next morning they could hardly wait for the children to come to breakfast and begin interrupting.

When at last they had all assembled, on purpose Mr. Franklin began a long dull story about the value of getting up early. Before the children had a chance to see how long and dull the story was going to be and while they were all turned toward Mr. Franklin, Mrs. Franklin took her little blower and blew the magic powder on them.

Then Mr. Franklin began, "When I was a boy I loved to get up early. Nobody ever had any trouble getting me out of bed. I used to get up early every single morning. At first I used to get up late, about six-thirty. Then I started getting up at five-thirty, then I decided that that wasn't early enough so I began getting up at four-thirty—"

Benji started to interrupt. "There's a boy at school—" he began but that was as far as he got. His mouth opened and closed like a goldfish but no sound came out.

Mr. Franklin looked at him, smiled and continued, "at four-thirty so I could see the beauty of the sunrise and hear the early morning sounds—"

Stevie tried to interrupt. "My teacher says—" but that was as far as he got. His mouth snapped open and shut and snapped open and snapped closed like a spectacle case but no sound came out.

Sally began to laugh and to point at the boys. "Hey, look," she began, then her mouth just stayed open, wide open. She looked like a board with a knothole in it.

Mr. Franklin looked around at his gaping children, smiled with pleasure and continued, "sounds of bird song and peace; could smell the delicious fragrance of flowers drenched with dew; could watch the sun come up and give the gray earth form and color." He finished his story in complete uninterrupted silence.

Then Mrs. Franklin said, "John, do you think I should have the Weavers to dinner Friday night. They are terrible bores but we do owe—"

Benji tried to interrupt. He said, "Today is the—" But no one ever found out what today was because his mouth just stayed open like Sally's.

Mrs. Franklin continued, "owe them a dinner and the Chalmers are not too—"

Sally started to say something, "You told me not—" the

sound stopped but her mouth snapped open and snapped shut and snapped open and snapped shut like a spectacle case. There was no sound.

Stevie said, "Whatsa matter—" but the words seemed to choke in his throat and his mouth opened and shut and opened and shut like a goldfish.

Mrs. Franklin continued, "Chalmers are not too bright themselves so it would really be killing two birds with one stone."

"Which is a fine way to talk about your cooking," said Mr. Franklin, laughing. The children didn't say anything, they just sat there like a knothole, a fish and a spectacle case.

That afternoon Mrs. Franklin had some of the ladies from her garden club for tea. She asked Sally to pass the sandwiches and the boys to keep the kettle boiling and to wash the cups. Sally had on her best ruffly white pinafore and the boys washed clear above the water marks on their wrists and everything went very smoothly until Mrs. Wintersmelt began explaining the value of chicken wire in flower arrangements.

All the ladies were listening in a most eager way when suddenly the kitchen door was flung open and Benji and Stevie came racing into the living room.

"Isn't it water crest, Mother?" Stevie said.

"Aw lissen to that dummy," said Benji. "Anybody knows it is water cresk."

"Boys," said Mrs. Franklin. "Go out to the kitchen. You have INTERRUPTED Mrs. Wintersmelt." The boys went sheepishly out to the kitchen and Mrs. Franklin excused herself, picked up her little blower from the hall table and followed them. Just as they turned the corner from the pantry to the kitchen she covered them with the magic powder, then gave them a short firm lecture.

Then just for safety's sake she called to Sally, who was listening outside the door anyway, hoping the boys might be slapped a little, and told her to fix some more lemon slices. When she was getting the lemons out of the cooler and had her back turned, Mrs. Franklin sprayed her with the magic powder, then went back to the living-room to catch the end of Mrs. Wintersmelt's advice on chicken wire.

When Mrs. Wintersmelt had acknowledged the clapping that followed her talk, Mrs. Backscratcher began a talk on how much more effective flower arrangements are when you don't use flowers at all. She was well into her subject and was describing a lovely flower arrangement she had brought with her made of toothpicks and bottle caps, when Sally tried to interrupt her to tell her that they made things out of toothpicks at school. She took hold of Mrs. Backscratcher's arm and began, "We make—" but that was as far as she got. Her mouth just stayed open.

Mrs. Backscratcher stopped talking and stared at her. "Does the child stammer?" she asked Mrs. Franklin.

"No," said Mrs. Franklin in a most exasperated way, "she interrupts, which is worse. Go out to the kitchen, Sally." Sally, her mouth still open wide, went.

Mrs. Backscratcher continued, "You know, ladies, that is a very funny thing. That little girl's open mouth reminds me of a lovely arrangement I saw in Chicago made out of a knothole and a bunch of grass."

The ladies all moved their chairs closer.

Mrs. Franklin from the corner of her eye saw the kitchen

door swing open. Benji and Stevie edged into the hall and began, "Mom, Stevie—" "Mom, Benji—" that was all. They just stood there, their mouths opening and closing and no sound coming out. The ladies all stopped listening to Mrs. Backscratcher and peered out at the children.

A Mrs. Wartsnoggle, who was deaf and wore an ear phone, thought the children were saying something and so she turned her ear phone up as high as it would go, then when she still couldn't hear anything she took out the batteries and tapped on them.

Mrs. Franklin got up and pushed the boys back into the kitchen. Mrs. Backscratcher continued, "two pipe cleaners and a vanilla cork put into an empty sardine can—"

Only to Mrs. Wartsnoggle it came out "TWO PIPE CLEANERS AND A VANILLA CORK PUT INTO AN EMPTY SARDINE CAN!" until she turned her ear phone down.

For the rest of the afternoon the children stayed in the kitchen but, just to be on the safe side, Mrs. Franklin kept the little blower in her knitting bag.

At dinner, Mr. Franklin blew so much magic powder on the children that they didn't even start to interrupt. Just turned their heads toward the person they hoped to interrupt and opened and closed their mouths, or kept their mouths open or snapped open and snapped shut like a spectacle case.

Finally Sally, during a pause in the conversation and when she was not interrupting, asked her mother and daddy what made Benji and Stevie and her suddenly stop talking and look like fish, so Mr. and Mrs. Franklin explained about the Magic Interrupter powder and showed the children the little blowers.

Benji said, "I think that's a good idea but I think you and Daddy should have some too. You interrupt lots of times."

Mr. Franklin said, "Benjamin, your mother and I are grown up."

Mrs. Franklin said, "I think Benjamin is right," and she blew a big puff of powder on Mr. Franklin. He grabbed his blower and blew some on her. Then everyone laughed.

A few minutes later, Mr. Franklin tried to interrupt Mrs. Franklin's rather long-drawn-out description of her tea and he was certainly surprised to have his mouth open wide and stay open and no sound come out.

Then Mrs. Franklin tried to interrupt Benjamin's night before last's dream which turned out to be a rehash of *Treasure Island*. Her mouth opened and shut and opened and shut like a cod. My, the children and Mr. Franklin laughed.

Of course the Franklins used up all the magic powder in two weeks, but its spell lasted and to this day nobody in that family ever interrupts anyone else. It is just a pleasure to tell a story at the Franklins' house. You can always count on uninterrupted eager attention, even if you are the biggest bore in the world.

THE HEEDLESS BREAKER

It was such a beautiful spring day. It had been dark and rainy in the morning when Sharon left the house for school but now at 3:15 the sun was shining, there was a nice little springy breeze to send the clouds tumbling and the big old peach tree in the Rogers' front yard was covered with fat pink buds.

Sharon Rogers said goodbye to her best friend, Mary Lou Robertson, banged open the front gate, and left it swinging, dropped her library book in the wet grass as she knelt down to hug her little dachshund Missy, forgot about the library book, went running up to the front door, banged it open and shut, tossed her galoshes and raincoat onto the floor of the hall closet, dashed into the living-room to kiss her mother, didn't notice that her mother had company and was drinking tea, grabbed her around the waist from behind in a big bear hug which sent the teacup flying across the room where it hit a little table and broke into a dozen pieces and it sprayed tea all over the rug.

Mrs. Rogers sighed as she kissed Sharon and said, "Sharon, dear, please try to be more careful. I love to have you hug me but won't you please look first to see if I have a cup of tea in my hands. Now say how-do-you-do to Mrs. Green then run and get the dishcloth."

Sharon's sweet blue eyes filled with tears and she said, "How-do-you-do, Mrs. Green. Oh, Mother, I forgot. I'm so sorry."

Her mother said, "I'm sure you are, dear. Now hurry and get the dishcloth before the tea dries and stains the rug."

Sharon ran to the kitchen and Mrs. Rogers sighed as she picked up the pieces of broken cup. This was the eleventh cup Sharon had broken this week, to say nothing of the seven plates, four vases, a blue sugar bowl and a mirror shattered the week before.

There was a splintering crash from the kitchen. Mrs. Rogers excused herself to Mrs. Green and still carrying the pieces of broken cup, hurried to the kitchen. She found Sharon sitting in the middle of the floor surrounded by broken spice jars and spilled spices. The little old spice cupboard which Mrs. Rogers had inherited from her grandmother was clinging to the wall by one nail, empty and with one of its fragile shelves splintered.

Mrs. Rogers said, "What in the world happened? I thought I sent you for the dishcloth."

Sharon said, "Well, the dishcloth was hanging on the

little rack by the spice cupboard and I was reaching for it when I remembered the hard candy you keep up there on that high shelf so I climbed up on the stove and just put one foot on the spice cupboard and I didn't know it would break. I'm sorry, Mother."

Mrs. Rogers sighed as she reached for the dishcloth still hanging on the little rack. She said, "Oh, Sharon, won't you please try to be more careful and not so heedless. Now pick up this mess and go up and change your clothes. Your cookies and milk are on the table." She took the dishcloth and went through the swinging door to the dining-room.

Sharon jumped to her feet, rushed over and grabbed the broom and began sweeping vigorously at the spilled spices, forgetting or not noticing in her heedless hurry that the largest and fullest jar of spice had been one of black pepper. Mrs. Rogers coming through the swinging door to return the dishcloth and fill the teapot, caught a large broomful of pepper square in the face. "Kachoo, kachoo, achoo!" she sneezed as the teapot lid rattled and Sharon continued to spread the pepper through the kitchen.

"Pepper! Be careful, achoo, achoo!" said Mrs. Rogers rubbing her smarting eyes. Sharon stopped sweeping. "Pepper, where?" She knelt down to look at the floor, carelessly letting go of the broom which fell down and rapped poor Mrs. Rogers across the instep.

"Ouch!" she yelled, bending down to rub her sore foot just as Sharon, who hadn't noticed that she had dropped the broom on her mother, grabbed a handful of pepper and without looking thrust it up over her shoulder and said, "Is this pepper, Mother?"

Mrs. Rogers caught this handful of pepper right in the left eye. She gave a yelp of pain, rushed to the sink and began throwing cold water in her face. Sharon instantly sorry said, "Oh, Mother, I didn't see you. I'm terribly sorry."

Mrs. Rogers said, "GO UPSTAIRS BEFORE I LOSE MY TEMPER!"

"Well, you don't have to be so cross about it," Sharon said, banging open the swinging door which caught Mrs. Green, who was just coming out to see if she could help, between the eyes and knocked off her rimless spectacles.

"My heavens, what happened?" said Mrs. Green, who couldn't see without her spectacles.

"Oh, I'm so sorry," said Sharon. "Did I hurt you?" She stepped forward solicitously and there was a loud crunch. "Oh," said Sharon, "look, I've stepped on something."

Mrs. Green said, "Oh, no! My glasses?" and Sharon said, "Oh, yes," and began to cry.

Mrs. Rogers, who was still at the sink trying to wash the pepper out of her eyes, called, "Sharod Rogers, kachoo! Go, kachoo! kachoo! right, kachoo, up kachoo, stairs, kachoo, and stay id your roob, kachoo!"

Sharon went.

Poor Mrs. Green knelt down and began fumbling around on the floor for the broken glasses. She was hoping that there might be one glass or perhaps a fairly good-sized piece of one glass that she could hold up to her eye and see to go home. She found the glasses at last, but they had been ground to dust by Sharon's heel. So Mrs. Rogers, her eyes red and swollen, and sneezing every five seconds, had to lead her friend home. Sharon from her bedroom window watched them grope their way along the street through the spring afternoon and it made her cry harder than ever because they looked like two feeble old ladies who had just been to a funeral.

At half-past-six Mr. Rogers opened Sharon's door slowly and carefully, then guarding himself with his arm he said, "Dinner is ready. You may give me one kiss, Careless Carrie, but be gentle and try not to black my eye or break my arm."

Sharon gave her daddy a hug and said, "Oh, Daddy, I don't mean to be so careless. I didn't mean to break Mrs. Green's glasses."

He said, "I know you didn't, Chickabiddy, but that doesn't help Mrs. Green see. You must learn to move more slowly. To look before you leap. You're only eight years old and I'd like to keep you for another twelve or thirteen years at least but at the rate you're breaking things I won't be able to afford it. Let's see, last week you broke eleven cups, there are fifty-two weeks in a year and 52×11 is 572 cups a year and we have at least twelve more years to go—that would be six thousand, eight hundred and sixty-four cups. Wow!"

They went down to dinner and Sharon was very careful and didn't jerk her chair or bang the table as she sat down. When she cleared off the table she moved slowly and carefully and only spilled a little French dressing in her mother's lap. She continued to be very careful while she was helping with the dishes and as a result didn't chip or break a single thing.

When the last dish was dried and the dishtowels were

hung up, her mother gave her a kiss and said that she was awfully sorry about the mishaps of the afternoon and now to give her father a kiss and hurry to bed. Sharon was so happy that she had not been heedless that she rushed into the den to tell her father, forgot that the door stuck, gave it a hard jerk, slipped on the rug, fell against the hall table and knocked over and broke the little red chinese bowl of white hyacinths. Mrs. Rogers cried because the red bowl had been a wedding present, Mr. Rogers shouted because the carpenter who was supposed to have fixed the door charged so much and didn't do anything and Sharon cried because her heedlessness had spoiled the whole evening for her mother and father.

After Sharon had gone to bed, Mr. and Mrs. Rogers sat up very late worrying about Sharon's heedlessness. Mrs. Rogers thought perhaps Sharon should have dancing lessons to make her more graceful. Mr. Rogers thought she should have a sound spanking every time she broke anything. Mrs. Rogers thought that elocution lessons were what Sharon needed to give her poise. Mr. Rogers thought Sharon should pay for everything she broke out of her 25¢ a week allowance. Mrs. Rogers wondered if Sharon's eyes needed testing. Mr. Rogers said that he thought that a good sound spanking *and* paying for everything she broke was the solution. Mrs. Rogers said that she had heard that trouble with the inner ear affected children's balance, perhaps this was a result of the chicken pox. Mr. Rogers said that as Sharon had had the chicken pox four years ago and had only been a heedless breaker for two weeks, he thought that theory was ridiculous. He thought that a good sound spanking, paying for everything broken and not going to the moving picture show on Saturday afternoon was the answer. Now when he was a boy, when he broke the little buck saw with which he had to saw great heaps of wood every single day after school rain or snow, his father had made him pay for it all himself and he had to earn the money after he had sawed the wood. Mrs. Rogers said that she thought she would go to bed and read. Mr. Rogers said that that was the trouble with Sharon, Mrs. Rogers refused to face facts.

The next morning Sharon wakened to find sunbeams in her eyes and a fat robin sitting in the tree outside her window and scolding her. Sharon said, "Oh, you darling robin, I'll get right up." She jumped out of bed and started for the window, forgetting that the night before she had been oiling her roller skates and had left them in a heap on the floor right in the middle of the room. The poor little robin was surprised and very scared when Sharon tripped over the roller skates and came banging against the window screen so hard she bulged it way out. The robin flew away and Sharon began to cry, which was a very poor way to start a lovely spring day.

Then Sharon jumped into the shower without her shower cap and got her thick brown hair soaking; then, when she was finally dressed and ready for breakfast, she just happened to find her favorite old golf ball and gave it one bounce on the stairs and it got away, bounced way up high and broke off three of the crystal danglers on the hall chandelier; then she sat down for breakfast, forgetting about the table leg (in spite of having been told about it every single morning for the last three years), and when her knees hit the table leg it joggled the table and slopped the orange juice, the coffee and the cream. Mr. and Mrs. Rogers just looked at each other. Sharon, very red in the face, began eating her cereal.

When she finally left for school, after shaking fountain-pen ink all over the hall carpet and turning the house upside down looking for the library book which was finally found all wrinkled and wet down by the gate, Mr. Rogers said, "I still think a spanking, paying for everything she breaks, and not going to the movies on Saturday is the answer."

Mrs. Rogers said, "If you tell me about that old buck saw which your nasty, stingy father made you pay for once again I'll scream."

Mr. Rogers said stiffly, "I had no intention of telling you about the buck saw. I was going to ask you if you had thought of calling Mrs. Piggle-Wiggle to see if she has any suggestions for curing our Little Heedless Breaker."

Mrs. Rogers said, "Oh, Herbie, darling, of course. Mrs. Piggle-Wiggle. Why didn't I think of it? She'll be sure to know of something. Oh, you're so smart, dear!" She gave Mr. Rogers a kiss and he went beaming off to work.

When Mrs. Piggle-Wiggle heard about Sharon's heedlessness she said, "Oh I have just the thing for that. It's a magic powder which you sprinkle in a Heedless Breaker's bed. The magic powder is absorbed during the night and the next morning when Miss Heedless Breaker gets out of bed she will find that she can only move very, very, very slowly. I'll send you enough for two days which should do the trick. Let's see, this is Thursday, I'll send the powder over tomorrow afternoon. Goodbye, Mrs. Rogers, and don't worry." Mrs. Piggle-Wiggle hung up.

Mrs. Rogers called Mr. Rogers right away to tell him what Mrs. Piggle-Wiggle had said. Mr. Rogers said, "Sounds fine, but if that doesn't work I still think my methods should be tried. A good sound spanking would at least make Sharon careful about sitting down." He laughed callously.

Mrs. Rogers said, "Ummm, ummmm. Don't be late tonight, dear, we're having cheese soufflé."

That afternoon, in spite of great precautions on Mrs. Rogers' part, Sharon tipped over her milk, stepped on Missy's foot, broke a basement window, and stepped hard on two poor struggling shoots of Mrs. Rogers' most prized delphinium. With each little accident, Sharon seemed truly repentant and promised tearfully to be more careful, but in five or ten minutes crash, bang and something else would be broken.

Just before dinner she whizzed up to the back steps to take off her roller skates, of course didn't look behind her and sat down splash in Missy's water dish. Mary Lou Robertson laughed until tears ran down her cheeks but Sharon was mad. She ripped off her skates, threw them on the porch and stamped upstairs to her room.

When Mr. Rogers came home early because of the cheese soufflé and found that it wasn't quite ready, he decided to do a little pruning. So, grabbing the pruning shears and with his cutting eye aimed toward anything in the garden showing signs of life, he threw open the back door, strode out into the spring evening, tripped over Sharon's roller skates, took a flying leap off the porch, landed with one foot in the garbage can and the other on the rake which Sharon had left lying by the steps after retrieving her ball

from the porch roof. As he stepped on the tines of the rake
the handle came up and hit him smartly in the nose.

Mr. Rogers was so mad he roared. "Marjorie! Sharon!
MARJORIESHARON!" When Sharon timidly opened
the back door he pointed at the roller skates and said, "DID
YOU LEAVE THOSE SKATES THERE? DID YOU
LEAVE THIS RAKE HERE?"

"Yes," said Sharon in a tiny little squeak of a voice.

"Well," said her daddy, "your careless heedlessness has
almost lost me my life. I am now going to give you a
spanking." And he did and so dinner was a snuffling red-
eyed meal filled with cold looks and long silences and the
cheese soufflé which was delicious.

Mrs. Rogers was secretly pleased to note that Friday, in
spite of Mr. Rogers' spanking, Sharon seemed more heedless than ever. She dropped the waffle iron and tipped over
the syrup at breakfast; she banged through the swinging
door into her mother who was carrying a platter of sausages
so that sausages flew through the air like little zeppelins
and a big blob of grease landed on Sharon's bangs; she
turned on the water in the kitchen sink so hard it sprayed
all over her clean middy blouse and soaked the front of her
nice clean pleated skirt; she banged the front door so hard
the house shook and Mrs. Rogers' new philodendron fell
off the window sill and the pot broke into a million pieces
and dirt scattered all over the hall.

The last the Rogers saw of their daughter she zoomed
through the front gate on one roller skate, banged into
Mary Lou, who was waiting for her, so that Mary Lou
went flouncing off to school alone, took off the roller skate,
tossed it over the fence into a bed of crocuses and ran after

her best friend. Mr. and Mrs. Rogers watched her until she rounded the corner then they went back to the breakfast table and had another cup of coffee.

Mr. Rogers said, "If Mrs. Piggle-Wiggle's magic powder doesn't work, I think we should move into an old bomb shelter until Sharon grows out of this awful Heedless Breaker stage."

Mrs. Rogers said, "I still think that dancing lessons might be the answer."

Mr. Rogers laughed. He said, "Yeah, I can just see her leaping around kicking the teacher in the eye and knocking down the other pupils. The only difference would be that she'd be busting things to music." They both laughed.

About four-thirty that afternoon, Larry Gray brought Mrs. Rogers a package from Mrs. Piggle-Wiggle. Inside the package was a small can, like a talcum powder can, with holes in the top. The can was marked "CURE FOR HEEDLESS BREAKERITIS" and the directions read: "Sprinkle powder thoroughly over Heedless Breaker's bed. Use two nights in succession."

Mrs. Rogers, who had been waiting for the powder before making Sharon's bed, ran upstairs, threw back the covers and dusted the entire bottom sheet with the powder. There wasn't much left when she got through but she thought, "The first day is the most important anyway."

That night Sharon went to bed, having no idea what was in store for her, and slept soundly, but both Mr. and Mrs. Rogers were restless and nervous and dreamed terrible dreams about magic and their poor little girl.

When Sharon woke up the next morning, she was very surprised to find both her mother and father standing by her bed staring at her. "How do you feel?" they asked anxiously. "Sleepy," said Sharon and yawned, very slowly.

"Hurry and get dressed," said her mother. "I'm going to make French toast."

"Goody," said Sharon and started to leap out of bed. Instead of leaping, she was very surprised to find herself moving like a queen, slowly and regally. Her body felt very, very heavy but smooth and sort of floaty. It was very pleasant.

Sharon's usual custom in the morning was to jerk out her bureau drawers so hard, they almost always came all the way out and dumped everything on the floor. This morning she went over to her bureau to get some clean socks, reached for the drawer handles and was surprised to see how slowly and carefully her fingers grasped them. She tried to jerk the drawers out but her arms moved back slowly and the drawer pulled out gently and just far enough for her to be able to reach her socks without any trouble. When she had finished she tried to give the drawer a shove, but her hand wouldn't come away. It pushed the drawer all the way in, carefully and slowly.

When Sharon sat down in her little rocking chair to put on her socks, she found that she moved slowly and as though controlled by strings, like a puppet.

Usually Sharon jammed her feet into her socks so hard that often her toes would go poking right through the end. This morning her foot wouldn't poke. It moved forward slowly and gracefully and Sharon found herself pulling on her socks with as much care as her mother put on her nylon stockings. Her socks looked nice too, the tops were turned down and even and the heels were on her heels, not in front as they often were.

It actually didn't take Sharon any longer to dress this new careful way, because she didn't have to stop and get other socks after poking holes in the first ones and she didn't have to stop and cry and rub her knees, her toes or elbows after tripping over, bumping into or knocking down the furniture.

She saw her old golf ball on her desk and carried it down to breakfast but she didn't bounce it on the stairs because she was moving slowly and had time to remember what had happened before, how it had bounced and broken her mother's crystal chandelier. When she walked slowly into breakfast, carefully pulled out her chair, sat down gracefully without bumping the table leg, and daintily unfolded her napkin, her mother and father looked at each other and beamed. Breakfast was a gracious, quiet, pleasant meal and the French toast was delicious.

After breakfast Sharon washed the dishes for her mother and her new slow careful way of doing things made it seem like an easy job. She was through in no time with nothing broken and everything put away in the right place. Her mother was so surprised and pleased when she opened the ice-box door to find that Sharon had not, as was her usual practice, put in big plates with tiny dabs of food on them, had not balanced the syrup jug on a glass of milk, had not crowded things so that when Mrs. Rogers opened the door at least three dishes jumped out at her and crashed.

Sharon was sweeping the back porch and Mrs. Rogers peeked out the door and watched her in amazement. Instead of standing in the middle of the porch and sweeping from side to side with big careless sweeps so that dog bones, dust, crumbs and leaves went flying in every direction including her hair, Sharon was sweeping with small careful strokes, and everything was in a neat little pile. Her mother tapped on the door and waved at her. Sharon slowly raised her head and smiled.

After a while when Mary Lou, Molly O'Toole and Susan Gray came over to roller skate, Mrs. Rogers was terribly pleased to see that Sharon was the most graceful skater of all. Mrs. Rogers used to be afraid to watch Sharon skate because she skated like double-greased lightning and banged into trees, tripped over stones and fell flat on her face and used to do very dangerous heedless things like skating down a hill backwards. Now she sailed down the street on one foot, as airy and graceful as a leaf. She even won when they had a race because her strokes were long and she watched where she was going and avoided rough places.

When she came in for lunch, Mrs. Rogers almost fainted to see her carefully unlatch and open the gate, then close it after her. She was carrying her roller skates and she put them in the hall closet where they belonged, instead of tossing them on the porch.

At lunch, instead of gulping a mouthful of hot soup, giving a yell and spraying it around the kitchen, Sharon waited a little for the soup to cool, then ate it slowly and daintily. When she had finished she said to her mother, "You know, Mother, I feel so funny today. Sort of slow and floaty and everything seems so easy. I don't bump into things, I haven't broken a single thing, and I can roller skate just beautifully."

Mrs. Rogers said, "I've noticed it, Sharon. You move slowly and gracefully like a queen. It must be that you had a very restful sleep last night."

Sharon said, "I think that must be it." She kissed her mother and went upstairs to change her clothes.

Instead of whamming through the swinging door so that it clanged against the wall on the other side, clumping up the stairs and crashing open the door of her room, Sharon slipped through the swinging door, went up the stairs on tiptoes and gently clicked open the door of her room. Mrs. Rogers had tears of joy in her eyes as she got out all her nice little knick-knacks and put them back on the shelves and tables. She even called Mrs. Green, explained the wonderful change in Sharon and invited her over for tea.

Mrs. Green came but she approached the Rogers' house warily and with great caution as though it were a bomb.

Sharon was just leaving for the moving-picture show but she stopped and greeted Mrs. Green, apologized again for breaking her glasses, and was so quiet, gentle and charming that Mrs. Green couldn't believe it was Sharon and thought that probably it was really a secret twin sister.

When Mrs. Rogers explained about Mrs. Piggle-Wiggle's magic powder, Mrs. Green was terribly interested and asked if she could borrow a little to use on her husband when he played golf. "If he misses a shot," she told Mrs. Rogers, "he roars like a lion and breaks the clubs over his knee. He's broken two sets already and it is only April."

Mrs. Rogers ran upstairs to get the magic powder because she knew she wouldn't need it any more.

THE NEVER-WANT-TO-GO-TO-SCHOOLER

Seven-thirty, time to get up." called Mrs. Jones loudly and cheerfully from the foot of the stairs. Julie and Linda jumped out of bed and began to race getting dressed. From Jody and Jan's room there was the sound of one person getting up and loud groans.

"I feel terrible," groaned Jody from the upper bunk.

"Aw," said Jan, "you just don't want to go to school. You did the same thing last week. Groaned and moaned and felt sick until the rest of us left for school and then you felt fine."

"Oh, is that so? And how do you know so much, Dr. Jones?" said Jody, leaning out of the upper bunk and forgetting to groan.

"I know," said Jan as he tied his shoes, "because somebody was using my toolbox while I was at school. Somebody who nicked the chisel and left the hammer out on the sidewalk by the maple tree."

Jody said, "I was fixing the treehouse and I did not nick your old chisel. Dick Thompson nicked it and you know he did."

Jan said, "Dick nicked it just a little, now it has a bigger nick in it, I measured."

Jody said, "When I'm ten and get my own toolbox I won't let you even walk past it. I'll never ever even let you see inside it."

There was the sound of brisk footsteps on the stairs. Jody threw himself back in bed and began to groan. Mrs. Jones appeared at the doorway. She said, "I have made waffles for breakfast this morning. Hurry, boys."

Jan said, "I'm all ready as soon as I wash my face and hands. Ole-pretend-he's-sick-Jody is groanin' up in the upper bunk so he won't have to go to school."

Mrs. Jones walked over to the bunk, reached up and felt Jody's forehead. She said, "You haven't a speck of temperature, Jody, so stop playing possum and get up."

Jody groaned loudly and agonizingly. He said, "My stummick hurts awful. It feels like I swallowed ten knives."

Mrs. Jones looked worried. She said, "Where does it hurt, dear?"

Jody said, "Oh, all over. All over my stummick!"

Jan called from the bathroom where he was splashing a tiny little bit of water on his face. "Don't believe him, Mom, he was all right a minute ago."

Mrs. Jones said, "Jody Jones, get out of that bunk this instant! If you are sick I want a good look at you."

Jody started to sit up then crumpled in apparent agony. "Oh, oh, oh," he moaned. "My stummick is killing me."

Mrs. Jones climbed part way up the little ladder that led to the upper bunk and peered anxiously at her eight-year-old son. His eyes were closed and in the reflected light from the pine ceiling he appeared pale. Mrs. Jones patted him on the shoulder and said, "Just lie there quietly, Jody, until I get the other children off to school, then I'll bring you some tea."

Then she went downstairs and told Mr. Jones she thought they should call the doctor. Mr. Jones said, "Perhaps you had," but Jan said, "Oh, Mom, don't be dumb. There's nothing wrong with Jody at all. Just a minute ago he was leanin' over the bunk talking to me about my tools. He stayed home yesterday and the day before and he's getting so ignorant I don't even like to play with him any more."

Twelve-year-old Julie said, "Miss Robinson asked me about Jody yesterday and I told her that we thought he had amœbic dysentery."

"Amœbic dysentery!" said Mrs. Jones. "Where in the world did you get an idea like that?"

"We're studying about amœbic dysentery in hygiene," said Julie, "and personally I think Jody has all the symptoms."

"Personally, I think Jody has hydrophobia kleptomania," said Mr. Jones.

"Really?" said Julie. "What are the symptoms?"

"Pain in all cartilege and a slight stiffening of the esophagus," said Mr. Jones, solemnly buttering his waffle.

"Is Jody going to die?" wailed Linda, who was only five and didn't know what they were talking about.

"Of course not," said Mrs. Jones. "Now hurry with breakfast or you'll be late to school."

After the children had left for school and Mr. Jones had gone to the office, Mrs. Jones carried a tray up to Jody. On it were a pot of tea, two poached eggs and three pieces of toast. Between groans Jody ate every crumb.

At exactly 9:02 he came pattering down to the kitchen in his pajamas and announced that he felt a tiny bit better and thought he'd go outside for a breath of fresh air. Mrs. Jones looked at him suspiciously but he widened his large blue eyes and—as he was only eight years old, a little small for his age and seemed even smaller in ten-year-old Jan's pajamas, which he had swiped the night before because he had forgotten that he had stuffed his own in the window seat when he was cleaning up his half of the room—Mrs. Jones convinced herself that he wasn't fooling and let him go out to play.

After he had dressed, Jody helped himself to as many of Jan's tools as he could carry and went out to work on the treehouse. My, it was beautiful up there in the old maple tree! The sun made little speckles on the floor of the treehouse and two fat gray squirrels ran up and down the branches and chattered at him when he hammered.

"This is the life," said Jody happily to himself. "I'm never going to school. I'm going to be a carpenter and that's certainly something ole Miss Robinson doesn't know anything about."

"Cuttacuttacuttak," said one of the gray squirrels.

Just before the other children were due home for lunch, Jody climbed down out of the tree, went in the house and told his mother he had a little headache and felt weak. She told him to lie down on the couch with the afghan over him.

Even Julie and Jan, who came rushing in to sneer at him, thought he looked quite frail and left the room on tiptoe. Linda kissed him stickily and told him that he could take a nap with her after lunch, which made him feel slightly ashamed.

Jody had only intended to stay on the davenport until after Julie and Jan left for school, but it was so quiet in the living-room, and so comfortable on the davenport, that he fell asleep and didn't wake up until two o'clock. Twice while he was sleeping Mrs. Jones tiptoed in and felt his head. As it was cool and moist, she decided that Jody had just had a little stomach upset and it wasn't necessary to call the doctor.

As soon as he waked up, Jody got up and worked on the treehouse until ten minutes past three. Then he skinned down out of the tree, rushed in and put away Jan's tools and was again lying wistfully on the couch when Julie and Jan came home.

Jan said that he was going to work on the treehouse and did Jody want to help him. Jody said, "I'll just climb up and watch for a while. Thanks anyway, Jan." Jan watched suspiciously as Jody shinnied up the tree faster than a squirrel but he didn't say anything until he had climbed up into the treehouse himself and had seen how much work Jody had done.

"I just wish Mother could climb up here and see how

sick you are," he said, carefully examining his tools for scratches and nicks.

Jody said, "I did feel sick this morning but I got better after lunch. Hey, do you think this roof's going to be high enough?"

Jan said, "Let's make it high enough so we can have a window. Wouldn't it be fun to look out our window at the ole girls playin' in the street below?" Jody's sickness was forgotten.

Having had no lunch, Jody was starving for dinner and had two helpings of everything. When Mr. Jones passed him his second plate-full he said, "Your hydrophobia kleptomania seems to have cleared up. You'll certainly be well enough to go to school tomorrow, eh, Jody?"

Jody, making his eyes as big as he could over a mouthful of baked potato, said, "I certainly hope so, Daddy. I hate to miss school." Jan choked on his milk and Julie said that she thought all boys were disgusting and should eat out of troughs.

Mr. Jones said, "From now on, conversation at this table is to be limited to current events," and so the children had nothing to say until dinner was over.

After dinner, Linda went to bed and the other children were sent to their rooms to study. Jan went right to work on a theme he was writing entitled, "My Most Interesting Experience," but Jody got out an old magic-dot book and began filling in the pictures.

"How do you spell dangerous?" asked Jan.

"I dunno," said Jody.

There was silence for a while.

"How do you spell Africa?" asked Jan.

"I dunno," said Jody.

Silence.

"How do you spell leopard?" asked Jan.

"I dunno," said Jody.

"Gosh, don't you know anything?" said Jan.

"Sure," said Jody. "Lots of things but not spelling and I don't notice you're so good at it either. How do you spell dangerous, how do you spell Africa, how do you spell leopard?" He mimicked Jan.

Jan said, "It's just that I happen to be writing a theme and I don't have time to stop and think how to spell every single word."

"What are you writing a theme about?" asked Jody.

"My most interesting experience," said Jan.

"*Your* most interesting experience," jeered Jody. "Ha, ha, ha! What do you know about Africa and leopards?"

Jan looked embarrassed. He said, "Well, I'm pretending that one of Dick Thompson's Uncle Charlie's experiences was mine. Miss Hatfield's never been to Africa. She won't know the difference. Anyway it'll be a lot more interesting than 'The Time My Dolly Broke Her Front Tooth' or 'The Time I Found My First Crocus,' like the ole girls write."

Jody was busy filling in the last dots. He said, "Hey, look at this. It's an elephant and I thought all the time it was going to be a football field." They both laughed loudly just as Mr. Jones called that it was bedtime.

The next morning when Mrs. Jones called, "Breakfast, boys!" Jody began to groan. "Oh, oh, oh," he groaned.

"My stummick!"

Jan said, "Oh, oh, oh, my stummick, I mean I hate to go to school."

Jody ignored him. "My stummick hurts awful!" he moaned.

Jan said, "You stay out of school all the time and you won't pass. You'll be just like that old Lemmy Carson that's fourteen and in the third grade."

Jody closed his eyes and yelled louder than ever, "Oh, oh, oh, my stummick!"

Mrs. Jones came in and felt his forehead. It seemed a little hot, which could have been from the fact that Jody had his underwear on under Jan's pajamas and it could have been from his groaning.

Mrs. Jones said, "Just exactly where does it hurt, Jody?"

Jody said, "It's a sort of all-over, terrible stummick ache."

Mrs. Jones said, "You're sure you aren't just fooling, Jody?"

Jody said, "Oh, Mom, don't be silly. My stummick's killing me."

Jan said, "Don't bother with old Lemmy Carson, Mom. He's not going to school any more."

Mrs. Jones said, "Who's Lemmy Carson?"

Jan said, "Oh, he's a kid in school who is fourteen and only in the third grade."

Mrs. Jones said, "Is there anything wrong with him?"

Jan said, "Nothing except he never goes to school."

Jody said, "Oh, oh, oh, my poor stummick! It aches awful."

Mrs. Jones and Jan went downstairs. On the way down

Mrs. Jones said, "Jan, do you really think that Jody is just pretending?"

"I know he is," said Jan. "He says he's going to be a carpenter and he doesn't have to go to school."

Mrs. Jones said, "We'll just see about that," and went in to breakfast.

She didn't carry Jody any tray and so at 9:01 he came down to the kitchen and said, "Mom, dear, I feel a little better but I thought I should maybe have some er, uh," his eyes strayed toward and became glued to a large bowl of ripe bananas, "some bananas and cream and toast," he finished.

Mrs. Jones said, "Not with that stomach ache. A little tea, perhaps, but nothing else. Now march right upstairs and get back into bed." Jody went slowly and meekly.

At 9:30 he asked his mother if he could get up. She said no, loudly and firmly. At 10:00 he asked again for food. "No," said Mrs. Jones. At 10:30 he asked to get up. "No!" said his mother.

Unfortunately at 11:00 Mrs. Jones sat down to have a cup of coffee and happened to glance at the morning paper. On the front page was a heart-rending story with vivid pictures of some little starving Greek children. Mrs. Jones read the entire story twice then called to Jody to come down and get his breakfast.

He came down to the kitchen all dressed in his play clothes, in about seven seconds. Mrs. Jones gave him two shredded-wheat biscuits with sliced bananas and plenty of rich cream, two scrambled eggs, three pieces of bacon and a cinnamon bun. Jody ate it all then went out to work on the treehouse.

When the other children came home for lunch, Julie told her mother that Miss Robinson had told her that Jody was getting very far behind in his work and that if he was going to be sick long, Mrs. Jones had better go up to school and get his assignments or else arrange to have the teacher who traveled around and taught invalids come to the house.

Jan said, "Honestly, Mom, I don't see how you can be so dumb about Jody. He's just pretendin'. His ole stummick never gets sore except on school mornings."

Mrs. Jones said, "Now don't worry, children, I'll handle Jody. Julie, tell Miss Robinson I'll call her tomorrow morning."

After she had put Linda down for her nap and had washed the lunch dishes, Mrs. Jones called up her friend Mrs. Armadillo. She said, "Mrs. Armadillo, have you ever had any trouble getting Armand to go to school? I mean, does Armand like to go to school?"

"Oh, my yes," said Mrs. Armadillo. "You know Armand is only eight years old and he is in the high seventh. The teacher told me only yesterday, that actually Armand could do high-school work but I don't like to force him."

"Oh, no?" said Mrs. Jones to herself. "You started teaching him to read when he was about four months old and you started him in a private school when he was three." Aloud she said, "Well, I'm not so fortunate. You see Jody has decided that he doesn't want to go to school. Every morning he has terrible stomach aches and pains and actually seems to be suffering until after nine when he knows the bell has rung. I just can't understand it."

Mrs. Armadillo said, "Perhaps he is having trouble in school. Perhaps he isn't happy with his teacher."

Mrs. Jones said, "Oh, I'm sure he likes Miss Robinson. All the children have had her and they have all loved her."

Mrs. Armadillo said, "Well, you know some children are high strung and sensitive and the confusion of a large public school is too much for their little nervous systems. That's why we took Armand out of public school and put him in Miss Walkinshaw's School for Exceptional Children. I'll call Miss Walkinshaw right now if you wish."

Mrs. Jones said, "Oh, no, please don't bother, Mrs. Armadillo. I'll talk to Jody and see if something is troubling him. If I should decide to take him out of public school I'll let you know." She hung up. "That little earwig of an Armand," she said angrily to herself. "Imagine that, high seventh and he was only eight last month."

She called to Jody, who quickly shinnied down the tree trunk and came loping into the kitchen, beaming and expecting more food. Mrs. Jones took him on her lap. She said, "Jody, dear, is something at school bothering you?"

Jody said, "Uhh, uhh. Say, do we have any of those big ginger cookies? That kind Mrs. Maxwell bakes?"

Mrs. Jones said, "Jody, I want to talk to you about school. Do you like Miss Robinson?"

"Sure," said Jody. "She's all right. Mrs. Maxwell bakes those big ginger cookies every single Saturday."

Mrs. Jones pushed Jody rather rudely from her lap. She said, "Oh, go out and play."

Jody looking puzzled went out but called from the front gate, "I'll go down and ask Mrs. Maxwell how to make those ginger cookies if you want me to."

Mrs. Jones said, "Don't bother!" and shut the door firmly.

Then she called her friend Mrs. Wheeling and asked her if she ever had any trouble making Kitty go to school. Mrs. Wheeling said no but she knew plenty of mothers who had had trouble with Not-Want-To-Go-To-Schoolers. She told Mrs. Jones to call Mrs. Piggle-Wiggle, and Mrs. Jones did.

Mrs. Piggle-Wiggle said, "Oh, so that's where Jody's been. I wondered why I hadn't seen him pass the house lately. Well, what he needs is some Ignorance Tonic. I'll send a bottle over with Jan. Give Jody a tablespoonful right away, another after dinner, another in the morning, before lunch and before dinner tomorrow. Keep it up until he asks to go back to school." Mrs. Jones thanked Mrs. Piggle-Wiggle and hung up.

At 3:15 Jan handed his mother a package from Mrs. Piggle-Wiggle. It contained a large black bottle marked "IGNORANCE TONIC." Mrs. Jones measured a tablespoonful into a small glass, called Jody in and handed it to him.

"What's this?" Jody asked.

"Something for your pains," said his mother.

Jody said, "But they're gone now."

His mother said, "This is to prevent their returning tomorrow morning. Now drink it."

Jody did. He said, "Ummmm, tasted just like chocolate syrup."

He went out to play. He climbed up into the treehouse, sat down and began pounding in a nail upside down and with the pliers instead of the hammer.

Jan said, "Hey, what are you doing?"

Jody said, "Pounding" only he really said "Poudig" because his throat had suddenly become thick and choky.

Jan said, "Why don't you use the hammer?"

Jody said, "What's a habber?"

Jan said, "Don't try to be so funny. Here!" and handed him the hammer.

Jody took it but began pounding with the handle.

Jan grabbed the hammer away from him. "What's the matter with you, anyway?" he said.

"Duthig," Jody said and laughed a high silly giggle.

Just then Julie called from below, "Hey, boys, come on down and play Kick the Can. There's Molly and Larry and Susan and Kitty and Anne and Joan and Dick and Hubert and Patsy and Mary Lou and everybody."

So Jan and Jody climbed out of the tree and Julie began to count them out, "Ibbity, bibbity, sibbity sab. Ibbity, bibbity, casaba." Jody was it.

They told him to count to five hundred by fives. He leaned against the maple tree and closed his eyes but he couldn't think.

"Five," he said. "Let's see what comes next." He couldn't remember. He decided to count to one hundred by ones. He began in the funny thick voice he now had, "Ode, two, three," but that was as far as he could go. He couldn't remember what came after three. From all around, from one end of the block to the other he could hear the shouts of "Ready!" and he hadn't finished counting.

He decided to just stand by the tree for a while and pretend he had counted, the way Linda did. The tree trunk felt smooth and smelled spicy and delicious. He could hear the gray squirrels scolding the children from way up in the top branches. My, it was pleasant and dark behind his closed eyes. Jody fell asleep.

After about ten minutes of shouting "Ready" some of the children began stealing toward base. "Clank," Larry Gray kicked the can clear down to the corner then ran like mad. Jody did not move.

Julie come out from behind the hedge and yelled right in Jody's ear, "READY!" Jody jumped and rubbed his eyes. "Where abbi?" he said yawning.

"My gosh, Jody!" said Julie, stamping her foot. "You're too slow. You've spoiled the whole game. Now go and get the can, it's way down by the Thompsons'."

Jody ambled slowly down toward the Thompsons' but when he got down there he couldn't remember why he was there. He said good-afternoon to Mrs. Thompson, who was weeding her perennial bed, then just stood blinking in the afternoon sun. Up the street the children were all yelling. He wondered what they wanted. Mrs. Thompson said, "There's the can right there on the parking strip, Jody. Hurry and maybe you can catch them all." Jody picked up the can and ambled back toward the maple tree. As soon as he got near it the children all ran and hid. Jody put down the can and automatically began, "Ready or dot . . ." but then he couldn't remember the rest. "Ready or dot . . . Ready or dot—Ready or dot!" he said over and over again.

Julie came out from the hedge and pushed him rudely away from the tree. "Oh go and hide, dummy," she said, "I'll be it." She covered her eyes and began "Five, ten, fifteen, twenty . . ."

Jody sat down by the hedge and stared vacantly up at the sky. After a long time he noticed that there was no one around. That everyone had apparently gone home, so he went into the house. The family were at dinner.

His mother said, "Where in the world have you been? The other children came in a half an hour ago. Now go upstairs and wash and hurry." Jody went upstairs but couldn't remember what he had come up for so he went down again and in to dinner.

He sat down next to Jan, picked up a spoon and began eating. Jan said, "What are you eating with a spoon for, Baby?" Jody said, "What's a spood?" Jan and Julie laughed.

Mr. Jones said, "How do you feel tonight, Jody. Pains all gone?"

Jody repeated after him, "Paids all gode."

Mr. Jones said, "You sound as if you had a cold."

Jody said, "I'b warb edough."

Julie said, "Daddy asked you if you had a cold, dope."

Jody said, "I'b dot cold."

Jan said, "Gosh, what a dummy."

Mr. and Mrs. Jones looked at each other meaningly.

After dessert Mr. Jones said, "Let's all play 'What Johnny Has in His Pocket.' I'll start. Johnny has a ball of string in his pocket."

Linda, who was next, said, "Johnny has a ball of string and a worm in his pocket."

Julie said, "Johnny has a ball of string, a worm and an apple in his pocket."

Mrs. Jones said, "Johnny has a ball of string, a worm, an apple and a knife in his pocket."

Jan said, "Johnny has a ball of string, a worm, an apple, a knife and a nail in his pocket."

Jody said, "Joddy has a . . . Joddy has a . . ."

"Ball of string," prompted Linda.

Jody began again. "Joddy has a ball of strig, a . . . a . . ."

"And a worm," said Linda.

"Joddy has a worb," said Jody and looked around proudly.

Jan said, "Oh, let's leave the old dummy out. Come on, Daddy."

Mr. Jones said, "Come on, Jody. Johnny has a ball of string, a worm, an apple, a knife and a nail in his pocket."

Jody said, "I cadt rebeber all that. I dodt wadt to play."

He began to cry and Mrs. Jones sent him to bed.

The next morning Jody didn't have to pretend he was sick because when he waked up the other children had already gone to school. Jody got dressed and went downstairs but he couldn't find his mother. He called and called but no one answered so he went all over the house looking for his mother. He even looked under the beds and behind the furnace but he couldn't find her. When he came back to the kitchen he found a piece of paper sticking in the refrigerator door. It said, "Dear Jody . . ." and then there was some more writing but Jody couldn't read it. He began to cry.

There was a knock at the back door. Jody wiped his eyes on his sleeve and opened the door. The laundry man said, "Is your mother home, Jody?"

Jody said, "Do, I dod't know what habbeded to her," and began to cry again.

The laundry man said, "Didn't she leave a note?"

Jody said, "Yes, but I cadt read id."

The laundry man said, "Let me see it."

Jody handed him the piece of paper and the laundry man read,

"Dear Jody: I am going to the grocery store. Your medicine and your orange juice are in the refrigerator. There are sausages and toast in the oven. I'll be home in a very little while— Mother.

P. S. Be sure and tell the laundry man that the laundry is in the basement."

Jody thanked the laundry man, took his medicine and ate his breakfast.

Then he went out to the treehouse but he kept forgetting which end of the hammer to use, he couldn't remember where they kept the nails, he forgot where they were going to put the window, he couldn't measure the boards because he couldn't count or read numbers so he climbed down and just sat on the grass until Julie, Jan and Linda came home.

"Hi," said Jan. "How is old dummy this morning?"

Jody said, "I'b dot a dubby."

Julie said, "Let's hear you count to ten then."

Jody said, "I'd dodt wadt to."

Julie said, "You mean you can't, dummy."

Jody said, "I'b dot a dubby."

Linda mocked him, "I'b dot a dubby. I'b dot a dubby."

Jody began to cry so the other children went in to lunch, just as Mrs. Jones came back from the store.

Seeing Jody crying under the maple tree, she asked him what the trouble was. Jody said, "The other kids tease be."

His mother said, "What do they tease you about?"

Jody said, "They call be dubby. I'b dot a dubby, ab I?"

His mother said, "I hope not, dear," and went in to fix lunch.

All afternoon Jody just sat in the sun because he couldn't think of anything to do. When the children came home from school they played Kick the Can but they didn't ask him to play, so he just watched and dozed.

At dinner the family all played What Johnny Has in His Pocket again but they didn't even try to include Jody, so after eating his dinner with his spoon, he just sat and watched the candle wax drip down the candles in the middle of the table.

After dinner Jan and Julie went up to study, Linda went to bed and Jody climbed up into his bunk and looked at the ceiling. There were two knotholes that looked just like owl's eyes. Jody looked at them until he fell asleep. At eight-thirty Mrs. Jones came in with the bottle of Ignorance Tonic but finding Jody asleep decided to wait until morning before giving him any more.

The next morning Jody woke up so very early he could hear the paper boy whistling as he threw the papers, thump, thump, thump onto each porch. Jody climbed carefully down out of his bunk, got dressed in his school clothes, went into the bathroom and washed thoroughly, brushed his teeth, combed his hair and then looked carefully at himself in the mirror. He looked just the same as always. But he certainly felt different. He felt quick and light. He tested his voice—he said, "I'm not a dummy," and it came out of his mouth, "I'm not a dummy" not "I'b dot a dubby," the way it had for the past two days. He went downstairs. It seemed very peaceful in the early morning sunlight.

Jody decided to squeeze the orange juice for his mother. He went to the cooler for the oranges and found stuck under the box the note his mother had left for him the day before. He picked it up and was surprised to find that he could read it. Every word. He began to hum a little as he cut and squeezed the oranges and poured the juice into the six glasses.

There was a gentle scratching at the back door so Jody opened it and let in Chlotilde the cat. Chlotilde rubbed against Jody's legs and purred until he stopped squeezing oranges and warmed her some milk.

When Jody had finished the oranges he decided to make some coffee. He read the directions on the can and was very pleased to see how easily he could read the hard words and fine print. He decided to make boiled coffee in the old granite picnic coffee pot. He measured the water as he filled the pot—twenty-four cups of water seemed quite a lot but Jody remembered how his mother always filled the pot at picnics. Then he measured twenty-four scoops of coffee. Then he found the coffee pot was so heavy he couldn't lift it out of the sink so he dipped out half the water into a saucepan, put the coffee pot on the stove, poured the rest in and turned the burner on high. Then he set the breakfast table, putting on a nice clean cloth.

Then he looked at the clock and found it was only just seven o'clock. He gathered up some stale bread and took it out to the squirrels. They came down out of the tree and got on his shoulder and he stood very still and watched them pick up the pieces of bread in their funny little hands and take bites out of it.

After a while Jody went back into the house to see if his coffee was boiling and was very surprised to find his mother breaking eggs into a blue bowl.

She said, "Oh, so you're the good fairy who did all this work for me. Thank you, Jody," and she hugged him.

He said, "I woke up way early, even before the paper boy."

His mother said, "How do you feel this morning?" She had noticed the neat hair, washed face and school clothes.

Jody said, "I feel just wonderful. Think I'll go to school."

His mother said, "Fine, dear, your father will be so pleased and so will Miss Robinson."

Jody said, "Miss Robinson doesn't have to worry. I'll make up my work. I'm no dummy."

His mother kissed him and said, "I should say you're not."

"Say, Mom," Jody said, "do you think I made enough coffee?" His mother looked at the enormous granite picnic coffee pot, filled clear to the brim, then at Jody's sweet anxious face. "Just right," she said. "Just exactly right. Now call the others to breakfast, dear. Tell the children to hurry or they'll be late for school."

THE WADDLE-I-DOERS

This was Saturday and the morning of the hike to the big rock. Lee woke up very early, ran into Mimi's room and jerked back the covers.

"Hey, Mimi," he said in a hoarse excited whisper. "Get up quick, this is the day we go to Big Rock to have the picnic."

Mimi turned over and opened her eyes. She said, "We can't go to the rock today because its raining."

"Oh, it is not," said Lee running to the window.

" 'Tis too," said Mimi. "I woke up in the night and heard it. I was so mad I cried."

Lee pulled up the shade and sure enough, a hard spring rain was streaming down the window, pelting the bedraggled tulips and bouncing on the roof like popcorn. Lee was almost eleven but he felt like crying too because he had been counting on this hike for weeks.

So had all the other children. Mrs. Piggle-Wiggle was going to take them all to the Big Rock and they were going to walk behind the waterfall, climb up on the rock and take turns looking through Mrs. Piggle-Wiggle's very powerful spy glass, build a big bonfire and roast potatoes and weenies. They had planned to leave at six-thirty this very morning.

"Oh, how I hate rain," said Lee pounding on the window seat. "I'd just like to go out and kick it."

Mimi pulled the covers up around her chin. "I don't think I'll get up at all," she said. "It'll just be another rainy Saturday with nothing to do." She closed her eyes so Lee shuffled disconsolately back to his room and got back into bed. He lay and stared at the ceiling and listened to the pitta-patta-pitta-patta of the rain on the porch roof and hated everything and everybody in the whole world.

When his mother finally called him to breakfast, he came downstairs scowling and hitting at the furniture with his belt.

"Put on your belt, Lee dear," said his mother, "and stop snapping it at things. The buckle might scratch something."

Lee said, "Gosh, I hate rain. Why does it always have to rain on Saturday, why does it, huh, Mom?"

Mrs. Wharton said, "It does seem very unfair, I know, to have nice weather all week long and rain on Saturday, but you'll just have to learn to take the bad with the good. Where's Mimi?"

"Oh, she's not gettin' up," said Lee, picking at his egg and still scowling.

Mr. Wharton said, "As long as it's raining and you can't go on your hike, this would be a good time to clean the basement."

"Oh, Daddy!" wailed Lee. "What a horrible idea!"

"Not at all," said Mr. Wharton. "You must learn to make the best of things in this world and the best possible thing you could make of this rainy Saturday is a good job on the basement. 'Something attempted, something done, has earned a night's repose.' Now run upstairs and arouse your lazy sister."

"Now, Boyd dear," said Mrs. Wharton when Lee had left, "let's not overdo things. Remember this rainy day is a dreadful disappointment to the children and I hardly think that cleaning the basement, which is really your job, is any compensation for their disappointment."

Mr. Wharton said, "The trouble with all children today is that they are spoiled. Now when I was a boy if I got an easy job such as cleaning the basement I thought I was most fortunate. The cool dark basement seemed very pleasant to a boy who had spent hours and hours and hours hoeing cabbages in the red hot sun."

Mrs. Wharton said, "Your mother told me that from the time you were seven years old, your winters were spent in boarding school and your summers in the San Juan Islands, swimming, fishing and playing on the beach. Just when did you do all this grubbing around in a musty cellar and hoeing of cabbages in the red hot sun?"

"I spent one summer on my grandfather's farm," said Mr. Wharton stiffly, getting up from the table. "And I was only eleven years old and I worked very hard and enjoyed it. Modern children are all spoiled."

Some time after Mr. Wharton had left the house, Mimi came clumping downstairs, wearing her jeans and her mother's blue satin mules. She was as cross as two sticks and her hair looked as if she had combed it with an eggbeater.

"I hate rain," she said, grabbing a piece of toast and spreading it thickly with peanut butter.

Mrs. Wharton said, "Please put down that toast, go upstairs and take off my best bedroom slippers, comb your hair and then say good-morning."

Mimi stuck her tongue out at Lee and clumped back upstairs. Mrs. Wharton sighed. What a problem this day was going to be. She said to Lee, "This would be a fine day to work on your model airplane."

Lee said, "I don't wanna."

Mrs. Wharton said, "What about fixing the chain on your bicycle?"

Lee said, "I don't wanna."

Then Mimi came back, in her own shoes and combed a little, said good-morning not too sweetly, and began eating her toast and peanut butter. Mrs. Wharton went out to the kitchen. Lee followed her.

He leaned against the drain-board of the sink and said, "I hate rain. Waddle I do?" His mother suggested everything she could think of, but he "didn't wanna" do anything but lean against things and say, "waddle I do?"

Pretty soon Mimi came out and leaned against Lee and said, "Waddle I do?" She didn't want to make doll clothes, she didn't want to paint, she didn't want to play games, and most of all she didn't want to wash the breakfast dishes.

Mrs. Wharton got so desperate she was just about to send Mimi up to clean the attic and Lee down to clean the basement, when the telephone rang. It was Mrs. Piggle-Wiggle and she wanted both Mimi and Lee to come over to her house right away. She said she had something very important to tell them and could they stay for lunch and dinner. Mrs. Wharton said they certainly could, in fact she would just as leave not see them again until the rain stopped. Mrs. Piggle-Wiggle laughed and said that every mother in the neighborhood felt the same way.

So Mimi and Lee put on their raincoats and galoshes and started for Mrs. Piggle-Wiggle's house. The rain blew in their faces, ran down the gutters in rivers and went glurnk, glurnk, down the drains. In front of the Burbanks, the street drain had gotten clogged with leaves and the whole street was flooded. Mimi and Lee took sticks and poked until they found the grating, then with their hands they scraped away the leaves and pretty soon the water started gurgling down the drain. The children watched it for a while then glup—it stopped. Mimi reached down and felt around. Something was stuck in the drain. She jerked and jerked and finally pulled up a large black silk scarf. It was wet and torn and she was just about to throw it away when she noticed something tied in one corner of it. She worked on the knot and Lee worked on the knot but the scarf was so wet they couldn't untie it, so they decided to carry it to Mrs. Piggle-Wiggle's and cut the knot with scissors.

When they got to Mrs. Piggle-Wiggle's all the other children were there, and there was a huge stack of galoshes and umbrellas on the porch and all the hooks in the front hall were filled with dripping raincoats. Mrs. Piggle-Wiggle opened the door for Lee and Mimi, told them to hurry and take off their things and to come into the living-room as she had something very important to tell them.

Mimi showed her the black silk handkerchief and Mrs. Piggle-Wiggle said that while Mimi was taking off her things she would take the scarf to the kitchen and cut the knot. She did and in a minute came back and handed Mimi a round gold coin. She said, "Mimi, I am quite sure that this is a pirate lucky piece. Mr. Piggle-Wiggle used to have one and as I remember it also was gold and had a skull and crossbones on it. You'd better take very good care of it. Now let's see, do you have a hanky?"

Mimi said, "No," so Mrs. Piggle-Wiggle loaned her one of hers, tied the lucky piece in the corner, put the handkerchief in Mimi's back pocket and pinned it fast with a safety pin.

"Now," said Mrs. Piggle-Wiggle, "we'll just go in the living-room with the rest of the children and perhaps later on today we'll be able to test and see if that really is a pirate's lucky piece. That certainly looked like a pirate's black silk handkerchief. I hung it up to dry in the kitchen and after a while you can iron it."

Sitting around on the floor in the living-room were Mary Lou Robertson, Kitty Wheeling, Kitty's little brother, Bobby, Bobby's friend Dicky, Hubert Prentiss, Ermintrude Bags, Gregory Moohead, Susan Grapple, Molly O'Toole, Chuckie Keystop, Dick Thompson, Patsy, Prunella Brown, Paraphernalia Grotto, Cormorant Broomrack, Bobby, Larry and Susan Gray, Catherine and Wilfred Grassfeather, Worthington and Guinevere Gardenfield,

Allen Wetherill Crankminor, Pergola Wingsproggle, Anne and Joan Russell, Jasper and Myrtle Quitrick, Sharon Rogers, Julie, Linda, Jan and Jody Jones, Wendy and Timmy Hamilton, Christopher Brown, Darsie, Bard and Alison Burbank, Armand Armadillo, Pamela, Percy and Potter Penzil, Mimi Wharton, Dicky Williams, Marilyn Matson, Benji, Stevie and Sally Franklin, Terry and Theresa Teagle. Everyone was drinking tea and eating cookies and being surly and quarrelsome in a damp rainy Saturday sort of way.

Mrs. Piggle-Wiggle sat down on a little stool by the fireplace, made room for Lightfoot the cat, Wag the dog and Lester the pig (who should have been at the Grapples' but had stayed home for the hike and picnic) by her feet, took a sip of tea, clapped her hands for quiet and began:

"I know that this horrid rain has been a great disappointment to all of you children—I know because I was very very disappointed myself last night when I heard raindrops tiptoeing on the roof and tapping at the window. I also know because almost all of your mothers have told me that you children were terrible Waddle-I-Doers this morning. However, this rain and our not being able to have the picnic is actually the luckiest thing that ever happened because I need all of you to help me, today, here in this house.

"You see a long, long time ago, when Mr. Piggle-Wiggle and I decided to build a house upside down, because when I was a little girl I used to lie in bed and wonder what it would be like if the house were upside down, we couldn't get anyone to build it for us because carpenters and contractors thought that building a house upside down was crazy, so Mr. Piggle-Wiggle built it himself. He said it wasn't too hard, he just took the plans of a regular house and used them upside down. As you all know, Mr. Piggle-Wiggle, before he retired, was a pirate and had collected quite a sizable treasure. Part of this he buried very deep somewhere in the yard, the rest of it he hid in the house, in secret cupboards and drawers.

"I didn't know anything about these secret cupboards and drawers until the house was all finished, then Mr. Piggle-Wiggle told me about them and said that there were enough secret drawers and cupboards filled with treasure to last me the rest of my life. He would not tell me where they were because he said he wanted me to experience the joy of seeking and finding treasure.

"I didn't even look for any of the treasure until after Mr. Piggle-Wiggle died. Then one day when I had used up the very last of my money, I hunted and hunted and finally found a little secret drawer filled with money. This money lasted me for almost a year. Then I hunted for and found another secret drawer with gold pieces in it. I have been doing this for ten years and have, as you know, been living very comfortably. But now I seem to have reached the end."

Mrs. Piggle-Wiggle's sweet brown eyes filled with tears but she blinked them away and went on. "You see, if it hadn't rained today we wouldn't have been able to have a picnic anyway because I used the last of the flour yesterday to make these cookies and now there is nothing at all to eat in the house. All my money has been gone for days and days and days and I have looked and looked until my eyes hurt for another secret drawer or cupboard but I can't find one. I stayed up all night long last night looking and hoping I'd find one before morning so that I could buy the supplies for our hike, but I had no luck. Of course, the money may be all gone, but I just can't believe that. I have never been extravagant and Mr. Piggle-Wiggle knew that I was very healthy and would live a long time. No, I think I've lost my feeling for secret cupboards and drawers and that is why I have asked you children to come over and help me because I know that there are no better lookers and finders in the world than children and you all know this house, how peculiarly it is built, and I'm sure that if anything was hidden in it you would find it.

"Now you must all promise me on your word of honor that you will not mention this to one soul—not even your mothers and fathers, because if word ever got around that I had money hidden in my house, the burglars would be as thick as thieves. I'm certainly hoping that you will find something before lunch but if you don't we'll just have a cup of tea and keep on looking. Fortunately I have plenty of tea and water. Now, if you don't mind, I'm going up to my room and lie down for a little. I'm very tired."

Lester got up and helped Mrs. Piggle-Wiggle to her feet, then Mrs. Piggle-Wiggle, Lester, Wag and Lightfoot went up the stairs to her room and shut the door.

For a minute or two the children just sat and looked at each other. Then Jody said, "Boy, I'll bet I can find that old money. I bet it's in the cellar." He jumped to his feet and he and Jan raced for the cellar door. Chuckie Keystop, Wilfred Grassfeather and Kitty's little brother Bobby followed.

Mary Lou Robertson said, "I think we girls should wash

the tea cups and tidy up the kitchen. Come on everybody bring your cups to the kitchen."

Hubert Prentiss said, "I think we should organize this search. Give everybody a certain territory and have reports."

"Oh, that's dull," said Joan Russell. "We don't want report cards."

"I didn't say report cards, bonehead," said Hubert, "I said reports like soldiers do."

"I think we should just stack up the cups and immediately start hunting for secret panels," said Molly O'Toole. She put her cup and saucer in the sink and skipped into the pantry. "The pantry's my territory," she said.

"I choose the dining-room," said Hubert.

"You can't have a whole room, pig," said Kitty Wheeling. "You can just have one part of the dining-room. I dibs the buffet." She rushed through the door and put her arms out in front of the old-fashioned built-in buffet, which was in the wall between the kitchen and the dining-room and arranged so that you could put dishes in the cupboard on the kitchen side and take them out on the dining-room side, a fact that Kitty didn't know but Hubert did. He climbed into the lower cupboard through the kitchen side, carefully and quietly opened the door on the dining-room side, reached out and pinched Kitty's leg. Kitty gave a terrible yell as though a cobra had bitten her and Hubert laughed and said, "Oh, pardon me, I thought I had found a cupboard of old bones."

Just then Jody came breathlessly up from the basement. He said, "Say, did you know that Mrs. Piggle-Wiggle's basement is flooded? The water is terrible deep and we're lookin' for the money in boats. Ole Wilfred Grassfeather was rowin' around in a dishpan and it tipped over and he looked just like an ole beaver swimmin' around with his ole beaver teeth."

Jan called from the basement, "Hey, hurry up, Jody, and bring some dry clothes for Wilfred."

Jody said, "Where will I find something dry for ole Wilfred?"

Mary Lou said, "There are some old clothes of Mr. Pig-gle-Wiggle's in the attic. Here, I'll get them." She ran up to the attic and got a suit of red woolen underwear out of the old trunk, then called to Wilfred to come upstairs and dry off in the bathroom.

Then she went down to the basement and told Jan and Jody to row over to the woodroom and get some wood so she could build up the fire and dry out Wilfred's clothes. The basement was certainly flooded. The water was up to the fourth step and getting higher all the time. Wilfred was dripping on the stairs and Jan and the other boys were rowing briskly around in washtubs, wash boilers and dish-pans, tapping the walls and hunting for the money. Dick Thompson came down and told them to look for the base-ment drain but they said they were going to look for the money while the water was high and they could see up by the rafters.

By this time every child was crawling, tapping, peering, poking and feeling around in Mrs. Piggle-Wiggle's house. By noon they had found seventeen secret drawers and cup-boards, all empty. Patsy found the first one. She went to pull out a drawer in the kitchen and pulled too hard and it came all the way out and lo and behold, way in behind it was another drawer. Patsy screamed with excitement and everybody came running, even Wilfred looking just like a giant firecracker in Mr. Piggle-Wiggle's long red underwear.

Then Jody came yelping up from the basement with one leg soaking wet clear to the hip, and he had found a secret cupboard in the tool bench. He just happened to lean hard on the end of the bench to keep his boat from bumping into Jan's, when the end of the tool bench came open and there was a secret cupboard, but empty. Then Molly found a little door in the ceiling of the pantry and another empty secret cupboard. Then Mary Lou found that one of the bedposts in the spare bedroom unscrewed and underneath it was a tiny drawer that pulled out, but it was empty. Then Armand Armadillo, who of course happened to be looking at the Encyclopedia, found a little sliding panel in the bookcase and when he opened it there was a tiny little cupboard, empty. Then Lee Wharton found a brick in the fireplace that came out on little hinges and behind it was a tiny drawer that pulled out, but it was empty. Paraphernalia Grotto found a board in the living-room floor that lifted up and there was a little cupboard, empty.

Mimi stood by the window, looked out at the driving rain and thought, "Everybody but me. Everybody but me is finding the secret cupboards and drawers. I'm just an old dummy. Poor Mrs. Piggle-Wiggle needs the money so much and I don't even know where to look." Tears of self-pity stung her eyelids. She reached for her handkerchief, remembered she didn't have one and wiped her eyes on the back of her hand.

"What's the matter, Mimi?" said a soft little voice.

Mimi looked down and there was Linda Jones, standing forlornly behind the curtain with her thumb in her mouth. Mimi said, "Everybody's finding the secret drawers and cupboards but me."

Linda said, "And me. Every time I find a good place to look, one of the bigger, faster children has already looked there. Anyway, I'm hungry. It must be way past lunch time."

Pergola Wingsproggle, who was sitting sadly in a chair nearby said, "It's almost two o'clock and I'm starving. Are there any cookies left?"

Mimi said, "Not one, but we can make some tea. I'll bet poor Mrs. Piggle-Wiggle would like some."

"How do you make tea," said Linda.

"Oh, you just put some tea in the pot and pour in some hot water," said Pergola, who had never made any.

"All right, then, you make it," said Mimi. "Linda and I are going to take a look at the attic."

They went up the little winding attic stairs, but Mary Lou Robertson, Anne and Joan Russell and Julie Jones were already up there poking around and arguing. "This trunk's mine," said Anne.

"No, I already chose that trunk," said Julie.

"I'm going to look in this old desk," said Joan.

"Go ahead," said Mary Lou, "Dick Thompson and Gregory Moohead already almost tore it apart."

"Oh, boy, I'm going to look in this old toy box," said Linda.

"People don't hide money in toy boxes," said Anne.

"I do," said Linda. "I hid twenty-five cents in my toy box last Christmas."

Mimi went over and stood by the chimney. It was warm and she felt cold, a little damp and very sad. "Ouch," —something stuck her. She felt her back pocket and found the safety pin pinning Mrs. Piggle-Wiggle's handkerchief in her pocket had come undone. Mimi tried to fasten it but it wouldn't fasten. It seemed to be broken. She took it off and threw it away. Then suddenly the wind gave a big howl and the lights went off. It wasn't dark outside but it was completely dark in the attic, except for a little bit of milky daylight that squeezed in through the one small cobwebby window.

The children all began scrambling around, bumping into each other and the furniture trying to find the stairway. Little Linda Jones fell over the toy box she had just been searching through and began to bawl. "Somebody pushed me. There's a ghost up here."

Mimi said, "Don't be silly, Linda. The lights were on just a second ago and there wasn't any ghost up here. Here, give me your hand."

But as she bent over to help Linda her jeans caught on a loose board back of the chimney and suddenly she was as scared and panicky as Linda. She knew that it was only a loose board that snagged her back pocket, but in the darkness it felt like a strong bony hand. Everything else up in the attic seemed to have changed too. The big old-fashioned dresser now looked like a great monster with paws raised ready to pounce; Mr. Piggle-Wiggle's shabby old trunk looked like a coffin; the old broken rocking-chair looked like a witch kneeling by her cauldron; the desk looked like the opening to a big cave. Mimi jerked her pocket off the board and she and Linda stumbled across the attic and down the stairs.

Down in the living-room, Mrs. Piggle-Wiggle was lighting big fat white plumber's candles and distributing them to the older children. "Be careful," she warned each one. "Don't put your candle down—just give it to someone to hold for you. Has anyone had any luck yet?"

"I did," yelled Patsy. "I found a secret drawer, but it was empty." The other children all told her of their finds, but added every time, "it was empty."

Mrs. Piggle-Wiggle said, "Don't worry about finding only empty secret cupboards and drawers. The important thing is that you found them. That your eyes and ears are so sharp that you found in a few hours what it has taken me ten years to find. Now everybody get busy. I just know we're going to find a new secret cupboard before the lights go on again. Isn't it fun to hunt for secrets in the dark? Aren't you glad there's a storm?"

The children all said yes in scary hushed voices, took their candles and again began to search.

Mimi was the last to get a candle and when Mrs. Piggle-Wiggle handed it to her she said, "Hasn't your lucky piece helped you find the secret yet, Mimi?"

Mimi said, "Oh, no, Mrs. Piggle-Wiggle. I'm just terribly dumb about finding things. I've looked and looked and I haven't even found one secret cupboard."

Mrs. Piggle-Wiggle said, "Take out your lucky piece and rub it hard between your thumb and first finger. We'll just see if it really is a real Pirate's lucky piece."

Mimi reached in her back pocket but Mrs. Piggle-Wiggle's hanky with the lucky piece tied in the corner was gone. She reached in the other pocket. It wasn't there either. She said, "It's gone, Mrs. Piggle-Wiggle. I've lost it."

Then she remembered how she had caught her pocket on the board behind the chimney in the attic. She said, "I think I know where it is, though. I think I left it up in the attic."

Mrs. Piggle-Wiggle said, "Do you want me to go up with you?"

Mimi did but she didn't want to admit that she was afraid, so she said, "Oh, no, I'll take my candle and go up, I know just where to look."

She ran up the stairs and to the door to the attic so fast, her candle flame leaned way over to one side and threatened to go out. Mrs. Piggle-Wiggle called to her, "Better take some extra matches, Mimi; it's draughty in the attic. There are some on that little shelf there by the landing." Mimi grabbed a handful of the matches and then started slowly up the attic stairs.

Her candle flame grew very high as if it were trying to peer over the stairway, then ducked down as a sudden gust of cold air flew at them from under the eaves. The sounds of the storm were much clearer up here. The wind moaned and whined around the eaves and the rain lashed furiously at the window and hammered hard on the roof, demanding to get in. Mimi held the candle high and looked around. There was the trunk, there was the rocking-chair, there was the toy box, and there was a terrible monster, oh, no, the bureau.

She picked her way over to the chimney. Ooh, it was dark over there. A gust of wind blew her candle out. It was a big gust of wind, almost like an open window. Mimi hurriedly struck one of the matches—it blew out, too. She struck another—it also blew out. Another and another. Finally she had only two left. With trembling fingers she lit the next to last one. The flame held and the candle sputtered and then flared cozily.

Mimi bent over and peered behind the chimney. There was the board and there hanging to a corner of it was Mrs. Piggle-Wiggle's handkerchief. Mimi reached for it but it seemed to be caught on something. She jerked hard and slowly a big piece of the attic wall opened. Mimi held her candle higher so she could see better. Behind the piece of wall, which was hinged like a little door, there were six drawers with little handles. Mimi opened one. It was stuffed full of green paper money. Mimi opened another —it was filled with gold pieces. She opened another—it was filled with silver; another held jewels; another held more paper money; another more gold.

Mimi rushed to the stairway and yelled, "Mrs. Piggle-Wiggle, Mrs. Piggle-Wiggle, I've found it! I've found it! Money! Jewels! Hurry!"

Everyone came running but the first to poke his head over the attic stairway was Lester. Mimi knelt down and hugged him. "Oh, Lester, dear!" she said, "Mrs. Piggle-Wiggle's rich. Isn't it wonderful?"

Lester smiled.

When Mrs. Piggle-Wiggle came up she walked over to the secret cupboard and just stood with her arm around Mimi and with tears streaming from her eyes. Mimi opened the drawers one by one and Mrs. Piggle-Wiggle looked at the treasure and wiped her eyes. "Dear Mr. Piggle-Wiggle," she said. "I knew he wouldn't forget me. I just knew it."

As each one of the children had to see the cupboard and examine the treasure, hear over and over exactly how Mimi had found it, and see and feel the wonderful magic lucky piece, it was dark before they finally went downstairs. Then Mrs. Piggle-Wiggle said, "My goodness, how selfish I've been. Here you poor children are all hungry and I've been so excited over the treasure I forgot all about dinner. What do you say we have our picnic after all—we'll roast potatoes and weenies in the fireplace, we'll get chocolate ice cream and I'll bake a cake to celebrate. Now first I'll go to the store and while I'm gone you boys can row to the woodroom and get a lot of wood so we can have a nice roaring fire. And Dick, would you please go down and see if you can find the basement drain? Mimi, you and Mary Lou and Kitty come to the store and help me carry the groceries, and you Molly and Hubert see that everyone has on dry clothes and that the house is picked up a little."

Just then the lights went on. "Hooray, hooray!" shouted everyone but Jody and Lee. They said, "Oh, darn the ole lights. It was lots more fun down in the basement rowing around with candles. We pretended we were in a flooded mine and we used our candles to test the air for oxygen."

"When you go down again, use your paddles to test the floor for a drain," said Mrs. Piggle-Wiggle, laughing.

Just then Dick Thompson came running up from the basement. He said, "Say, Mrs. Piggle-Wiggle, I found the drain and there was something over it and so I scraped it off with this stick and look, it seems to be a letter to you."

Mrs. Piggle-Wiggle took the soggy piece of paper and read:

"Dear Wife:

My last secret cupboard is very hard to find so I am leaving this letter on your gardening shelf in the basement as I am sure that before too many years this shelf will become so crowded and cluttered you will have to clean it off and then you will find this letter. The last secret cupboard of treasure is behind the chimney in the attic. Just jerk hard on that old loose board.

Your loving husband,
Mr. Piggle-Wiggle"

"Well, for heaven's sake," said Mrs. Piggle-Wiggle. "I looked on that gardening shelf last night and I remember when that letter fell to the floor. I thought it was an old empty seed package and didn't bother to pick it up. I never would have found it if it hadn't been for you, Dick, and I never would have found the secret drawers. This rain certainly has brought us luck. It clogged the drain by the Burbanks' so Mimi would find the pirate's lucky piece and it clogged the drain in my cellar so I would find Mr. Piggle-Wiggle's letter. I guess from now on I'll always have to like rain, even on picnic days."

The End